Taming Brooklyn

THE CLUB KINGS
BOOK ONE

CHARLOTTE ST. PIERRE

Contents

To the authors that have inspired me to reach for more.

Author Note

Reader friends - this is a "why choose" romance, where the main female character will end up with multiple romantic partners. In this book there are descriptions of child abuse, domestic violence, rape, attempted murder and detailed sex scenes. If these subject are difficult for you, this may not be the book for you.

If you are still reading...I hope you love Brooklyn and The Club Kings as much as I have enjoyed bringing them to the page!

CHAPTER
One

Brooklyn

"BROOKLYN REEVES, you better not even think about trying to ditch me tonight!"

My best friend was standing at the door of my bedroom, staring at me. I couldn't help but visibly cringe which just tells her I was absolutely thinking about finding an excuse to not go out. I sighed and rolled out of bed. Granted, it was still early, but I was content to curl up with Netflix on my laptop and a glass of wine.

"I'm just not sure I want to be around so many people," I started to explain.

Ash had been my best friend since college. There was no one on the planet that knew me better than her. No flimsy excuse was going to work on her. Right then, I knew I was in trouble by the way her eyes narrowed at me.

"I leave in two days. I will be gone for months. You are coming out to celebrate with me," she demanded.

With that, I was caught. She was right. Ash had won a fantastic promotion at her job and they were sending her to Europe to train in the main office for three months. It was an opportunity of a lifetime, I repeated in my head for at least the millionth time. I was happy for Ash, really, but I was heart-broken over the idea of her being gone for so long.

I trudged to my closet and looked around. Ash came to stand next to me and rub my shoulder, as I took a deep breath, trying to convince myself I could do this. Ash's company had given her VIP access to Club 4, one of the hottest clubs in the city. She had always wanted to go, but with her schedule, and being best friends with a hermit, she never got the chance.

Now, I somehow had to convince myself that I could handle the crush of a drunken crowd. I turned and grabbed my red wine, downing the rest of the glass in a few gulps.

"That's the spirit!" Ash exclaimed as she raced out of the room, presumably to get herself pretty.

I was left with my doubts and future regrets I knew I would have. I pulled a black halter dress from the closet. It was club attire, which means I hadn't worn it in months. However, the high front with halter, would cover almost all of my most insecure feature.

In the bathroom, I slipped the dress on. I couldn't wear a bra, which didn't bother me. My breasts weren't so large that they couldn't handle a night without security. The dress stopped mid-thigh, though with every step it liked to crawl up just a bit. I wore lacy hipsters underneath, just in case. I liked how the dress showed off one of my favorite assets, my toned legs. All the running I did was evident in them and that was the only reason I kept doing it.

Standing in front of the mirror, I traced the scar that started below my right ear and crossed across my collarbone, ending just above my cleavage. I adjusted the halter a few times and most of the scar was hidden by the material. Leaving my long blonde hair down also helped. Looking at it made my stomach turn, but I looked at my face, smiled wide and walked into the apartment living room.

Ash was waiting, in a fire engine red tube dress. She squealed when she took in my dress and silver stilettos I was slipping my feet into. I figured I'd regret the choice later, but Club 4 was the place for all the upper class to party. I didn't want to be a complete sore thumb in that crowd. With no bra, Ash carried my ID and debit card in her strapless bra. I had plans to dance tonight.

We convinced the Uber driver to put on some hip hop as we drove and by the time we pulled up to Club 4, we were both giggling and ready to have a drink. The line outside was ridiculous, but Ash grinned and flashed her VIP pass. That got us right in the door, much to the complaints of some in line. My best friend was eating up all the special attention.

"Bar first?" She said, moments before our senses were assaulted by the inside of the club.

I nodded, knowing my voice would be lost as we stepped into the large open space filled with smoke and noise.. My eyes tried to take everything in as Ash led us to the nearest bar. The center of the club was a large dance floor, which was packed full of bodies moving and grinding to "She's a Goddess" by Cut One & Spruce Bringstein. It was a slow song for dancing, but it was clear the crowd enjoyed the sensual beat and lyrics.

There were two bars on the main floor, on either side of the dance floor. It was dark with lights strobing throughout. For some reason I was already struck with how sexual it felt inside. Standing at the bar next to Ash as she worked to catch the eye of the bartender, I looked up. There were at least two stories above the dance floor, with balconies overlooking the main floor. Ash caught me looking and pulled on my arm.

"The second floor is the VIP area, I think. We can go up there for some space," she yelled near my ear.

I nodded and continued to look around. I saw a man at the other end of the bar staring hard at me, so I immediately turned to face Ash. I wanted to have fun and a man wasn't required for that. Ash shoved a pink shot into my hand. I raised an eyebrow and she just shrugged before clinking glasses and downing the shot. I followed her lead and let the sweet liquor flow down my throat.

Two more shots down and Ash was ready to hit the dance floor. I started to feel warm and finally stopped fidgeting with my halter, trying to ensure it stayed over my scar. Ash had told me so many times that it wasn't gruesome and maybe it wasn't. I just didn't like to answer questions. How am I supposed to introduce myself with the remains of the long gash clearly visible? "Hi there. Oh that? It's nothing, I survived a murderer."

Maroon 5 came across the speakers with "Girls Like You," which caused Ash to grin and drag me toward the moving mass of people. With a bit of alcohol induced courage and Ash protecting me from being trampled, we found ourselves in the middle of the dance floor.

After dancing enough that I had started sweating, we decided to head up to the VIP section and take a break and find more alcohol. Ash was beaming with joy and I knew it's not only the dancing and liquor. She was really very excited about her new opportunity. I pasted a smile on my face to hide all of my turmoil.

Ash flashed her VIP card again and we were allowed to climb a set of stairs that took us to an area with booths sectioned off by black curtains. The hostess at the top of the stairs showed us to an empty booth and placed Ash's name on the table so we could hold it and still dance.

I waggled my eyebrows at Ash comically, neither of us knew what it was like to be treated with such importance. I slipped off my heels and massaged my feet for a moment, before a waitress appeared. Ash ordered us two rounds of the shots we had been taking and I threw in waters at the last minute. My friend just laughed and nodded before the waitress left.

Scooting into the center of the too large booth, we sat together in the center. Ash leaned on me and I wrapped an arm around her. A man passed by our booth and I saw his gaze land on us for a moment longer than necessary.

"Mark that one. He's coming back," I said in Ash's ear.

"He was hot, so that's ok," she replied with a laugh.

I looked at her incredulous. "You're leaving in two days!"

"What's that gotta do with a one nighter?"

We both cracked up laughing at our conversation and the waitress arrived with our drinks. The shots were gone in the blink of an eye. I had enough thought left to sip the water, while shoving the open bottle into Ash's hand as well. She rolled her eyes but sipped, used to my caretaker ways at this point.

Holding hands, we made it back to the dance floor and carefully made our way back to the center. "I Don't Wanna Live Forever" by Zayn came on and I couldn't help but sway with the crowd, my arms above my head. I twisted so Ash was dancing along my back.

A shiver passed through me and for a moment I could feel eyes on me. I looked around, but didn't see anything to worry about. Looking up, on the third floor, I saw them. The dark club didn't hide that they were beautiful men. One with short blonde hair and the other with dark spikes. Beyond that, I couldn't make out all of their features. And for some reason, I knew it was me they were watching.

The feeling made me feel emboldened and sexy in a way I had never considered myself. Ash was still with me, but there was a man trying to get her attention. It only took a moment to realize it was the hot guy from the VIP section. I caught Ash's gaze over his shoulder, and she gave me a megawatt smile.

She spun around the guy, so her and I were still dancing together. The guy definitely didn't care as his attention was one hundred percent on my friend. I was sure a last minute fling would be happening. I would just try to not catch the walk of shame in the morning. The idea had me laughing to myself.

When I got the courage, I looked back up to the third level balcony. My heart stuttered and sank a little when I realized my admirers were gone. It was a strange fleeting feeling. I mentally shook my drunk self. Quit it, Brooklyn.

CHAPTER

Two

Jaxon

THE BLONDE CAUGHT my eye the moment she came to the lower VIP level. From our owner's booth, we could see the entrance. This was done with a specific purpose. If there was a VIP we needed to interact with, we could easily be aware of their arrival without anyone knowing.

However, the blonde wasn't someone we were waiting for. Her hair, so pale, hung almost to her ass. The color caught my eye and then I couldn't stop staring. She had legs for days that were shown off very well in the black halter dress she was wearing. Once she and her companion were taken to a booth, I lost track of her.

Though, I didn't stop watching the stairs. The moment she came out again, I was at the balcony, watching her make her way into the crowded dance floor. She lifted her arms above her head and I was pretty sure she was dancing with her eyes closed, swaying to the music. The way she moved exuded freedom and sensuality. I couldn't stop watching her.

Oliver joined me at the rail, bumping me with his shoulder. When I didn't look up, he looked down into the club and we didn't have to speak, he immediately saw what had my attention. When she lifted her face, I could feel her eyes on us. My skin tingled as she stared and continued to dance, as if it was for us. I knew she couldn't clearly see us, but the zap of electricity I felt, told me she knew we were here.

Her body moved with the music, her hips gyrating perfectly with the beat. She threw her hair to the side and I could see her dress had an open back. Her skin was smooth and pale and my hands immediately itched to touch her. The strong desire wasn't normal for me. I fisted my hands against the rail, trying to figure out where the strong rush of desire was coming from.

"Who is she?" Oliver asked.

"No damn idea," I replied.

"Seems you want to know, brother," he said, smacking my shoulder.

When the blonde looked back at her friend, who was now dancing with a guy, I decided Oliver was right, I needed to know. The blonde's dress was barely covering her ass and something told me I needed to be the one to press against her. I pushed away from the rail and started for the stairs.

"Jaxon, really?" Oliver called after me.

"You coming?" I called over my shoulder.

I couldn't hear his response, but I wasn't surprised when I saw him at my side. We made our way down the stairs to the dance floor. This was unusual for us. As owners of Club 4, too many of the cubbies knew who we were. We didn't like the attention, so we very rarely came to the main floor when the club was open.

Unlike my brothers, I didn't normally partake in the offers that came to us every night. Even the most uptight of us, Aiden, accepted an offer once in a while. I knew he only did it to scratch an itch. I didn't like women throwing themselves at me, because they knew I had money, so I avoided them like the plague. At least in the club.

This is why, as we made our way through the throng of people, Oliver caught my eye and gave me a quizzical look. I just looked over at the blonde, who hadn't looked up as we were working our way through. I continued to stare and people around me seemed to peel away when they realized who we were.

The shift in the crowd caused a confused to look to cross the woman's face and she looked up, meeting my eye. I almost choked, her beauty almost knocking me back a step. I saw the moment she recognized me, her plump red lips parted in what I was sure was a surprised sound.

Her friend was still dancing next to her, but when she saw that the blonde had stopped, she touched her arm. The blonde looked over at her and shook her head, a brilliant smile crossing her face, reassuring her that everything was ok. When she turned to look at me again, I was right in front of her and the crowd was starting to move around us again.

I held out my hand to her and she only hesitated for a second before slipping her fingers into my palm. Carefully, I pulled her to my chest and she looked up at me in surprise. "Impatient" by Jeremih came through the speakers and the bass vibrated through our bodies.

I saw when Oliver's hands swept over her hip and she turned to look over her shoulder. She went stiff for a moment, but as we moved to the music, cradling her body between us, she began to relax. I took her hand and put it around my neck, and on her own she lifted her other and reached back to pull Oliver closer.

Oliver's eyes met mine and we both shared a smile. I knew he was thinking the same thoughts. The woman fit like a puzzle piece between us. As I slipped my hand around her waist, I let my fingers dance along the exposed skin of her back. She closed her eyes for a moment, arching into my touch.

As the songs changed, we turned her, so Oliver could look into her eyes while we danced. His knee slipped between her legs and for a moment she moved her hips against his, before moving back against me again. I was rock hard and I'd barely been near her. The way she seductively slid down my body and back up told me she knew exactly what was happening.

As she slid back up my body, her hands ran up Oliver's torso and I saw his mouth part. He couldn't hide what this woman was doing to us either. Bending my head down, I ran my nose along her cheek and she turned into me. When I got to her ear, I let my teeth nip just a moment before pulling back.

Lavender, the smell of lavender enveloped me. Normally, I wasn't into floral scents, but for some reason the sweet smell was perfect for our blonde beauty. She was smiling up at Oliver now. The song "Closer" by Nine Inch Nails came on and I swore I saw a seductive sparkle in her eye.

She slipped around again and gyrated her hips perfectly with the strong beat of the music. Throwing one arm around my neck, she leaned back into Oliver as he ground against one of her hips. I slipped a hand behind her, taking a chance and letting it stray across her ass. She looked at me with a playful smile that made my heart thud in my chest. I was losing myself fast.

Aiden

I WATCHED my brothers dancing on the main floor. Swirling dark liquor in my tumbler, I scoffed at how the two of them were drooling over one woman. There was a sea of offers that fell at our feet nightly. And these two went after one they'd never seen.

"What's the problem, Aiden?" Gideon asked, joining me at the railing.

I looked over at one of my best friends and brothers. We weren't blood related, but that didn't matter. As soon as we were old enough, we changed our last names and became our own family.

Gideon was always looking out for us. Tonight was no different. I watched his shrewd gaze go over the crowd and stop on Jaxon and Oliver. His eyebrow quirked up, which was the only sign that he was interested in what was happening.

"No problem. Just wondering what those two are up to," I replied.

"Celebrating, no doubt," he said.

We were all celebrating tonight. Our newest club opening had gone better than anticipated, our brand gaining us the attraction we needed. We had attended the first few nights there, but we handed the club off to management and we would watch from a distance. Club 4 was our number one place and we liked to spend our time in it.

At least, my brothers did. I would have liked to be in the office, going over budgets and some new proposals we had to review. But Gideon insisted I relaxed and celebrated too. We didn't go out as a group as often as we did early in business. They called me stuffy and serious. I saw it as keeping us grounded and successful.

I looked over at Jaxon and Oliver again. The way their bodies moved with the blonde, made it fairly clear what they wanted from her. I had no doubt she knew who they were and would easily give in to it at some point.

She was beautiful, I could admit that. And there was something about the way she moved between them, that was sensual in a way I didn't normally see in the club. I didn't come to the club all that often these days, so I couldn't be sure, but this one didn't seem like a normal clubbie.

With one last long gaze, I turned and went back to our owner's booth. Either the boys would be bringing her up here, or they'd find a dark corner to have their fun. I didn't need to watch them like a parent. Gideon was still riveted at the rail, so I just relaxed on my own.

Our dedicated waitress came and left us another round, without saying a word. Most of our staff was loyal and knew their roles. We paid better than any other club employers in the city and had generous benefits packages. Rarely did we have anyone we had to reprimand. I couldn't remember the last time we had to fire someone.

I scrubbed my hand along my jaw, rubbing at my 5 o'clock shadow. I was tired. The opening of our new property had taken a lot of work on my part. My brothers filled their roles and did fantastic work. I couldn't imagine working with anyone else. But the numbers and business came down to me. And it could be exhausting.

Gideon finally sat down opposite me and a deep frown was on his face.

"What gives?" I asked.

"Nothing," he replied absentmindedly.

He was in deep thought, so I was going to leave him to it. Throwing back the last of my fresh drink, I stood. It took Gideon a beat to realize I was getting ready to go home.

"Celebration over?" He asked.

"I could use an early night. Not going to work. Just to bed," I said, with a deep sigh.

Gideon nodded and walked me to our back exit. He often did that, as if to ensure we made it to the place we were destined. Our driver was parked in our designated parking in the back of the club. And we exited through a stairwell no one else had access to. It was the best way to avoid the crowds that often tried to get our attention.

When we got to the door, Gideon clapped me on the shoulder, but didn't say anything as the door shut behind me. I slowly took the stairs down, thinking about going home to my big cold bed. Going to be alone was my normal routine, but why did it feel so heavy tonight?

CHAPTER
Four

Brooklyn

IN ALL OF MY LIFE, I had never caught the attention of men that looked like these two. When I saw them making their way toward me on the dance floor, it was as if the Red Sea parted and allowed them to get to me. I gave the alcohol buzzing through my system all the credit for me not completely freezing up and panicking.

When they pressed their bodies against me, my heart fluttered and goosebumps broke out all over my skin. They're both tall, taller than me even with my heels. And close up, they are even more attractive than I originally thought.

The dark haired one, had his hair shaved tight on the sides with wild spikes on the top. I wanted to touch it, but decided against it. I thought at first that his eyes were a deep brown but when the light hit his face, I realized they were more maple syrup. He was wearing a white v-neck shirt and a full sleeve of tattoos showed. I wanted to run my fingers over the art, so when he touched my hip, I let my fingers dance on his skin.

The other did have light colored hair, but now that he was close to me I realized it was a mop of curls, carefully controlled by product. His eyes were a bright blue and I couldn't stop staring into them. His lips tipped in a small smile when he sees I'm staring, but I don't look away.

They didn't speak to me with words. The movement of them against my body was like a language all of its own. I hadn't been out dancing in forever, but my hips and blood recall the sensation. I easily fell into a rhythm with them and closed my eyes for a moment, losing myself in the sensation of their proximity and touch.

I didn't get a look at the DJ of the club, but it seemed that every song that played was about sex. It was clear the mood was meant to be sensual and hot. The music pounded through me and it only added to the high I was riding with my two dance partners.

I used to love to dance, but the crowds weren't my thing anymore. Somehow, tonight I was finding myself again. With the heat of the crowd pressing in, the bass of the music thrumming through my veins, I could almost forget everything. Almost.

Looking around, I realized Ash was still dancing with the hot guy she had found. She made eye contact with me and fanned herself letting me know how hot this all was. I had to agree. As dark hair's hips ground behind my ass, I pushed back just enough that I could feel how turned on he was.

I had never had a one night stand. Hell, I hadn't had a boyfriend in months. Besides my own fingers and vibrator, I hadn't gotten off with a man in years. Somehow, at this moment, on the dance floor with these men, I was experiencing the most sensual moment of my life.

Mr. Blue Eyes had his hands on my hips. He pulled me forward toward him just a fraction, sliding me along his thigh before he began to sway with the music. The friction felt delicious and dangerous. I pushed my hips forward, lifting one leg to hook around his hip as we swayed. His hand went to my knee and the touch was electricity directly to my core.

I had no idea what I was doing. Why I was pushing all of the lines I had drawn for myself. But something about these two, something made me want them to touch me. I saw them make eye contact over my shoulder and blue eyes quirked an eyebrow. They seemed to have some sort of full conversation without words.

The next thing I knew, a heat touched my shoulder and I realized dark hair was kissing my skin. And holy shit, when his tongue danced out across my sweat drenched shoulder, I shuddered. He must have felt it, because his hand snaked between blue eyes and I, anchored my back to him.

Blue eyes followed and every scrape of his chest against my breasts, reminded me I didn't have a bra on. My nipples were pebbled and I was thankful no one could tell in the darkness of the club. Part of me wanted these men to know though, to know how they were turning me on just by dancing dirty with me.

I let my fingers trail down blue eyes' chest, digging in my nails just slightly and I saw his eyes widen. Without warning, he grabbed me by the throat and crushed our lips together. His lips were surprisingly soft, but there was a demand behind them that I hadn't experienced before.

When I felt his tongue along the seam of my lips, my body responded without any conscience thought. As his tongue swept into my mouth, I felt like I was suddenly drowning in him. Each caress sent zaps of electricity down my spine. His hand still held my throat, which should have been a warning sign, but instead his thumb rubbed gently along the material of my halter.

Blue eyes leaned back and his eyes held the same sort of shock I was feeling from the connection. It was just a kiss, I chided my alcohol addled brain. So why did I want him to do it again. And as often as I could possibly get it.

Not to be left out, dark hair behind me continued his kissing up the back of my neck. When his fingers moved to the right side of my neck, sliding under my halter, I froze. Suddenly, all I could think of was the raised scar I was trying to hide. The two men didn't realize right away that I had stopped moving. However, the moment dark hair leaned toward my right ear, shifting my halter, I spun out of their embrace.

I could see Ash behind them, dancing her heart out with the man that had approached her. I needed her, but I didn't want to interrupt the fun she was having. Blue eyes and dark hair were frozen in spot, watching me, as if they were waiting for me to explode. However, the ripe fear in my gut had turned my body to ice.

Without another word, I turned and started to push my way through the crowd. I wasn't sure I was going the right way, I just needed to get away. I had been feeling better than I had in such a long time. I wanted to lose myself in the feeling, the touching and electricity. But, I couldn't. There was too much baggage locked up inside me.

When I reached the edge of the dance crowd, I took the chance to glance back and saw that the men were coming after me. I gulped in air as panic struck me. Their eyes were locked on me as if I were prey to catch and there was no way I could explain my sudden freak out. The feel of them against me, I knew they saw me as something I wasn't.

Turning away, I saw the bar that we had gotten our first drinks at. I rushed that way until I saw the front door. I burst out without another look back and started walking down the street. A taxi rolled slowly by me and I cried out with my arm up. The cab had barely rolled to a stop before I was jumping in and slamming the door.

The driver looked back at me in alarm.

"Miss, you ok?" He asked.

"Yes. Please drive," I said, rattling off my address.

Looking back, I could see my dance partners in the distance. They were looking up and down the street, trying to figure out where I had gone. I slouched in the seat as the cab pulled away from the curb. Once we were out of sight of Club 4, I sat up straighter and took a few deep breaths to calm my nerves.

I watched as the city passed by. Mentally, I felt exhausted. I was always hiding, always avoiding. I didn't know how not to feel scarred, ugly and worthless. There had been very few people in my life that made me believe anything more.

The last thing I wanted was two hot guys to look at me with pity in their eyes. And they would, the moment they realized just how damaged I really was. I worked hard to keep my mask on around those I worked with. Even Ash rarely saw the truth of things unless I was having a really bad time.

At my apartment building, I realized Ash had my debit

card. I begged the cab to wait and I would run and get my credit card from my wallet. Luckily, Ash and I had hidden a spare key in a light fixture, so I was able to unlock the door.

After paying the cabbie and tipping him extra for being kind, I locked myself in our apartment. I shot a quick text to Ash, letting her know I was home and not to worry. Of course, her response was quick and she was worried. After letting her know I was just super tired and didn't want to interrupt her fun, she let me off the hook.

I stripped off my dress and got back into my comfortable pajamas. In bed I pressed my fingertips against my lips and closed my eyes for a second. No matter how the night ended, that kiss was the hottest thing to ever happen to me. I allowed the heat I felt earlier roll over me again.

I had to admit, I was hot and bothered. I dug out my vibrator from my nightstand. Slipping my toy into my panties, I pictured the men from the club. I pictured the sleeve tattoo of dark hair and how he pressed his lips to my back and shoulder.

I closed my eyes and switched on the vibrator as I replayed the kiss with blue eyes. I could still feel the hot brand of his fingers on my throat. My orgasm was swift and released some of the tension I was feeling. But, as I sank into bed and my eyes started to close, I knew it was nothing compared to what it could have been with those men.

CHAPTER
Five

Brooklyn

SAYING GOODBYE TO ASH, as she was leaving for her red eye flight, was harder than I had anticipated. There were plenty of tears. Ash refused to let me go with her to the airport, knowing I had work in the morning. It wasn't forever and it was a wonderful opportunity for her. I had to keep reminding myself.

"And you're gonna be fine while I'm gone, right?" Ash asked for the tenth time.

She knew that she was the only person I had in the city. Ash was my person. We had been through all the highs and lows together. She knew more about me than anyone else. I guessed her concern was valid. I hadn't been alone in a long time. My anxiety was high, but I was sure to hide it behind a smile.

"I've got this. Just a few months, right?" I replied.

Ash hadn't seemed convinced, but she had to go or risk missing her flight. I walked her down the stairs and waited as her Uber arrived. I probably stood longer than necessary, watching the tail lights in the distance.

Alone, in the apartment, getting ready for work the next day felt awkward. Usually, Ash and I had coffee and a small breakfast together as we both got ready. But today, it was just me. The apartment felt empty and lonely. I turned on my Bluetooth speaker, hoping to comfort myself a bit while I got ready.

"Sway" by Danielle Bradbery came on my shuffle and I paused for a moment thinking about the irony. As she sang about how life sucked sometimes, I swayed my hips while brushing my teeth. I had always connected music to my emotions and as I listened to the lyrics, I found myself smiling a little bit.

Like most mornings, I got to my office early. As the Director of Operations and Marketing for the non-profit KidsUpFirst, my plate was normally quite full. Today was no exception. I had back to back phone calls and then an in person meeting with a company called 4K, that was wanting to host a fundraiser for us. The company President had already come up with the idea and today was a brainstorm session on what would be most successful.

KidsUpFirst was near and dear to my heart. We provided safe havens for kids in the foster care system. Ones that struggled with finding homes they fit into. Often these kids felt that they were rejects in one way or another. With a safe home, therapy and caring adults, we found a way to keep kids off the streets, improve their graduation chances and lower the suicide rates. All of this took funds which we usually got from fundraisers or private donors.

During college, I had taken an internship with the company. It opened my eyes to the non-profit world and what good could really be done when money was applied in the right place. After I graduated college, they offered me a position and I worked hard to get to the director position I was in now.

The phone call monotony of the day felt like it droned on. When my in person meeting came up, the call I was on didn't end promptly. I shot my assistant a quick ping to let my team know I would be running a few minutes behind and to apologize to the owners of 4K. I hated to be late, so I quickly wrapped up the donor call I was on. It was where the money came from, so I had to do things delicately.

I rushed into our conference room, looking at the papers in my hand. I hadn't done as much research on 4K as I wish I had. I knew they had a property they wanted to open for us to hold our largest annual fundraiser. We switch the event up yearly, so we were open to suggestions this year.

I took my seat and raised my eyes with an apology on my lips.

"I'm so sorry I'm late. Please continue," I say in a rush.

I smile at my team but my eye is caught by one of the men at the other end of the board room table. Blue eyes bore into mine and I choke on air. My assistant rushed to get me a glass of water and I see the man smile slightly. As I drank, my hand flutters to my neck. I always hide my scar carefully in the office. Today I wore a high collared button up shirt, with a necklace that obscured my open skin on my chest. I decided I would analyze my immediate self consciousness later.

Sitting across from me, in a navy blue business suit, with a white button up, unbuttoned at the throat, was my blue eyes dance partner. Panicked, I look at the other faces and immediately recognize brown hair, who has one eyebrow raised at me. They both recognize me and they aren't unhappy to see me.

I squirm a bit in my chair, as my events manager goes on with our brainstorming ideas. Blue eyes leans over to whisper to the man sitting next to him. I didn't see this man, or the fourth while I was at the club. They were all vastly different in appearance. The one blue eyes whispered to has short black hair, swept back in a professional cut.

Whatever blue eyes says to him, has him focusing his gray eyes on me, and I can feel a blush racing up my neck to my face. His gaze is fierce and hard, giving me pause, and nerves that I haven't felt in business in a long time, settle in my gut.

"Excuse me, can I stop you there? May we have the room?" He said.

Gathering my papers, I nod and we all start to stand.

"Not you," he said, pointing at me.

I couldn't help the audible gulp that came from my throat. This caused blue eyes to grin at me. I looked over at my team and nodded to let them know to go. How could I have the inevitable conversation that was about to happen with them in the room?

When the door shut, the room was silent enough to hear a pin drop. I sat back down slowly, waiting, not knowing where this was going.

"So, you knew who we were the other night,"

I'm taken aback by the comment and I focus on the man with the dark hair. I look to the fourth man, who I definitely knew I would have remembered, had I seen him, he dominated the space around him. He had a full thick beard and hair that was pulled back in a bun. He looked at me with a frown, but his gaze wasn't harsh. It almost felt like he was analyzing my existence and somehow that made me uncomfortable.

"I don't think I understand what you're asking," I finally said.

"You came to our club and knew we were the owners. That's why you were flirting with Jaxon and Oliver," gray eyes said.

"Aiden," a warning came from one of my dance partners, though I still wasn't sure which name belonged to who.

The man named Aiden didn't seem done however.

"I just think we should know what we're getting into here. You know the types we deal with at the club," Aiden continued.

It took me a moment to get over being dense and under-standing what he was insinuating. I took a deep breath and controlled the switch in my head. I went into business mode. Because in that mode, I was in control. What happened at the club hadn't mattered. It didn't matter that seeing the two men again made me hot and bothered, just sitting across from them.

"Sir, I'm not quite sure what you mean. I've never seen the two of you before," I said, pointing to him and the bearded one.

Aiden opened his mouth, but I held up a hand to stop him. I flipped open the file that was in front of me. I knew that my event manager and assistant had all of the paperwork in order as they always did, so I didn't need to search for the donor application or email stating they wanted to host our yearly fundraiser.

When I looked back up, Aiden's face was stone and I knew he wasn't one that was usually told to be quiet.

"What I see here is, you reached out to us. Not me directly

of course, but the proper channels to donate. Which we thank you for. And in this email I see that you offered to host our annual fundraiser. This was all before, well, the other night," I said, the last few words coming out a little quieter than the rest of my speech.

I could see blue eyes grin and shoot a sideways glance at Aiden.

"I'm not sure this is an appropriate business arrangement any further," Aiden said, standing and preparing to leave the room.

I shoot to my feet as well. We have new donations coming in all the time. It's not that we're ever swimming in funds, but we do well enough. Losing this donation wouldn't kill the company, however, I would be the one to explain to the President why the fundraiser was no longer being held at a 4K property. I didn't exactly have the words to do that.

"Aiden, you're being hasty," blue eyes said, his gaze on me.

Aiden stopped and glanced back at his business associates. He nodded to blue eyes, but didn't say anything before leaving. My mouth dropped open, shocked at how badly the meeting had turned. The bearded man, stood and I realized he was gigantic. He frowned at me again, as if he was puzzled, before following Aiden.

Blue eyes sighed and looked at his remaining business partner.

"Well, never did I see this meeting going this way," he said.

I sat down again, closing my file and tapping the papers to line everything up. I avoided their gazes. If I looked at them, without any other distractions, I couldn't think of anything but the night in the club. I blushed again as I thought about the number of times I got off thinking about the kiss.

Vanilla wafts over me as blue eyes moves to my side of the conference table. I can't avoid him any longer without looking like a complete idiot. And when I do, my breath tries to catch in my throat. It's not really fair for these men to be so attractive. When I told Ash about what had happened in the club, she sympathized with my breakdown. But most of all that I would never get it on with men that looked like them.

"I'm Oliver. That's Jaxon," Oliver said.

"Brooklyn," I replied, finally exchanging one of the missing pieces from the night of the dance club.

He sat in the seat right next to me, not crowding me, but not letting me escape easily either. I had a feeling this was about me running out on them and I didn't have a ready excuse to give. I never expected to see their faces again.

Jaxon, with his dark hair more controlled today, sat with an interested look on his face and his arms crossed over his chest.

"So, is Aiden right. Did you know who we were? And before you answer, it's not some sort of ego asking. We tend to get more attention than we like. You have to admit this coincidence is quite...interesting," Jaxon asked.

I flipped my gaze to him, shaking my head immediately.

"Before I walked in here, I didn't know the names of the business partners that ran 4K. I'll be really honest, I was running late today as you saw. I didn't get my normal read through of the paperwork. And even if I had your names, well, we didn't exactly exchange information the other night," I said quietly, shifting my gaze to the table top, wondering why I had to explain when they were the ones to approach me.

"She has a point," Oliver said, a light laugh coming from his mouth.

"I believe her," Jaxon replied.

"Me too," Oliver agreed.

I look between the two of them. It was incredibly difficult to not feel like I was under some sort of microscope as they both looked at me. I knew there were questions. I decided the best way to go, was to pretend it didn't really matter. Even if inside me, I knew kissing Oliver was the sexiest thing I'd ever experienced to date.

"Well, that's great. Perhaps you could let Aiden know, before this whole agreement goes up in flames. Also point out that you two approached me at the club. Once you guys get a chance to discuss, we can reschedule this meeting," I said, flipping back into business mode.

The men study me again and Jaxon nods, moving to stand. He straightens his suit jacket and I can't help but watch as the shirt under stretches across his chest. They are all well built, even if I've only seen them with clothes on. Men shouldn't be allowed to look that good in business suits.

Oliver hadn't moved. He continued to sit next to me, watching my profile, as I politely watched Jaxon. When I don't turn my attention, I feel a warm palm over my hand. I freeze, and look down where Oliver is touching me. I don't pull away, but I don't melt into him like I'm dying to.

"Dinner," he said.

The synapses in my brain weren't really functioning as all I said was "Huh?"

Jaxon

I WAS close to embarrassing myself. The moment Brooklyn walked into the conference room, my cock jumped. Even in business attire, her body was perfect, curves in all the right places. I wondered if she knew the power she could have over men.

Before she recognized us, I studied her from head to toe. She was wearing a white, high collared button up shirt. It was tucked into a black pencil skirt that ended at her knees. The one thing that didn't feel all business was her sky heels. They made her legs look fabulous and I stared.

I saw the moment she recognized us and it was delicious to watch her cheeks turn a shade of pink. Her hand fluttered around, checking her appearance. It wouldn't have mattered if a hair was out of place in the twist she had on the top of her head. She was drop dead beautiful.

Even though Aiden was harsh before he left the room, I couldn't really blame him. We had been burned a few times because of the fame we garner and the money we had earned. But, Gideon's face was interesting and I planned to ask him about that later. The man could be a stone sometimes.

When Oliver invites Brooklyn to dinner, I freeze in my movements to leave the room. Aiden would think that this was a random fling for Oliver and I. But I knew it wasn't. After Brooklyn had bolted on us, we were both in shock. We of course followed, but we also didn't want to seem like we were chasing her.

I would be embarrassed if she knew that he and I had studied the outside surveillance multiple times, just trying to find a clue to who she was. We were able to connect her to another woman she had arrived with. But we hadn't gotten to matching names to credit card receipts. If we hadn't just stumbled on our blonde goddess today, we may have started really digging.

My memory of her was streaked with her smell and taste. The feel of her grinding against me, her hands on my neck, my mouth on her skin. I wouldn't admit it to anyone but I was damn jealous that Oliver kissed her. The look on his face afterward, told me it was worth every second we searched for her.

"Huh?" Brooklyn replied to Oliver's invitation.

I had to smile. She was definitely flustered and Oliver was

touching her, only making it worse. Oliver looked over at me and I gave a small nod.

"Have dinner with us both. We can discuss business over a meal, can't we?" He pressed.

"What about Aiden and the other partner?" She asked.

"The big guy is Gideon. Aiden trusts us to work this out. I'm sure we can come to an agreement," I replied.

Her ice blue eyes flashed over to me again and I button my jacket to make sure I don't look like a complete fool. My body responded to the presence of this woman like no other. Whatever it was, I wanted to try and get it out of my system. I couldn't handle getting hard every time a woman walked into the room.

"So, just the three of us, dinner?" She asked.

"I think that's best right now," Oliver replied.

I could tell by Oliver's tone that he was trying to be businesslike to get Brooklyn to agree. After what we had been through since she rabbited on us, I knew his mind wasn't on business in anyway. We both had obsessed over her in one way or another.

"Ok. Well, my schedule is fairly open. When works for you?" She asked.

She flipped back into business mode. She picked up her phone and started tapping away, presumably looking at her calendar. Oliver looked over me with a smile. I could see the wheels turning and knew this dinner was about much more than business.

I didn't even care what was on my calendar. Any night Brooklyn found available for us, I was dropping everything to be there. If I didn't think it would overwhelm her now, I'd be sitting on her other side, just to be close to her, to smell her again. God, I was such a creeper.

As I was tuned out, thinking about how lavender was such

a delicious smell, Oliver stood and was holding out his hand to help Brooklyn up. I saw her indecision and she hesitated before she allowed her fingers to slide into his palm. Oliver in his way, grinned goofily at her and bent over her hand, placing a kiss against her knuckles.

"Until tomorrow, Brooklyn. We'll pick you up. Text me your address," he said as he handed her his card.

His card was just like the rest of ours. A simple white, satin finished card, with our names, cell and the 4K logo at the bottom. Brooklyn stared at it for longer than was really needed to read the few lines of characters.

"Wait, your last name is Knight?" She suddenly asked.

Her mouth snapped shut as soon as the words were out, telling me she hadn't meant to say a word. I couldn't stay away any longer, so I took the few steps needed to get around the table. I handed her my card as well. Something in me wanted my number in her hands.

"All of us have the last name Knight," I said, as she studied my card as well.

She didn't reply right away, but her mind was flipping things over in her head. When she looked up at me, the blush was back and she fidgeted. I realized I was standing fairly close, but I couldn't force myself away.

"There's a story there, I'm guessing," she said quietly.

Oliver stepped up behind her, caressing her bare arm. Brooklyn jumped and the blush on her face deepened.

"You can ask your questions at dinner," he said quietly in her ear.

She just looked up at me and nodded. I took her other hand and placed a kiss on her palm. When I released her, she held her hand near her chest and I smiled. I had no idea why I did it, but damn I wanted my mouth on her again.

I stepped away and Oliver followed me to the door. We

both glanced back at her and I couldn't help smiling at the lost expression on her face.

"See you tomorrow night, love," I said before we made our way through the office.

We stood at the elevators and I tried to control my breathing. Oliver clapped me on the shoulder as the doors dinged open.

"Me too, brother. Me too," he said.

Just as the doors shut, our phones both dinged. Digging mine out of my pocket, I saw the Brooklyn had created a group text, sending her address to us both. I grinned and showed Oliver, who also smiled wide.

"What is it about her?" I asked.

"Fuck if I know. But I've never been so hot just being near a woman," Oliver said.

"Same. Aiden isn't going to be happy about this. But we can't just drop the non-profit. We all care too much about the work. And I have a feeling she knows what she's doing," I said.

We exited in the underground building parking garage. Oliver had driven separately to the meeting as he had a liquor emergency for the new club. We each had our area of business to handle and we saw each other as equal partners. It had been this way since we were kids, all of us knowing our lane, but working as a team.

Oliver handled all of the supplies, shipments, distribution to our clubs and pricing. He was good working deals with the vendors. Gideon was over security and the employment of people we could trust with the safety of the clubs and ourselves. Gideon had been our muscle since we were kids getting into scrapes, so it was a natural progression. Aiden was the business minded one, working with the finances and overall business operations.

My role was natural for me. I tended to be quiet and even with people. So I handed all of the human relations and employment with all employees other than security. I also handled any complaints that came in from our properties. I rarely allowed my emotions to get the best of me, knowing that if I stayed quiet the solution normally made itself known.

Oliver drove like a demon through the city, heading straight for home. We knew that was where Aiden and Gideon would be. We were going to have to break this plot twist to Aiden. I had no intentions of just giving up the chance to spend time with Brooklyn. Convincing him would take some work and likely some drinks.

CHAPTER
Seven

Oliver

THE TENSION of the meeting at KidsUpFirst was completely unexpected. I liked having a plan in place when I walked into something. Offering a property for a fundraiser was a no brainer for us. Not only would it be great publicity for 4K, it was also a cause close to our hearts.

I hadn't expected Aiden to react the way he did when I leaned over and whispered that the blonde Jaxon and I had been searching for had just walked into the room. She was looking ridiculously hot and flustered the moment she recognized us. That was a sign that our evening at the club affected her just like it did us.

Pulling up to our house, Jaxon just sits and stares out his window. I pulled my black, classic 1969 GTO into its space inside the garage and shifted into park. Jaxon still didn't make a move to get out of the car.

"He's gonna be unreasonable," he finally said.

"You know how he can be. He's always trying to protect us, the family. You can't really fault him for that," I replied.

"I really want to spend more time with her. I don't get it," he said.

"Me too. We'll convince him. She's professional. I think we can do both."

"She must care, to be working for the non-profit," Jaxon said.

"I have no doubt. Come on, let's go in and face the one man firing squad," I joked.

Jaxon rolled his eyes, but climbed out of the car. Our house was large, custom built after much discussion and searching for something that was perfect for all four of us. When we couldn't find what we wanted, we hired someone to design it with our ideas in place and then had it built. I was very proud of our home.

We entered through the garage, which led to a mudroom. I could already hear glasses clinking in the kitchen and knew we'd find Gideon doing dishes. He would become damn domestic when things didn't go right.

We had staff that handled a lot of the household chores. It was needed since we worked so much. But when Gideon was feeling a sort of way, he'd give them the evening off. Then you'd find him washing dishes, vacuuming and cleaning windows. Weirdo.

I walked into the kitchen and leaned against the counter to watch Gideon. He was elbow deep into a sink of water and soap.

"We have a dishwasher I think," I said.

Gideon just grunted.

"What's going on, brother?" Jaxon asked, as he grabbed a beer from the fridge.

Gideon didn't answer, just shrugged.

"Are you worried about Brooklyn too?" I asked.

"Who's Brooklyn?" Gideon asked.

"The blonde bombshell, our club mystery and now apparently a director at the non-profit we want to work with," Jaxon said.

Gideon just nodded in response to the information.

"We think she's fine. Business will work out with them. Jaxon and I are going to have dinner with her tomorrow night," I said, throwing in the last bit of information to get a reaction.

Gideon froze for a moment in his washing. He looked at me for a second, before diving back in with vigor. Water sloshed slightly and he cursed, jumping back before soaking his sweatpants.

"I think she gets to him too," Jaxon finally said, clapping Gideon on the shoulder.

"She doesn't get to me," Gideon mumbled.

I looked at Jaxon and we silently communicated for a moment. Gideon was less likely than either of us to find a woman to satisfy any cravings. He was more serious and usually looking for a connection before jumping in with a woman. If he was acting like this, there was definitely something going on. But he would have to come to it himself.

"Where's Aiden?" I asked.

"One guess," Gideon replied.

Of course. The only place Aiden went when he was worked up, was his home office, likely with a glass of something dark and strong. I didn't bother knocking when we got to the door. We didn't stand on formality in our home. When we entered, Aiden barely looked up.

"You guys work this all out? We pulling out of the event?" Aiden asked.

"Nope," Jaxon replied.

That got Aiden to look up. He took a sip from his glass tumbler and studied us over the rim.

"Nope you didn't work this out? Or nope we aren't pulling the event?" He asked.

"We believe her. She didn't know who we were in the club. Come on Aiden, if she had, do you think she would have seemed so shocked today?" I asked.

"She could be a good actress. We've seen it before," he shot back at me.

I cringed. He seemed to always bring Missy up whenever it would cut the deepest. In our home, we didn't talk about what I referred to as the Missy mishap. It was years ago, early on in our business. We hadn't made it big yet, when Missy came into our lives.

Looking back at it now, I knew we were young and impressionable. We had just purchased our first home together, a condo in an up and coming high rise in the city. It felt incredible to feel successful. We met Missy in the lobby of the high rise.

In the beginning, her attention was evenly spaced on each of us. We had never shared a woman before, but it came easily for us. We're brothers in all the ways that mattered and it just seemed to come naturally. Each of us fulfilled different needs Missy had.

However, it didn't take long for things to feel nefarious.

The idea of sharing her, had been Missy's idea to start. A few months into the relationship, some of our personal information was showing up on the internet. Things about our relationship with Missy, that made us look like we were using her or abusing her.

It was a definite bump in our early business success. Aiden hired a PR manager to wrangle the situation. Even then, he was still reassuring Missy that we would protect her and her reputation. It didn't take long for the PR manager and a private detective to realize where the private information was coming from. Directly from the source.

Missy had hoped to garner some sort of popularity through charity and sympathy in the public eye. We were not prepared for the emotion backlash from the relationship. I think Aiden was the most hurt, he thought he loved Missy. I knew I didn't, but I had thought it was possible I would grow to love her.

I moved to Aiden's wet bar and poured myself a drink. Turning to face him, I leaned back sipping the alcohol. The silence stretched between us. Jaxon stood and watched the two of us until he finally cleared his throat.

"We learned our lesson the same time you did. This is different. I can feel it," he said.

Aiden just grunted disapprovingly and turned back to his paperwork.

"Do you trust us?" I asked.

"That's not the point here and you know it," Aiden replied immediately.

I knew the answer before I asked the question, but I wanted him to say it out loud.

"So then, you should trust us to not fall into a trap. We're taking her to dinner. We'll discuss business, work out the details of this event. But I for one, need to know more about her."

"Need?" Aiden asked.

Frustrated, I run a hand through my hair. I glance at Jaxon, but he's not adding anything. I know he's feeling the same pull, but I'm typically the one that can talk to Aiden. I lighten things, joke, make things not such a big deal. Talking about Brooklyn, I couldn't think of any jokes to make.

"I don't know how to describe it, brother. She caught my eye immediately at the club. When I touched her, it was like there was a sizzle between us. I've never felt anything like it. I have to know why," I explain.

Aiden doesn't respond, just stares at me.

"I felt it too, man. Her skin, her smell, everything was so attractive. I really want to be around her again," Jaxon added.

Scrubbing his face with his hands, Aiden huffed and sat back in his office chair. He looked older all of a sudden, worn down. I knew he was working hard, but I realized it had been a while since I had checked in with him on business stuff. We always just stayed in our lanes, unless something crossed lines and we needed to have a company meeting.

I wanted to believe this didn't all connect back to Missy. But I couldn't remember a time since then that Aiden was close to a person that wasn't in our family. Not that the rest of us had been rushing to have committed relationships. We all were too busy to really try. So it was a revolving door of short stints with women who mostly just wanted to feel like they were with a powerful man.

"Look. If we get the feeling that this isn't going to work for business, we are both smart enough to recognize it and with-draw our application with KidsUpFirst. Trust us," I said.

Aiden doesn't look up, just nods his head and goes back to typing on his laptop. I looked over at Jaxon and sighed.

He shrugged his shoulders and walked out of the office. In the hallway, he paused and looked back at me.

"We're doing this?" He asked.

"Most definitely."

Getting ready for the dinner date, my hands were shaking as I buttoned my shirt. I chose a simple charcoal suit, with a white dress shirt. As I was tucking it in, Jaxon came in, wearing a lighter gray suit. He looked at me and cursed with a smile.

"Well, we're quite the pair," I said.

"I'm not changing," he replied.

I laughed and just shook my head as I shrugged into my jacket. I couldn't quite figure out why my stomach was all over the place. We didn't even know Brooklyn yet. But when I pictured her eyes and how they shifted through her emotions, I got excited to see her again. I wanted to watch every emotion I could evoke to play out across her face.

We decided that having a driver would be best for the evening. Neither of us admitted we were trying a bit too hard to impress her. Jaxon even appeared with a bouquet of flowers. I was pretty sure never in his life had he given a woman flowers. But here he was, cradling the bouquet on his lap, with his leg bouncing up and down.

"Nervous?" I asked.

I didn't want to feel like the only one completely overwhelmed. Normally, Jaxon was cool, calm and collected. But he couldn't seem to sit still in the back of the limo.

"A bit, yeah," he replied.

"What do you think it is about her?" I asked.

Jaxon looked over at me thoughtfully. We were silent for a long moment.

"I can't even pinpoint it. Was it the moment I saw her and couldn't help but notice how beautiful she was? Or was it the way she felt in my arms? Or how about the fire she had when she put Aiden in his place during the meeting? I have no idea," Jaxon replied.

I nodded. I didn't say anything. Because I couldn't argue any of the points. I didn't know when it started. At first, I thought her being the only woman that had ever run from me, made her interesting. That hadn't happened to any of us since we became well known and normally people wanted something from us.

However, I watched the security video more times than even Jaxon knew. I would watch her profile as she looked up and down the street for a cab. When she got into the car, I traced the shape of her leg as her dress slid up her thigh. When she walked into the conference room, all business, I could have choked on my tongue.

The limo slid to a stop outside a nondescript, nicely maintained, apartment building. We both climbed out of the limo, giving the driver quick instructions to just keep it running at the curb. At the door, we pressed the buzzer for her apartment and her voice came through the intercom. She confirmed who was there before buzzing us in.

I forced myself not to take the stairs two at a time. Jaxon seemed to have the same thought. We didn't want to look like we were chasing her again. When we got to her apartment door, I straightened my jacket and Jaxon knocked. When she opened the door, my mind went completely blank.

Brooklyn

REGRET WAS the first thing I felt. I was sure this dinner was the worst idea ever. But my brain was frazzled after being faced with the stars of my personal wet dreams. I had gone back into my office and buried my face in my hands, until the manager of events came in to find out what was going on.

The rest of the day was a drag of finalizing a few donor gifts and filtering through some new board member applications. We had two open spots and it was my job to come up with the best candidates to give to the President and the board to evaluate. By the time I left the office it was dark and I was feeling jumpy on the city streets alone.

When I got to my apartment, I rushed up the stairs and locked the door behind me with a slam. It had been almost a year since I moved in with Ash. Partially due to need and due to safety concerns. But I hadn't been completely alone since then.

I had leaned against the door and breathed through my unnecessary panic. I pushed scenes from my past out of my mind and focused on the exercises my therapist had given me. My cellphone rang at that moment and I almost dropped my purse when it startled me. When I saw it was Ash's name on the screen I was so happy to answer the call.

She was elated to have arrived to what would be her home for the next few months. She excitedly told me about her flights and how she somehow scored a first class seat for the longest leg and I laughed as she recounted all of the perks she made sure to take advantage of. Then, she asked me about my day.

I hesitated and she immediately knew something was up. When I told her the hotties from the club showed up for a donor meeting, I had to pull the phone from my ear as she squealed.

"This is a freaking sign!" She screamed.

"I don't believe in signs," I replied.

"Yes, I know. But you can't deny this. How insane that they are two of the Four Knights," Ash said.

"Four Knights? So that's what 4K stands for?" I asked.

"Brooklyn, do you live under a rock? I know you work way too much. And getting you out into the world is about impossible. But the Four Knights, yes the business is called 4K, are some of the hottest business men out there. They are called the

Club Kings of the city. I didn't actually know what they looked like, but I'll be Googling that now. I've just heard about them by reputation," Ash said.

I pulled off my heels and put them in our hall closet as she spoke. I had never heard of the Knights. But I found it interesting they all had the same last name. Was that for business purposes or something else?

"So is that a good reputation? Bad reputation?"

"Hot reputation. Like real hot. Business wise, they are super professional and successful. With women, well there's not much clarity around that," Ash said.

"What does that even mean? And why do you even know this?" I asked.

"Tabloids my friend, tabloids. They're all over them. But when it comes to relationships, there's never anything confirmed. So either they're celibate, gay or they don't do relationships," Ash replied.

Silence stretched on the call. I wasn't sure what to say to any of that. What did I even think this dinner was supposed to be?

"Brooklyn, did I lose you?" Ash finally asked.

"I'm here," I said into my cellphone. But I really wasn't there.

"Wait, why are you so interested in this? What's happening?"

"Well, I sort of, agreed to a dinner with Oliver and Jaxon," I replied.

The squealing started again and I pulled the phone from my ear. I waited until I heard it quiet down again before putting it back to my ear. When I did Ash was running through all of the things I needed to do, like shave my legs and pluck my eyebrows. She then started listing off the clothes I should wear.

By the time we said goodbye, I was exhausted from just thinking. After changing into sweats, I sat on the couch with my cellphone in my hands. I stared at it, debating texting Oliver and Jaxon that I needed to cancel. We could always reconvene the meeting in the office, keep it completely business and work out the event details. This dinner wasn't really necessary.

But, I couldn't even unlock my phone. My mind got lost in their looks when I walked into the meeting. They were both very pleased to see me. Even though I had run away from them like they were a house fire I was escaping from, they were still happy to see me. I would be lying to myself if I didn't admit to the hunger I saw in both of their eyes when they studied me. Did I want to deny myself that?

I spent the next day in my office, avoiding any heavy conversations. Every time I thought about seeing the guys for dinner, my palms would start to sweat and I would swear I was going to hyperventilate. Yet, I still didn't cancel. I just couldn't bring myself to being that girl, hiding away.

At home, I tried on almost every dress in my closet. Some were too business like. Some were too casual. I wanted to feel that I could be all business, in case this dinner was exclusively that. But I wanted to feel sexy and beautiful. I wanted Oliver and Jaxon to look at me like they did at the club.

I chose a sleeveless black sheath dress, that had a high collar but low V neckline. I wore a fancy necklace to hide the scar that ended just above my cleavage. I felt sexy and smart when I looked at myself in the mirror. I decided to twist my hair up on the top of my head, with a few pieces curled around my face.

As I was slipping on my heels, the buzzer rang and I almost fell over. Nerves shot through my system. When Oliver's deep voice came across the intercom, I had a split second feeling of indecision, of just not buzzing them up. But I shook myself out of that and hit the button.

I stood, fidgeting at the closed door, just waiting for them to knock. It felt like an eternity and when they finally did get to the door, I jumped a mile from the sound.

"Deep breaths, Brooklyn. It's just dinner," I whispered to myself before opening the door.

My mouth went completely dry as soon as the door swung open. Oliver and Jaxon were standing casually, right within reach. They wore different shades of gray suits, which made me smile. Delicious was the word that came to mind as I studied the exposed skin they each showed with a few buttons open at their necks.

Oliver stepped forward and kissed my cheek. His subtle vanilla scent flowed over me and he hesitated just for a moment, running a finger along my jaw. I had to fight the urge to close my eyes and lean into his touch. Part of me wanted a second act to the kiss we shared at the club.

Jaxon held out a beautiful bouquet of flowers, before kissing my other cheek. I shiver from the feeling of his 5 o'clock shadow against my skin. For a split second I wonder where else on my body I could feel that sensation. When he pulled away and meets my eyes, it's almost as if he can read my mind as a slow sexy smile crosses his face.

"Thank you for the flowers. They're beautiful. I'm going to put them in water really quick. Come on in," I said in a flurry.

I walk to the kitchen to dig out a vase and started to fill it up in the sink. I could see the men looking around the apartment. I didn't have much in the way of personal items in the main living room area. This was Ash's place before I moved in, so most of it was decorated already. There were a few photos of her and I in frames on our bookcase and that was the extent of me in the room.

Nerves struck me, suddenly feeling very self conscience having these men in my apartment. I tried to remember they invited me to dinner, they insisted on seeing me again. I put the flowers on the small dining table we rarely ever used. After fidgeting with the arrangement for a few moments, I knew I was running out of time.

For a moment I felt that same electric feeling from the club, the sensation of eyes on me. I spun to find both men watching me from near the door. Jaxon was relaxed with his hands in his pockets, though Oliver was looking a bit more tightly wound. I smoothed my hands down my dress and went to grab my clutch.

When I reached the guys again, Oliver reached out and took my free hand in his.

"You look beautiful," he said quietly.

"So do you," I said, meeting his intense gaze.

I watched as his eyes flicked down to my lips and back up to my eyes. At that moment we shared the same thought, remembering how it felt to be pressed together, our mouths fused, heat flowing through us. Without thinking, I licked my lips and a smirk appeared on Oliver's face.

"We should go," he finally said.

Jaxon opened the door for me and once we were all in the hall, I turned to lock my door. I double checked it like always and when I turned, Jaxon held out a hand to help me down the stairs. I walked the stairs in my heels everyday, but I couldn't stop myself from taking his hand.

Outside, a black stretch limo idled at the curb. A driver was standing at the backdoor and once we appeared, he opened the door. I looked at the guys with a surprised look. Oliver smiled and placed a hand on the small of back, guiding me to get into the limo first.

Inside, I chose a spot on the center of the seat that faced

forward. There were additional seats on either side of the vehicle. However, when the guys climbed in, they sat on either side of me, instead of sitting on a different bench seat. Their heat and scents were almost immediately overwhelming.

As the limo pulls away from the curb, Jaxon casually picked up my hand and laced our fingers together. Not a word is said, they both just sat casually as if this isn't the craziest thing that's happened to them. That was probably just me, knowing nothing like this could possibly happen to a woman like me.

I don't pull my hand away, enjoying the way his thumb sweeps over my skin. It actually calms the anxiety I'm feeling and I appreciate him seeming to understand. Oliver's leg pressed against mine and I try not to audibly gulp.

Thankfully, the drive to the restaurant wasn't a long one. The limo pulls up and Jaxon helps me out of the car. I freeze on the sidewalk in front of one of the most exclusive restaurants in the city. Ash once mentioned wanting to try it and we discovered if you weren't "somebody" your name wasn't getting on any list.

"We're eating here?" I asked.

"Is that alright?" Oliver asked, as his hand lightly touches my lower back again.

"Oh of course. It's just funny. My best friend always wanted to come here. She's going to be pretty annoyed with me," I replied with a smile.

Oliver's eyes light up with humor as Jaxon leads me by my hand toward the door.

"Well then I guess we better order a little of everything, so you can really tell her," Oliver joked.

Inside, the atmosphere was dim and romantic. It wasn't the type of place I would normally hold a business dinner. The guys were throwing off my control of the situation, both acting like this was a date and not a business dinner. Which was it? I wasn't even really sure.

As soon as we walked through the door, the maitre'd approached with a large smile and menus in hand.

"Mr Knight," He said, bowing slightly to Oliver, then turning to Jaxon with a bow as well, "Mr. Knight. We have your requested table ready. Please follow me."

With Oliver's hand never leaving the small of my back, we followed the maitre'd to a quiet, private table in the back of the restaurant. Jaxon waved off the maitre'd as he tried to pull out a chair for me. Instead, he did the duty himself, helping me slide into place. His hand brushed down my arm as he stepped aside to his seat.

I was handed a menu and Oliver ordered a bottle of wine without even checking the list in his hand. The maitre'd bowed again and rushed off. I had to laugh quietly behind my menu. Both men looked at me with bemused looks on their faces.

"Are you some sort of royalty I wasn't aware of?" I asked.

Oliver grinned and Jaxon just shook his head.

"I guess there are benefits to working as hard as we have," Jaxon replied.

I nodded, agreeing that hard work should be rewarded. I wasn't sure I could get used to the treatment I was seeing, but I could imagine it was nice. What I did know was hard work. I had done that most of my life.

Pushing away negative feelings, I studied the menu. There were so many unknown options to me, I felt overwhelmed. The wine was brought back and I watched as Oliver did the opening taste. I couldn't help but notice as his throat moved with the swallow. His skin was dark and smooth and I had the desire to touch it.

I had studied my menu for too long when Jaxon spoke up.

"How about we order some of all the best dishes. We can share, if that works for you?"

I shot him a grateful look and nodded. Wine was poured for each of us and I took a long sip, hoping to soothe the rolling in my stomach. The silence was heavy, but not exactly uncomfortable. It felt charged with unasked questions and desires.

"Should we talk about the event you're proposing?" I finally said, wanting to get the business accomplished.

"Getting to the point, huh?" Oliver asked with a smile.

"I mean, sure. That's why we're here, right?" I asked, uncertainty lacing my voice.

"Brooklyn, do you believe business is the only reason we asked you to dinner?"

CHAPTER
Nine

Brooklyn

SUDDENLY, I was feeling unsure of myself and what I had gotten myself into. What was I doing at dinner with not one, but two men. Powerful men, who were used to getting what they wanted. Two men that turned me on in a way that made me feel like a spotlight would break through my skin. And two men, that did all this to me, and I was supposed to be discussing business with them.

I fell back onto what I knew I could do, business.

"I wanted to reassure you that KidsUpFirst appreciates your generous donation. We would also like to continue the partnership with our annual event. Once you give us the details of the property you'd wish to allow us to use, we can plan the event around that," I said, repeating the speech I had practiced all day in my office.

Both men watched me and Oliver nodded finally.

"All of that works for us," he said.

"And Aiden?" I asked.

"We've discussed it with him. This is an important cause to us all," Oliver said.

"Can I ask why you chose KidsUpFirst?" I asked.

Oliver and Jaxon shared a small look. An understanding passed between them and Jaxon sighed before speaking.

"Aiden, Gideon and the two of us grew up together basically. From the time we were young teens, we had fallen in together. Our lives weren't what you would consider easy or healthy. It took a lot for us to figure out how to get out of the life we were all born into. Many kids don't figure it out, don't have opportunities to leave. They die, or spend lifetimes in prison. Education wasn't something most kids we knew actually appreciated or wanted. But the four of us, we had each other. And in that, we knew we could work together to make a better life for ourselves."

"We've been together ever since. So, when we decided to find a non-profit to support, our thoughts went directly to kids that are growing up the way we did. KidsUpFirst does things for kids, that we would have died to get. We never got that help when we were kids. So, if we can make a difference for any of them now, we want to," Oliver added.

"Is this why you all have the same last name? You aren't really related by blood?" I asked.

"That was Aiden's idea when we first got into business.

Maybe it was a silly symbol. But for us, we're brothers in the ways that matter. And we wanted a way to show that," Jaxon replied.

"It's not silly at all," I said.

The men smiled at me and hearing a little about them was doing funny things to my thoughts. I hadn't assumed they were born with a silver spoon in their mouths, they seemed too rough for that. However, I hadn't expected them to be more like me than I knew.

"And you? Why do you work there?" Jaxon asked.

I studied him over the rim of my wine glass. I quickly swallowed the last sip and slid the glass toward Oliver, who had the bottle.

"I'll need some more wine for that conversation," I said.

"Oh, by all means," Oliver replied with a laugh.

With a full glass back in my hand, the men both looked at me, waiting for my explanation. Just as I was going to open my mouth, a waitress brought a number of plates. Once she settled them in the center, she stood and smiled at the men. I watched her with interest, imagining the Knights likely received more attention than they wanted.

When the waitress continued to fuss with the plates and trying to lay napkins in the laps of Oliver and Jaxon, I sat silently. I kept my face neutral, but as I watched her lean too close to Oliver to help him with his napkin, I was shocked at the feeling of jealousy that went through me.

Who was I to feel jealous about these men. We shared a few dances, one hot as sin kiss and some business. I sucked the feeling back and waited. Both of the men were kind but cool to the woman. She eventually took the hint and left the table.

Looking at all of the foods, I wasn't even sure where to start. Jaxon, clearly someone that was used to taking care of people, pushed a plate my way where he had put one of everything. I smiled at him and took a bite and my smile widened as flavor exploded in my mouth.

We ate in silence for a while, and as the plates became empty they were quickly cleared away.

"You were going to tell us why you work for the non-profit," Oliver reminded.

I cleared my throat with a drink of water and tried to think of the best way to answer their question.

"I guess I'm a bit like you all. I grew up in and out of foster care. I know how much of a failure that system is. I had to figure out life for myself when I turned 18 and it wasn't an easy path. Working with KidsUpFirst, helping build it from the time I was an intern, to now, makes me feel like I'm doing something to help kids that are like me," I finish.

There's so much more I could say. Like the fact that my mother was a raging alcoholic and there were days I worried I would end up just like her. That I was taken away from her and given back more times than I could count. That I barely even remembered what my father's face looked like, nor did I have any idea of where he was.

It was all too heavy for a business slash dinner date. Especially with two of the most successful men in the city. It was easier to look at them, knowing they came from similar beginnings as I did.

"What ideas did you have for the event you would hold at Club 4?" Oliver asked.

"We've done a number of things in the past. Auctions, parties, art galleries. Now that I know you're suggesting Club 4, I'm thinking a masquerade party," I replied with a wide smile.

"So masks and dancing? This could be fun," Oliver joked.

"I have an idea for a fundraiser, if you'd humor me," Jaxon said.

"Of course. I welcome all of your ideas," I replied without hesitation.

I found that it was true. I was at ease with the men. They were successful and well known, however they acted personable and interested in KidsUpFirst. A little more of me warmed toward them knowing the cause was as important to them as it was to me.

"How about auctioning dances off to well known actors or members of society? I have a list of people that I think would bring in good money. And with the masks, it would be all fun and games," Jaxon explained.

We spent the time between our main course and dessert continuing to work out the details of the party. I was excited to get the information to my manager of events. I knew she would be over the moon with something so creative and out of the box from our normal events. Our president would appreciate the attention it would bring, especially being held at Club 4.

The act of sharing a meal with the guys, felt intimate and personal. As promised, they had ordered a few meals and we shared them family style. Each of them found ways to casually touch me or feed me a bite of their food. Jaxon reached over as if to wipe something from my lip, and his thumb lingered longer than necessary. Oliver's hand brushed my bare knee and a slight squeeze pulled my gaze to his.

Each brush of skin, every sensual gaze, their attention to our shared time, had my blood buzzing. In the back of my mind, I appreciated that I wasn't drunk this time. I could focus on how my body reacted to them and the reality of what I was truly feeing and not the effects of alcohol and a dark club. It was just as intense, if not more, now.

As dessert was being served, I excused myself to the ladies room. Both men stood as I did, and I was speechless at the respectful gesture. My dating experience was very limited. However, I had never been treated as if I was this important by anyone. I smiled shyly at them and escaped for a moment to the bathroom to allow myself to cool down.

Alone, I leaned on the marble bathroom counter, hanging my head. Taking deep breaths, I avoided the need to splash cold water on my face. I didn't want to have completely ruined makeup when I went back to the table. Once I felt like I was slightly under control, I walked briskly from the bathroom.

Jaxon was leaned against the wall in the dark bathroom hallway. I pulled up short when I saw him, looking around trying to figure out if he was waiting in a line for the bathroom.

"I'm waiting for a beautiful woman to come out of the bathroom," he said in response to my unasked question.

Without hesitation I smiled and said, "Well I was alone in there, so you're out of luck."

He returned my smile and slowly walked toward me. He crowded me with his body and I couldn't stop myself from stepping back. My back hit the wall and Jaxon leaned an arm above my head. He dips his head and runs his nose along my cheek, to my ear.

"I can't stop thinking about it," he whispered roughly.

"Can't stop thinking about what?" I asked.

My voice is a breathy whisper, that I don't recognize. Without thinking, I run my hands up his chest, under his suit jacket, to grip his shoulders. When I dig my nails in slightly, a growl comes from his throat.

"That kiss that Oliver got to share with you the other night. You ran off, before I got a taste," he answered.

Pulling back, he rubbed his nose along mine for a moment before meeting my gaze. His eyes were dark with desire and heat pooled deep in my belly. I licked my lips in anticipation and his gaze caught the movement. But he didn't move in closer.

"What are you waiting for?" I asked.

"The moment when I know I am capable of stopping at just a kiss."

Those words undid me and I crashed my lips to his without another word. His hand tangled in the hair at the nape of my neck, pressing me closer. Our tongues dueled, teeth scraping at lips, each of us swallowing the other's gasps and moans.

One of Jaxon's hands trailed down my side, along the side of my breast, over my hip. When he reached the bottom of my dress, his fingers danced along my bare skin, lifting the hem to reach further up. My mind misfired, wanting to forget we were in the bathroom hallway of an expensive restaurant, wanting nothing more than his dancing fingers to find their way to the place I needed him most.

A throat clearing, had me pulling away from Jaxon to look down the hallway. Oliver stood there, with a grin on his face. Jaxon didn't seem to mind the intrusion, as he began to kiss down the left side of my neck. I gasped when his teeth nipped my ear, but my eyes were on Oliver.

"You were right brother, she's delicious," Jaxon said, pulling his face from my neck.

Oliver made his way to where we stood, Jaxon still pressed against me, and I had a moment of insecurity. What was I doing kissing two brothers? What was Oliver thinking of me, finding me making out with his brother in this dark hallway?

As he got closer, I was able to see the heat coming from his gaze. There wasn't jealousy, or disgust on his face. Jaxon went back to my neck, his fingers still working their way up my thigh. When his fingers grazed over rough skin on my upper thigh, I grimaced and tensed. Jaxon's whole body went still, as he felt my response to his touch.

"What is it, love?" He whispered the question into my ear.

"I'm not...I have...scars," I said quietly.

Jaxon pulled back to look at me in the eyes. His gaze was intense and he searched for something I wasn't willing to explain yet. His other hand, came from the back of my neck to cradle my cheek. He then kissed me sweetly.

"We all have scars, love," he said against my lips.

A hand tilted my chin to the side, and Oliver's face lowered to replace Jaxon's. His kiss seared my lips and his tongue licked at the inside of my mouth. I moaned into him as one of his hands came up to cup my breast, his thumb sliding over the fabric where my nipple pebbled beneath my dress and lace of my bra.

"I asked them to pack up dessert. I think we should take this elsewhere," Oliver said.

His voice was deep and gravely. Pressing another rough kiss to my lips, he stepped back, making space for Jaxon to release me. I felt the absence of his heat immediately and my body yearned for it to come back.

Indecision warred with the need these men were creating in me. It was clear, if we were alone, things were going to go much further. I looked between the two of them, never wanting anything more in my life. If this was going to be the one chance I had, I knew I would regret not taking it.

I summoned the courage to speak.

"Let's go to my place."

Brooklyn

WHEN I SPOKE, Jaxon and Oliver looked at each other briefly, before nodding to me. My place felt like the right idea. I didn't know where they lived, but I didn't want to risk running into Aiden.

He didn't seem to believe I was separating business and pleasure, but I was quite capable of doing my job. My attraction to Oliver and Jaxon wasn't going to prevent me from running the masquerade event.

Oliver turned on his heel, I assumed to track down a waiter and pay the check. Jaxon threaded his fingers through mine, bringing my hand to his mouth. His lips were soft against my knuckles and the change in him warmed me even further.

Jaxon led me through the restaurant and I felt myself blushing. I knew my hair was probably disheveled from his hands. My make up was probably completely mused. I was thankful for the dim lighting as we wound through the tables of other diners.

Outside, the limo was already waiting for us and Jaxon opened the door for me before the driver could round the vehicle. Inside, he gave instructions to the driver and immediately put up the privacy screen.

It only took a few moments for Oliver to join us, a pretty white bag in his hand with dessert. Once inside, the limo pulled away from the curb and Jaxon pulled me into his lap. My arms went around his neck and he pulled me down to kiss. His free hand went back to the leg where he found my scarred thigh.

"Tell me, what happened?" He asked against my cheek.

Oliver moved to the floor of the vehicle, turning me on Jaxon's lap so he could push my dress up. My scarred thigh was barred and I froze, feeling insecurity well up. The limo was dim, but as we drove, the lights of the city lit up interior well enough.

Without waiting for me to answer, Oliver bent to my lap and began to feather kisses over the raised skin. His tongue snaked out and heat overwhelmed the worry I felt.

"Tell us, babe," Oliver whispered against my thighs.

I wanted to shift, wanted to pull Oliver to the place I needed him most. But it felt too bold, too beyond what I was experienced with. So I sat still and decided to just tell the truth.

"It's a burn. I was like five or six. My mom hadn't fed me in days. I can't really remember everything that happened that day. I didn't understand at that age that my mother was a raging alcoholic and drug addict. All I knew was there were days she didn't wake up. That day I decided to try and make mac n' cheese. Ya know, the box stuff with powder?" I explained.

Oliver nodded at my thigh, before returning his mouth to my skin. I gasped, as his head went higher, pushing my dress further up my thighs. Jaxon helped, by pulling the material from the top.

"What's wrong, love? Can't focus?" Jaxon asked, a chuckle in his voice.

I gulped and tried to remember where I was in the story. Jaxon moved me on his lap, spreading my legs on the outside of his. He then spread his legs wider, making room for Oliver between my thighs. I glanced up at the privacy screen, suddenly worried about someone seeing us.

"It's ok. Not only can the driver not see, but he's also very discreet," Jaxon said, reading my mind.

I nodded before continuing. "I was too short. I got the pot of water off the stove, but when I went to drain the boiling water in the sink, somehow the pot got caught and the water spilled back on me instead. My mother didn't wake up when I screamed and my skin continued to burn until a neighbor heard me and called the police. I think that was the first time I was taken away from her."

Both of the men had stopped and were just caressing me sweetly. I was a little stunned with myself for telling them the full story. I didn't often talk about my past. But if these men were going to see me without clothes, there would be questions. I had too many marks with stories behind them. And the burns on my thigh weren't the worst of them.

"So beautiful," Oliver muttered, as he began to kiss my

thigh again.

This time, he didn't stop his progression. I found myself arching toward his mouth and I heard him chuckle. I tried to not let my inexperience or nerves get in the way of what I knew was happening. I had imagined so many scenarios, starring these two men. I wanted what was happening badly.

Oliver's kisses arrived at the apex of my thighs. I felt his lips over the satin of my panties and I gasped. Jaxon turned my head toward him and his mouth captured mine. Oliver's fingers joined his mouth and his pulled my panties to the side. He ran one finger through my outer lips and he groaned.

"Brother, she is soaked," he said.

Jaxon smiled against my mouth, and one of his hands joined Oliver's. Jaxon ran a fingertip around my clit and dipped shallowly into my center before pulling away. He leaned back from me and I watched as he sucked my juices from his finger.

"She's delicious everywhere, brother," Jaxon said.

I sucked in a breath as my heart sped up in my chest. I wasn't sure I would survive this drive. Just as I was on the edge of begging Oliver to put his mouth on me, the limo stopped. I could just see my apartment building through the tinted window.

"Ah, saved by the driver," Oliver laughed lightly.

"I'm not sure I wanted to be saved," I said, boldness coming out as I looked down at Oliver, meeting his gaze.

With his eyes on mine, he lowered his mouth and ran his tongue along my folds. Before he pulled away he circled my clit and I threw my head back on Jaxon's shoulder. Oliver then sat back on his feet, pulling my dress down again. On his knees, he grabbed my chin, forcing my mouth to his.

"We aren't done yet, babe," Oliver said.

I could taste myself on his tongue and it was a sensation I

had never experienced before. All of this was so overwhelming and new. I was practically panting and feeling a need that I couldn't understand. My sexual experiences were limited and never adventurous.

Once I was covered, Oliver went to the door and climbed out of the limo. He held a hand out and helped me climb from Jaxon's lap to the sidewalk. Jaxon joined us and I saw him adjust himself. The driver came around the car, a professional look on his face, not indicating he had any idea what was going on in the back of the vehicle.

"Sirs, should I wait here?" He asked.

Oliver looked over at me, directing the question to me. His eyes burned with fire and I was lost in the lust he was creating in me.

"Should he wait for us, Brooklyn?"

I looked between the men, trying to decide if I was ready to throw caution to hell and drag them both upstairs. When Jaxon's fingers played along the shell of my ear, a shiver ran down my body and I decided to take what I wanted for once, without worrying about the consequences.

"No. You won't need the car tonight," I said quietly.

Oliver smirked at me before turning to the driver to share a quick conversation. Jaxon stepped closer to my body, pressing himself to my side.

"So, are you inviting us up, love?" He asked.

"Do you want to come up?" I countered.

Jaxon took my hand and slid it down his stomach to the front of his dress pants. My eyes shot up to his as I felt his hard cock, straining to get out of its restraints. I tightened my hand for a moment, and his breath came out in a hiss.

"I absolutely want to come up," he replied.

The power that I felt, knowing I made him feel that way, made my hips sway a bit more as I climbed the stairs. I could feel them both watching my body as they walked behind me. I knew that I was taking a risk by having them over, I was not the one night stand type of woman. But something about them made it impossible for me to turn away from knowing how hot being with them would be.

At the door, I fished my keys from my clutch, but almost dropped them, when Oliver pressed me to the door from behind. His hand came up and caged my throat and he pulled me against him. When his mouth went for the right side of my neck, I froze. He immediately felt the change and his movements stopped.

"Babe?" He asked quietly.

"It's nothing. Sorry. Let me get the door open before my neighbors start getting a free show," I said, stumbling over the words as I tried to get the keys into the door.

His hand slid down the front of me, until he had my hand in his, steadying it. With his help, we got inside the apartment and Jaxon closed the door and flipped the lock without taking his gaze off me. I dropped my clutch on the coffee table and turned to look at them, suddenly overwhelmed with nerves.

Oliver came toward me slowly and I willed myself not to move. His hand came up to softly massage my shoulders. He slid a hand to the back of my head and pulled my mouth to his. The kiss started softly, his tongue barely tracing my lips. I opened my mouth, allowing his tongue to find mine and he sensually licked at me. My hands came up to grip at his jacket, pulling him toward me.

Jaxon moved from behind me, gripping my hips, to pull my ass against him. It felt just as it was in the club, my body cradled between them, heat pulsating between us. The feeling was intoxicating and it gave me courage that I didn't think I had.

I released Oliver's jacket and slid my hands under, pushing

the garment off his shoulders. He released me to allow it to fall. I immediately went to the buttons on his shirt and yanked the ends from his pants. Bare skin appeared and I couldn't stop my hands from slipping along his chest and down his abs, his muscles tensing under my touch.

He was perfectly sculpted. I ran my hands over his skin, feeling the soft bristle of body hair as I shifted to touch his abs. He had the perfect V that women always drooled over, it was probably the first one I had seen in real life that made me want to drop to my knees and lick.

"Bedroom," Jaxon said against my ear.

Pushing slightly against Oliver, he didn't move. Instead, his hands went down to my hips, then under my ass, where he lifted me, until I had no choice but to wrap my legs around his waist. I leaned my mouth down and slanted it over his, kissing him deeply.

"Room," he muttered against me.

I nodded and pointed toward my door, dropping my face against the skin of his neck and shoulder, kissing and nipping. I reached an arm blindly behind me, and Jaxon caught my fingers.

"I'm here, love," he said, kissing my palm.

In my room, Oliver set me on the edge of my bed. He shrugged his shirt the rest of the way off and dropped it to the ground. Jaxon laid his jacket across the chair in my room. I stood to go to him and slowly unbuttoned his shirt as he watched me. Oliver's fingers found the zipper on my dress and he slowly pulled it down.

When the black material puddled around my feet, I stepped out of it. I stood in front of both men in my lace black bra, matching thong and stiletto heels. My hand slowly crept up, to cover the scar that was now bared for them to see, but Jaxon stopped me.

"Tell us about this one?" He asked, as he traced the scar lightly with his finger.

Blood, fear and nightmares flashed in my mind and I shook my head. I couldn't talk about that tonight. I couldn't let my past ruin what was happening right in front of me.

"Not right now," I whispered.

Jaxon didn't argue, just nodded. He leaned down and starting just below my right ear, he placed light kisses. When he followed the scar to near my breast, he ran his tongue along it as well. I couldn't help my hands when they came up to bury in his dark hair, pulling him against me.

His mouth closed over one of my taunt nipples, through the lace containing it and I arched into him. Oliver's fingers found the clasp to my bra and I allowed it to fall to the ground as well. Jaxon's shirt joined the bra and I ran my fingers down the tribal tattoo along his ribs that I had never seen. It connected to his tattoo sleeved arm and I found it extremely attractive. The black ink swirled and hugged his muscles as if he was born with it.

From behind, Oliver's hand skimmed up my stomach and cupped one of my breasts. I gasped as Jaxon leaned down to capture the other in his mouth. The heat of his tongue circling my nipple sent shocks through my body. I held onto Jaxon, in fear that my knees would buckle.

Oliver slowly moved us toward the bed. When my knees hit the mattress, I sat abruptly. Jaxon reached up and took my hair out of the twist it was in, allowing my hair to fan around my shoulders.

"Beautiful," he murmured.

I could feel a blush warming my skin and I fought the urge to cross my arms across my bare chest. Jaxon crouched to his knee and slipped off my heels. He kissed my ankle and up my calf. When he got to my thigh, he reached up and slid my thong down my legs, letting it fall to the floor as well. I was feeling incredibly exposed but the ache in my core was begging for release.

Reaching for Oliver, I fumbled with his belt and he helped me strip him of his pants. There was no hiding how badly he wanted me and I felt like a fool not knowing what I should do. He crawled up to lay next to me on the bed, kissing down my chest and sucking a nipple into his mouth. I cried out as I arched off the bed. At the same time, Jaxon pushed my thighs apart and kissed my outer folds.

I couldn't help the gasp that fell from my lips. My imagination and the porn Ash forced me to watch was all I knew about having a man go down on me. In my limited experience, sex hadn't been adventurous or incredibly fulfilling. I had never craved anything, the way I wanted Oliver and Jaxon. And most definitely, I had never been with more than one man at a time.

Using his thumbs, Jaxon spread me for him and his tongue flicked out and stroked along my sex. I gripped the blanket under me, shaking as he continued to explore with his tongue. When he dipped into me, I began to move my hips with his movement. I could feel the vibration of his groan as I did, making me feel like I was doing something right.

Oliver let my nipple pop from his mouth, before he lavished the other with the same attention. The sensation of two mouths on me, was almost more than I could handle. As if sensing the build up happening in my core, Jaxon flattened his tongue and found my clit, circling it and flicking it in rhythm with the movements of my hips.

As my pleasure rose and the peak was within reach, I couldn't stop the moans that left my mouth. I had never sounded so wanton before and I kinda loved it. As my orgasm ripped through me I couldn't keep my thighs from trying to close on Jaxon.

"Oh my god, oh god!" I cried out.

Jaxon looked up at me, grinning as he pinned my legs open. Oliver looked down at him and I saw how he adjusted himself in his boxer briefs. I reached down and ran my hand along his shaft and Oliver groaned as he twitched in my palm. Jaxon stood, dropping his pants in the pile with the rest of our clothes. My eyes widened when I realized Jaxon was commando and his cock sprang out, thick and hard.

Both men crawled up the bed and Oliver pulled me up to the center. They laid on either side of me and I looked back and forth, not sure what to do. I didn't have long to be confused, as Oliver's mouth crashed against mine and he pulled my hip so I was facing him. He pulled my leg over his hip and his hand slid to my center. He circled my clit with his fingertip and I jumped, feeling sensitive still from my release. Then he slowly slipped his finger into me.

Oliver pumped his finger once, then again before adding a second finger. I cried out against his lips and my hips flexed against his hand. Without losing our connection, Oliver shifted me to my back again, where Jaxon waited to capture my lips. My hand found his hardness and I circled it with my fingers, squeezing softly before slowly stroking him.

"Love, you can't keep doing that, or I'm going to embarrass myself," he said against my lips.

I had to smile, feeling powerful, having this effect on two beautiful men. I immediately knew I needed more. Turning to look at Oliver, I reached down to pull his boxer briefs off his hips. He helped by pulling them the rest of the way and throwing them across the room.

"I need you," I whined, as Oliver continued to finger me, building the pressure again.

CHAPTER
Eleven

Oliver

MY BRAIN WASN'T FUNCTIONING CORRECTLY, but I knew what she had said. I nodded to her, not even able to think about telling her no. I slipped my fingers from her dripping wet heat, bringing them to my lips. I let her watch me, as I sucked her desire from my skin. Her eyes widened, her pupils dilating as she watched.

I looked over at Jaxon and he nodded to me. We hadn't really discussed this, how we would do this with Brooklyn.

Sharing wasn't something we had a problem with, I just didn't realize it would be happening tonight. When I saw her with Jaxon in the hallway at the restaurant, I knew immediately we would end up here.

Now, she was begging for us. She turned to kiss Jaxon again and I fished a condom from my wallet. I threw another near Jaxon, because I knew he would likely need it before the night was over. I slid the condom on, before returning to Brooklyn.

She was on her side, facing Jaxon. He pulled her top leg over him and I nestled behind her. I kissed her back and shoulder, running my tongue along the shell of her ear. She moaned into Jaxon's mouth and ground her ass back toward me.

"Babe, you sure?" I said into her ear.

She pulled from Jaxon's kiss long enough to look at me over her shoulder.

"Yes, Oliver, please. Make me feel good," she begged.

I pulled her hips back toward me and I carefully nudged her entrance with my cock. She moaned and pushed back, pulling me into her. Slowly, I slid into her. She was so tight and clamped down hard on my cock. I had to breathe for a long moment to make sure I didn't explode immediately.

Brooklyn wasn't one for patience it seemed, as she started to rotate her hips and push back on me. I grabbed her to still her as I pulled out and slammed back in.

"Yes! Fuck," she cried out.

"I don't know if I can go slow, babe," I gritted through my teeth.

"Don't, oh god, please don't go slow," she whined.

With her permission, I slowly pulled out of her again and slammed deep. With each thrust she moved against Jaxon and he groaned as her hand pumped his cock between them.

"Brother, help her come," I said.

Jaxon reached down and I knew the moment he found her clit because Brooklyn's pussy pulsed around my cock and I could barely hold my own orgasm. Being inside her was the best thing I could remember ever experiencing and I never wanted it to end. I knew that moment I could die and be completely ok with it.

Brooklyn leaned her face into Jaxon's chest as she cried out with her release. The squeezing of my cock was the last thing I could handle and I thrust two more times before spilling myself into the condom. I sat buried in her for a moment, before I carefully slid out. I removed the condom and put it with a Kleenex on the floor.

She rolled over to me and I kissed her deeply, burying my hand in her long blonde hair. When I pulled back she looked up at me with a small smile. She then turned back to Jaxon, the condom in her hand. Without a word, she pushed Jaxon to his back and tore open the condom wrapper. Her hands shook as she slipped the condom onto him and Jaxon reached down to help her.

He took her hand and guided her to straddle him. She lifted herself up on her knees and reached down to position him at her entrance. Slowly, she lowered herself and Jaxon lifted his hips at the same time. She leaned down to kiss him and he pulled his hips down and then pressed back into her.

"Oh god, so deep," she groaned as he did it again.

When she leaned up again and began to slowly ride him, I knelt next to her, capturing her mouth with mine. She was so beautiful, her breasts rising and falling with each of her thrusts. Jaxon held one of her hands, helping her control her movements. Her other buried in my hair and pulled me closer to her.

I slid my hand down her pinched one of her nipples, causing her to gasp into my mouth. Jaxon used his other hand to rub against her clit as she continued to ride him. Her movements became more erratic as she got closer to orgasm. Her skin was slick and I kissed along her neck, down her scar to her breast, pulling her nipple into my mouth. She cried out and slammed down on Jaxon.

Jaxon thrust up once more before groaning and orgasming with her. Brooklyn collapsed on his chest and everyone was breathing heavily. I pushed down my desire that had started to build again. This wasn't the night to overwhelm Brooklyn.

Carefully, I pulled her to lay between us, spooning her from behind. She laid her head on Jaxon's chest and pulled my arm around her hips. I felt her body relaxing as she fell asleep.

"What are we going to do?" Jaxon whispered.

"Brother, I have no idea," I replied.

I knew what he was getting at. Neither of us had been looking for something real, something serious. Since Missy, everything had been just for fun. However, I knew Brooklyn wasn't that. And it wasn't just because we were doing business with her company. I didn't want tonight to be all we had.

I fell into a restless sleep, thinking about the unknowns. At some point, Brooklyn rolled in her sleep and I woke with her in my arms, her leg between mine. Jaxon was snuggled behind her, asleep with a quiet snore. I buried my face in her hair and fell back to sleep more soundly.

A buzzer woke us early in the morning. Brooklyn groaned and stretched. The buzzer went off again and I opened my eyes as Brooklyn started to climb out of bed. I reached out to pull her back into bed, but she dodged me and looked back with a shy smile.

"It's the door. I'll be back," she whispered.

I watched her walk around the room naked, until she was wrapped in a robe and heading to the living room. I heard the murmur of voices. A few moments later the door opened and closed. And then there was nothing but silence and Brooklyn didn't appear again.

Jaxon and I shared a concerned glance. We both climbed out of bed, sorting through our clothes. Once we both had pants on, we went into the living room. Brooklyn was at the dining table with her back to us. There was a large bouquet of flowers on the table and her shoulders were hunched.

"Do we have competition?" I asked in a joking tone.

Brooklyn spun and it was then I saw how pale she was. Immediately concerned I started across the apartment. Brooklyn didn't focus on me or Jaxon as she turned back to the flowers. She picked up the entire arrangement and took them into the kitchen. I got into the room just as she dropped the entire thing into the trash. When they didn't fit she started shoving the flowers down with her hands.

I pulled her away and made her face me. She was clearly upset by the flowers. When she turned her eyes to me, there was a wild look, of fear and panic on her face. I looked down at her hands and saw little red cuts popping up. I guided her over to the kitchen sink and turned on the water.

"Babe, you have a first aid kit around? We need to clean these," I said calmly.

"My bathroom, under the sink," she whispered.

Jaxon heard her and headed back to get the supplies. I carefully pulled Brooklyn's arms under the water. Using the soap by the sink, I softly washed the scrapes, finding most of them shallow and not in the need of anything. When Jaxon returned with the first aid kit, we dried her arms and put bandaids on the ones that didn't stop on their own.

We took her into the living room to sit on the couch. Her body trembled between us, but she sat ramrod straight. Her eyes darted everywhere, except to look at us. Her blonde hair was mussed and I wished we were back in bed, with her having that beautiful just had the best orgasm of her life look. Now she looked antsy, disheveled and far away from us.

Jaxon tried to reach out to take her hand, but she shot up to her feet. Her hands were clutching at her robe, closing it around her chest and her neck. For a moment, I noticed how her fingers touched her long scar and then she pulled the robe closed to hide it again. I had so many questions, but it was clear now was not the time to ask any of them.

"I'm sorry. Um, I need to get ready for work. You should go," she stammered.

Kicked out of bed the next morning, wasn't a typical reaction I got to staying over at a woman's house. Effectively, that was exactly what Brooklyn was doing. I stood and tried to go to her, but she stepped back and held out her hand, to ward me off. Freezing, I felt a weight on my chest I hadn't expected.

"Again, I'm sorry. But this isn't a good time. Last night was great. I look forward to our future work," she said, in the most business tone I'd heard from a woman I had been balls deep in just hours before.

I wasn't necessarily offended, but I was actually hurt. Which was strange for me. Something in the way she had given herself over to us, the way she had pleaded for me to make her feel good, it felt more personal than a one night stand. Brooklyn, perfect with all her self perceived imperfections, was burrowing under my skin and she didn't even mean to.

"We'll go. Maybe we can call you later?" Jaxon asked, as he moved to grab my jacket which had fallen on the floor last night.

"I'll be in the office. I have a lot of work and I'm already running late," she said.

Jaxon nodded, like me, realizing right then wasn't the time to argue. He disappeared into her room for a moment and came out with an arm full of clothes. We quickly sorted ourselves so we could leave, while Brooklyn stood, staring out the window. I stared at her back and Jaxon nudged me, to point to the door.

I couldn't just leave. It felt wrong. Quietly, I approached her, and when my hands touched her arms, she stiffened and started to pull away. I couldn't handle that, and against my best judgement, I pulled her back against my chest instead. Not turning her and not making her answer any questions, but wanted her to feel I was there for her.

Brooklyn didn't pull away, but she didn't melt into me like she had before. I did feel her body as she sighed, but no words were spoken. I kissed her temple before gently letting her go and joining Jaxon near the door.

"We're here for you, love. Call us if you want," Jaxon said.

Suddenly, she spun around and for a moment hope flared in my chest. Tears were shimmering in her eyes, but she had control and wasn't willing to allow them to fall.

"Could you do me a favor? I'm sorry to ask," she started.

"Anything," I replied, interrupting her.

"Could you take the trash with you?"

At the trash shoot in the hall, I held the offending bag away from me. It was light, the only thing in it the vase and flowers that arrived that morning. The flowers were gorgeous, even slightly expensive. However, it was clear that whoever sent them wasn't someone that would be threatening our relationship with Brooklyn. If you could even call it a relationship.

"Wait, don't toss it yet," Jaxon said.

He pulled open the bag and fished around carefully, trying not to cut himself on any thorns. He pulled out a small card, reading it and then motioning me to toss the bag. He handed me the card next and I read it aloud.

"Bee, You know how glad I am that I found you. - L."

"So we know they were definitely for her. Her roommate's name is Ash," Jaxon said.

"Found her, sounds like she was hiding from something," I added.

"I think there's a bit more to our girl, than we know," Jaxon said thoughtfully.

CHAPTER
Twelve

Gideon

SWEAT DRIPPED down my face as I continued to pummel the bag in front of me. The gym in our basement was completely outfitted with every piece of equipment we could want. The other guys did plenty of cardio and weight lifting. For me it was all about the heavy bag.

The door opened behind me and in the wall of mirrors, I saw Jaxon and Oliver step in. Both of them looked rumpled and were still wearing their suits from the night before. A pang of jealousy rose up inside me like a beast and I swung viciously at the bag before they came to stand next to me.

I could smell her on them. It was that lavender scent she brought with her when she came into the conference room. When I saw her at the club, dancing with my brothers, an interest came to me that I typically didn't have. Normally, I was worried about the security of our family and whether a woman was a threat. But this time, it was an attraction that I didn't really want to have.

My brothers also reeked of sex. However, their faces didn't look like they had the best night of their lives. Instead, they looked troubled. And that trouble brought them home and to immediately look for me.

"You both need a shower," I huffed out.

"Says the bear that's soaked in sweat," Oliver joked, as he took a mock swing at me. I easily evaded, as he expected me to.

"We need your help," Jaxon said.

"What? Couldn't make her happy?" I joked.

They didn't react and I realized my joke wasn't well timed. I started to unwrap my hands, while watching the two of them. Oliver's smile had disappeared and Jaxon paced near the doorway.

"What's up? You two are seriously tightly wound. What happened last night? You didn't kill anyone did you?" I asked.

The question might have seemed like a joke, but I was serious. I wasn't in the mood to deal with a dead body at the moment. And it would be my job to figure out the clean up for it. Jaxon just rolled his eyes at me and Oliver shook his head.

"Spit it out, what do you need?" I finally asked.

"A background on Brooklyn," Jaxon replied.

I raised an eyebrow at him and ran my hand down my beard. A background on a woman they were sleeping with was a bit drastic. If they were asking me to make this dive, they had a real reason for it. If that was because this woman meant more to them than I realized or there was a serious problem, I wasn't sure.

"Full? Into adolescence?" I asked.

"Whatever you can get. We know she was in foster care at some point and there were incidents with her mother. But something happened today that we need to get an answer to," Jaxon said.

Oliver dove into a story of flowers, a long scar on her body and her reaction to the card that was in the flowers. I agreed with them that it did sound like someone had been looking for her and she wasn't pleased with them finding her.

"If she's in trouble, we just want to know, so we can help," Oliver said.

"Help? You guys already stuck on this girl?" I asked.

The two of them shared a look, that was loaded enough for even me to read it. But I waited to see what they'd say.

"She's different, Gideon. I know that sounds ridiculous coming from me. But I can't get her out of my head. And after last night, I won't be letting her go unless she makes me," Oliver said.

"Same," Jaxon echoed.

"Aiden know this yet?" I asked.

Oliver was smart enough to grimace and Jaxon looked away. Aiden wasn't going to be thrilled with the crossover between business and professional. Though he hadn't said as much to me, I knew from his reaction at the business meeting, he didn't trust Brooklyn to not fuck us all over. One thing about the background check, we would at least know what we were facing when it came to her.

"Well, don't tell him until after I get this info. Then you'll have something to use to convince him one way or the other," I said.

"I don't care what he thinks. I'm not giving her up, not yet," Jaxon replied, his voice hard.

I held up my hands, not trying to start a fight.

"No one said he would make you do that. We've always been good with managing our personal affairs. He just doesn't like any sort of risks when it comes to business."

"Brooklyn isn't a risk. And if she's in trouble, well it's a risk worth taking," Jaxon said.

I nodded and agreed to do the check. The two of them left the gym and I cleaned up my mess before heading to my own room. I pulled my hair from the elastic, holding it back and it fell around my shoulders.

I wasn't as polished as my brothers by any means, but that didn't mean I was a mess. I had hair products all over my bathroom, including special shampoo from one of those online stores that created specific products for your hair type. I also had a number of different products for my beard, which I prided myself on. I was the only one of the four of us that could actually grow a decent beard.

I stepped into the hot shower and quickly cleaned up, enjoying the feel of the hot water against my sore muscles. I could have stayed under the spray longer, but my mind was now preoccupied. Who or what could Brooklyn be hiding from? She was somewhat prominent in the non profit world, but that didn't mean her name and photo were splashed all over publicly.

With a towel around my waist, I didn't wait to dry my hair, before I went to my desk in the corner of the room. We each had our rooms, as well as our separate offices, but I liked working in my room. Early on, we knew we wanted some space between personal life and business. Though often the two seem to completely bleed into each other. And I gave up the separation completely.

Sitting at my computer, I rubbed a second towel over my head, just to keep myself from dripping all over the place. I logged into my computer and switched over to my VPN. In addition to being the muscle of our family, I had picked up a number of skills that helped in the security of our businesses and home. Sometimes legal avenues didn't always get me the results I wanted.

I went with the basic search using her full name. A small news article, led me to searching police files. I grimaced as I looked at photos of Brooklyn. From there I was able to find a protection order she had, which was just a piece of paper and wasn't going to protect her from anything.

My printer whirled as I printed all of the pertinent information. I went to my room to get dressed before I took everything I had to Oliver and Jaxon. It wasn't everything about her, but it answered the most immediate question, what she was afraid of.

Brooklyn

THOUGH I WAS afraid to leave my apartment, I forced myself to go to work the next day. My skin prickled with the sensation of being watched. I told myself that in the middle of the day, on my way to work, or in the office, I was safe. It was when I was alone at night that I felt on the edge of a panic attack.

After the men had left the apartment, I had locked the door. Then manically checked each window throughout to ensure they were locked. We had a window that lead to a fire escape and that one scared me the most. I unlocked it, opened it, relocked it and tried to open it. I used more force than necessary, imagining someone trying to pry it open from the outside.

In the end, I sat on the floor in the living room, rocking back and forth. I couldn't stop touching the scar on my neck and chest. If someone wanted to get in, if he wanted to get in, breaking a window wasn't going to be a big deal. Hopefully, I would hear broken glass and be ready to get out before the intruder got hands on me.

I had avoided all calls and text messages from Oliver and Jaxon. I knew it wouldn't take much for them to learn what happened to me, the truth of how messed up I really was. I tried not to even think about our night together. It had been euphoric, feeling things done to my body that I had no idea were possible. But that was all it could be, one night.

This was why I had stayed single for as long as I had. I never dated. Never had one night stands, even though Ash tried to encourage me to get out there. I was broken, I had too many skeletons in my closet. I was embarrassed that I had even told them about my mother and my burns.

Then there was the fact that there was two of them. I had sex with two men, at once. The thrill of that fact was also mixed with the fear of being shamed. In the heat of the moment, it hadn't felt weird or wrong. It felt like pieces falling into place, where we were all connected in some way. But, that was over now.

I held my head in my hands for a moment, allowing myself just a bit of pity. There was not only one, but two men in my bed just a couple nights before. Now, I lived alone in fear, with no one around that cared about me. I couldn't even bring myself to tell Ash about the flowers. If she knew, I was afraid she'd leave her training and come home immediately. I couldn't be the cause of that.

A knock at my office door had me looking up. Breath caught in my throat as I found Jaxon standing in the doorway, as if my mind had conjured him at that exact moment. He was looking ridiculously delicious in a black pin stripe suit, with white dress shirt. As always, the shirt was unbuttoned at the throat. I couldn't help but picture the tribal tattoo that I knew went down his ribs.

"Jaxon, I mean, Mr. Knight. How can I help you?" I asked, standing up quickly.

"Mr. Knight?" Jaxon asked.

He stepped into the office and shut the door quietly behind him. Before I could object, he shut my blinds and turned back to me. He stalked toward where I stood and didn't stop until his chest brushed mine.

"You can call me that, in bed, if you'd like. It just might confuse my brother," he said quietly, his eyes searching mine.

"Uh, this is my office. I figured if you were here, it was about business?" I asked, confused.

"I think all of the details your event manager sent were exactly what we spoke about, there's nothing more to work through. I'm here on a personal matter," he said, reaching up to twist a piece of my hair around his finger.

I tried not to take a deep breath, his scent gave me flashbacks to his head between my legs and the insane pleasure he took me to. His fingers slid along my cheek, until his palm cupped my jaw. My eyes flickered up to his and I found emotions swirling as he looked down at me.

"You've been avoiding me," he murmured.

"I, well, I've been busy," I tried to explain.

He leaned down to press a kiss on my cheek before whispering in my ear.

"Was the other night, too much?"

I couldn't get my voice to work so I just shook my head. Then I nodded, but then shook it again. Confusion warred throughout me. Was it too much? My body was sore in the right ways the next morning. But receiving the flowers felt like a damper on everything and it was hard to separate the emotion.

Jaxon just chuckled as he pulled away. He ran a hand down my arm, until he could intertwine our fingers. He stepped toward the small loveseat that was in my office and pulled me with him. He sat, then pulled me to sit right next to him, our legs pressed against each other.

It wasn't until then that I realized he was holding a manilla folder. He set it on the small table in front of us and just looked at me. I looked at the file, then back at him, waiting to find out what the visit was about.

"These kill me by the way. Likely one of my favorite pieces of business clothing on a woman," he said, his finger running over my deep red pencil skirt.

He settled his hand on my bare knee, before taking a deep breath. I could tell he was nervous to talk to me today and it made me feel a little better about the turmoil I had raging inside me. I put my hand over his, on my knee and he looked at me with a smile.

"Oliver and I, we were worried about you the other day. Though I guess you're replaying everything that happened with us, I don't think that was what you were so freaked about the next day. So first I just want to say, what happened between the three of us, was perfect. We wouldn't have left without trying it again if the flowers hadn't shown up," he said.

He paused, waiting for me to speak. I just opened my

mouth, but no sound came out, so I snapped it shut again. He nodded and continued.

"We can talk about us later. I wanted to tell you, you can trust us. If you're in trouble, we can help you. It's been killing me just these two days, for you to ignore me, when all I want is to be there for you, should you need it. So yeah, two days was my limit and now I'm here."

I could feel warmth spreading through me at his words. Then I shut down the emotions. What did I really know about the Knights? I had Googled them as soon as I got to the office the day before. And it was amazing how light the information on their personal lives really was.

There was normal tabloid gossip about them dating certain women, but it never seemed to last long. There was never any real drama for the magazines to report. In business, it was clear they were vastly successful in all venues they touched, with Aiden playing the figurehead of CEO for 4K. It left me wondering, what were they hiding.

I couldn't think with Jaxon's warm hand on my knee or his body so close to mine. I stood up and paced the office a little, trying to clear my head. Jaxon's eyes watched me, and I didn't miss how he looked over my body more than once. That did give me a slight thrill and I wanted to tell him my closet was full of pencil skirts. It was my favorite business choice as well.

"There's a lot, to my past, that I have tried to bury and make go away. I'm not sure you really want all of that burden," I finally said.

Jaxon tapped the folder. I froze. Without opening it, I already knew what I would find. The public records are all tied to my name. It wouldn't explain how I got myself into the situation in the first place. That was only something I could tell.

I picked up the folder and opened it. Tears sprang to my eyes as I found not only the public records, but also the medical records attached to the police report. The photos of my injury before and after it was tended to by a plastic surgeon, bills of which I was still slowly paying off.

Jaxon said nothing, just sat on the edge of the couch and waited for me to speak. I went to my desk and took a sip of water because suddenly my throat felt like the Sahara desert and I was going to choke to death on sand. I finally found the courage to look up at him. His eyes were soft and kind. Everyone always felt bad for Brooklyn, the sliced up girl.

"Where did you get all of this?" I finally asked.

"When we got home yesterday, we talked to Gideon. He has sources, that he's built up over the years while he managed security for our businesses. He didn't dig further. We didn't want to violate your privacy completely."

"No, you only got my medical records," I replied, sarcastically.

"Only these. Because the police report referred to them."

I closed the folder and set it on my desk. I couldn't look at the pictures anymore. Not that it mattered, those images were burned into my brain. It had taken months of therapy to not see myself like that every time I looked in the mirror and saw my scar. The plastic surgeon had done an amazing job, so instead of a jagged line, it was mostly straight and clean. But for months, all I saw was how gruesome I looked.

Walking back around my desk, I settled against the edge of it. I couldn't sit down behind my desk, that felt formal. I couldn't sit next to Jaxon, his nearness threw me off. And if I kept pacing, I might walk right out of the office and just keep going. So, instead, I gripped the edge of my desk and took a deep breath.

"Do you know one of the biggest problems with the foster system and the process of CPS in general?" I asked.

Jaxon just shakes his head. I know he knows enough to

know the systems are complete shit. But he's going to let me tell the story how I need to.

"For the kids, they are often yanked back and forth through the system. The kid is taken when their parents get too drunk or high to care when they have third degree burns on their leg," I said, sweeping my hand around my thigh. Jaxon's eyes look down at my thigh and I see him adjust himself slightly and it bolsters me to think about the affect I have on him, even with my scarred thigh. I grabbed the little courage that gave me and continued.

"Then those kids are shoved into a foster home or a group home. Maybe the parents get clean and follow the rules for a while. So the kid is then forced to go back home. There are no relationships built. The child feels alone and abandoned. After the first few times, the child no longer feels excited to go home. Because inevitably, the parent is going to fall off the wagon again. Even the child knows that. But CPS just goes through the motions."

At this point, Jaxon stands and comes to lean against my desk next to me.

"Is this ok?" He asked, as he takes my hand.

I just squeeze his fingers in response, not wanting to look him in the eye as I tell my story.

"I was twelve I think, the first time I met Lyle. It was probably the fourth time I had been taken from my mom since I was five. This time, I was put into a group home, instead of an emergency foster home. It was the first night and I was told to change and come to dinner, but I didn't want to be around new people. So I stayed in my room, which had two sets of bunkbeds and I was one of four staying in the room. I just sat on my bed and was reading a book when the door opened. And this older boy stood there staring at me. He scared me at first, but then he put a plate heaped with food at the end of the bed. I said thank you and I'll never forget how my twelve year old heart did a flip when he called me Toots as he walked out. For the time I was there, I followed him like a puppy, soaking up any attention he would give me."

"Sounds like a normal childhood crush," Jaxon reasoned.

I shrugged. Maybe the beginning was normal, but I knew the rest was not.

"Over the next four years I guess, I was shuffled back and forth between my mother and this same group home. It seemed that Lyle was a permanent fixture there. The second time I came to the home, I was devastated when he acted like he'd never met me. My heart was broken because there was this attention I wanted to get so badly and he just ignored me. I even went out of my way to see him during meals, even though I'd rather stay in my room alone. But one night, I was in my bunk reading a book with my favorite stuffed animal. Lyle came in and sat down, acting like he was looking for something. He picked up the animal and told me he thought it was cute. I told him he could have it if he wanted it, because I would do anything for him to like me. Lyle talked to me everyday after that. I was so happy, even when I saw my favorite stuffed animal on the bed of another girl, it didn't matter. Lyle was paying attention to me," I explained.

"He was using you," Jaxon said, his hand tightening on mine.

I couldn't look at him. I couldn't see the pity in his face. Everyone always pitied the little girl with the alcoholic mother. I stared at the ground as I tried to figure out what else to tell him. Jaxon's free hand came up and he gripped my chin, turning me to face him.

It wasn't pity I saw in his face, it was anger. Without thinking, I ran my fingers over the angry lines between his eyes. He captured my hand and pressed a kiss to my fingertips that I felt throughout my entire body. I smiled softly at him and his face relaxed just a little.

"Well yeah. But where I was in my life, I didn't understand that. It was like that for years. I would pack things for the group home, just to catch his attention. I just knew I wanted someone to love me and Lyle was good at showing that attention when he wanted to. After my high school graduation we ran away together. I was seventeen and he was nineteen. I took out loans to go to college and he worked as a pizza delivery driver. As two young kids, we thought that was perfect because we had free pizza every night," I said with an ironic little laugh.

"You were a child. You couldn't have known any different," Jaxon said.

"Oh I know. Logically, I know that I grew up in shit and didn't know anything better. I was determined to make something of myself. So I loaded up on college classes and worked nights at a grocery store. It was exhausting. But I still made sure to clean and do whatever Lyle needed. Because that was how I got his love. Even when he took my virginity before I was ready, I rationalized it and made it ok. I mean of course he wanted sex, we lived together, slept in the same bed. Why did I think he would wait?"

I stopped talking when I realized Jaxon had gone rigid next to me. His grip on my hand was almost painful. I looked over in alarm and saw him staring off into the distance.

"Jaxon, you're hurting me," I said quietly.

"Shit, I'm sorry," he said.

He immediately released my fingers from the vice and rubbed at them with his thumb. Then he started to pace the room. He ran his hand through his hair, messing it up from the business like style he had when he walked in.

"So, what you're saying is, he raped you," he finally said. His voice was harsh and deep.

"I didn't call it that at the time," I replied.

"What do you call it now?" He asked, practically spitting the words.

"Rape," I said, hanging my head.

"No, absolutely not. You do not feel bad about this, love. This wasn't your fault," Jaxon said, as he stepped over to me.

His arms came around me, gathering me in, until I was surrounded by his woodsy smell. I breathed deep and let my arms slide around his waist. The comfort felt so good to take, I wanted to climb into the embrace like a cocoon. But I knew I had to tell this story once and get it out. Once it was out in the air, we could move on and forget that I was broken into pieces on the inside.

"As long as Lyle was happy, I got all the attention and love I needed, or thought I did. It was a constant cycle of me catering to his needs, to get my needs fulfilled. My therapist has explained that this behavior created an unhealthy under-standing of relationships in my head. I thought the only way to get love was to buy it with my time or money. If I didn't do as he wanted, I didn't deserve him."

"Such bullshit," Jaxon growled, hugging me tighter to him.

"I didn't know that then. And that was when he tried to kill me."

CHAPTER
Fourteen

Brooklyn

JAXON'S BREATHING had become shallow and harsh. Or maybe it was my breathing and slamming of my heart in my ears. I was getting to the worst of it, and internally I was freaking out. Having to reach back and retell this story, made my skin crawl and fear shoot through my system, almost like I was back there.

As if sensing all of this in me, Jaxon led us back to the loveseat. Instead of having me sit next to him, he pulled me right into his lap, adjusting me until I was laying against his chest. I could hear his heartbeat under my ear and I focused on it to try and settle my own.

"You don't have to tell me the rest. I can guess, from the reports," he said.

I shook my head. "I need to be the one to tell you. Get it out in the open. Those reports don't even cover it all. The police, well, they didn't take me all that seriously. At this point, Lyle had gone from pizza delivery, to gas station worker, to unemployed. Though he still brought money home. I tried to pretend I didn't know he was doing something illegal for the money. He was on the police's radar, so when they took my report, they figured I was just a dumb criminal's girlfriend and I would be back with him soon."

"They shouldn't even have jobs anymore. Maybe Gideon can look into that," Jaxon said, more to himself than me.

"I had graduated college with my degree in business administration. I was so proud of myself. I was making myself into something more than what I had come from. Even with all the issues at home with Lyle, I had hoped he would be at the graduation. I made sure he had a ticket and knew the time and place. But when it was all over, he was nowhere to be found. I thought maybe he had just run late or I couldn't find him, so when my friends invited me out for drinks I accepted. I texted Lyle to meet us, hoping he would show. He never did. I was happily buzzed when I got home that night. I never drank much because I was worried about being like my mother. But it was a big night and I was sad that I was alone."

"I'm so sorry," Jaxon said, interrupting me.

His hand stroked my arm as I spoke, but I was too far into the memories to feel the comfort now. Cold sweat broke out on my back as I remembered how I felt that night.

"All the lights were out in the apartment, so I was sure I

was alone. I stumbled and was giggling at myself like an idiot. The cold metal at my throat is what had me stopping immediately. I mean at that moment I thought maybe we were being robbed. Or whatever shady dealings Lyle was up to had found their way home. Lyle was in my mind immediately, worried for his safety. But when he spoke, it was Lyle holding the knife to my throat. I started crying, explaining it was me. But he knew. I hadn't been home to make his dinner or have sex with him like I was supposed to. With the knife to my throat, he ripped my skirt and panties to get at me. That was the second time he raped me."

"Jesus Christ. Brooklyn. Fuck. That's not in that police report," Jaxon said in a strangled voice.

His hand had stopped stroking my arm. Instead, he was holding onto me for dear life. I couldn't stop the words from spilling from my mouth now.

"It hurt so badly. I cried out, screaming for him to stop. Once he was finished, he collapsed on me. He used the knife to try and slice my throat as I screamed. My neighbors all came running. They were all used to Lyle screaming. But I was always quiet. When I saw them in the halls, I would put on a bright smile and no one ever asked me if I was ok. But they heard me screaming now and it was like a beacon for them. Lyle escaped before the police or ambulance arrived. Luckily his aim wasn't great, but I was treated to a scar that will never completely go away. He was eventually found and arrested on battery and domestic violence. But like I said, the police didn't take it too seriously. And since the cut wasn't across my throat, they didn't call it attempted murder. He was sentenced to five years in prison," I said.

I was shaking and Jaxon was doing his best to hold me against him. All of the fear and pain roared back into my mind and I felt like I was bleeding on the floor of that dingy apartment again. Tears began to spill down my cheeks and I leaned up to make sure I didn't make a mess on Jaxon's pristine white shirt.

"Nope. No pulling away now," he said, tightening me to him.

"I'm afraid to ask, but did Gideon look at where Lyle is now?" I asked.

"No one called you? The police? The courts?" Jaxon asked.

I shook my head. I knew this news was going to be bad. Getting the flowers only proved that he was out of jail. How it happened so fast, I had no idea. And how he so easily found Ash's apartment and that I was living there now, I couldn't even begin to understand. Being honest, Lyle wasn't the sharpest tool in the shed, his mind was better for getting away with illegal activities.

"I guess you already know what I'm going to tell you. It's in the file if you want to review it later. But he's out. Something about good behavior, first offense, and overcrowding at the prison. It's bullshit all the way around," Jaxon explained.

"He already found me," I whispered.

"Let us help. We can make sure he stays away," Jaxon said.

"It's not your problem. I won't have it become your problem. You guys are busy enough as it is."

"What if I say, I want you to be my problem?"

Jaxon shifted, pulling my face up so I had to look him in the eyes. Slowly, he came closer to me, until our noses were touching. His hands came up to frame my face and he thumbed away the tears on my cheeks. I couldn't stop myself from leaning into the warmth of his palm for a moment.

I realized then he was waiting for me. Waiting for me to make a move that told him I was willing to go there with him. I had just bared the horror of my past to him and I had expected him to run away. Who wanted a woman with not only physical scars, but mental ones as well. And that's not even to mention throwing in my sexual inexperience.

But looking at him, all I could think about was how soft his touch was. Or how he kissed my scarred thigh as if it was precious and beautiful. And here he was, even knowing everything that was wrong with me, he was still here. Not running for the hills or trying to make our relationship as business professional as possible.

I had a lot of hopes I had no right having as I softly pressed my lips to his. After a few soft kisses, I pressed further and slanted my mouth across his. I ran my tongue along his bottom lip and he didn't hesitate to open to me. He groaned as I slid my tongue along his. His hands left my face and roamed my body, until one tangled in my hair and the other gripped my hip.

It didn't feel like enough. All of my emotions had been rubbed raw and I was cracked open for him to see. And now I couldn't get close enough, couldn't get enough of him. Without breaking our kiss, I shifted and pulled my skirt up so I could straddle him. Both of his hands grabbed my hips, pulling me down to where I could feel how hard he was.

"Is this ok?" He asked.

"Stop asking me that. Don't stop touching me," I replied, kissing him deeply again.

He pulled away again and a whine escaped my mouth before I could stop it. He grinned at me before leaning over the loveseat toward the door. He pressed the lock and I realized how fuzzy my brain was, I didn't even think about someone walking in on us.

Jaxon leaned back to me and captured my mouth, as his hands went to my bare thighs, snaking up under the material of my skirt, until his thumbs found the edge of my panties. He stopped and pulled back again, but I spoke before he even had a chance.

"If you ask me one more time if this is ok, I will likely hurt you. Touch me, Jaxon," I said.

My voice came out more forceful than I had intended, but I could tell that he didn't mind me asking for what I wanted. He leaned forward, so he could find the skin of my neck. I was wearing one of my trademark, high collared shirts. It was buttoned almost up to my throat, to keep my scar hidden.

I ran my fingers through his hair, as I leaned into his mouth. One of his fingers moved my panties to the side, giving access to my soaking wet core. Softly, Jaxon ran a finger through my wetness, circling my clit at the end. I moaned quietly and Jaxon bit my ear.

"You're going to have to keep quiet, love," he said gruffly.

I nodded in agreement, knowing I didn't need my entire office to know I was on the verge of sex in my office. Never in my life would I have ever thought of doing this. But there was no way I could stop what was happening at that moment.

"Unbutton this," Jaxon said, using his teeth to tug on my shirt.

With shaky hands, I reached up and started to unbutton my shirt. I shrugged out of it and carefully laid it on the table, knowing I would need to put it back on before the day was over. I reached down to Jaxon's pants, undoing the belt, button and slid down the zipper. He watched me with heat in his gaze. When I slid my hand into his pants, I wasn't surprised this time to find him without underwear.

"Mmmm, easy access. I could get used to this," I murmured.

I circled his hardness with my hand and began to pump. He threw back his head for a moment, but his fingers went back to my core. I bit my lip to stop moaning as he pressed two fingers into me, fucking me slowly. His thumb rubbed on my clit at the same time and as he added more pressure, I fell over the cliff without warning.

Throwing myself forward, I pressed my face into his neck to make sure I didn't make any noise. I could feel his chuckle as his touch began to lighten, caressing me through my orgasm.

"I love how responsive you are," he whispered.

"Maybe you're just really good with your hands," I joked.

"Just my hands?" He asked, turning his head to nip at my ear.

I wanted more, badly. Without thinking, I pulled him from his pants, continuing to stroke him.

"I want you," I moaned against his mouth.

"Believe it or not, I didn't come prepared. This wasn't my plan for this visit," he said.

"I have an IUD and I'm clean," I said immediately.

"I'm clean. Are you sure about this?" He asked, pulling back from me, so he could meet my eyes.

"I'm pretty sure I will die if you don't fuck me right now."

CHAPTER
Fifteen

Jaxon

HER WORDS WERE DEMANDING and forceful, but I could see her eyes weren't as confident. I wanted to put the confidence in them, make her understand the beautiful woman she was. Hearing about her past hadn't changed the way I saw her. I knew she was worried about that. Instead, I only saw a strength I didn't know she had.

I stood up, gripping her ass in my hands. She muffled a squeal in my neck and I had to chuckle. I went to her desk and sat her on her feet. She looked up at me with a lust filled look that made me want to worship at her feet. Instead, I decided to show her how she should be fucked, all the time.

Before she could get comfortable, I reached down and palmed her pussy, pushing her panties out of the way again. Thrusting two fingers back into her, I kissed and licked at the skin along the column of her neck. Pulling back, I gazed back into her eyes.

"Turn around, put your hands on the desk, bend over," I ordered.

I watched as her eyes flared, her pupils blowing out further and I could feel her pussy clamp down on my fingers.

"Mmmm, you like that, don't you love?" I asked.

She nodded and I took my hand away, allowing her to turn and do as she was told. With both hands flat on her desk, she bent and arched her back. I just stared for a moment, wanting to memorize how delicious she looked with her pencil skirt hiked up her thighs, wearing her sky high heels, bent over for my taking.

Pushing her skirt up further, I slowly slipped her panties off her hips and down her legs. Once off, I slipped them into my pocket, thinking I'd be keeping that souvenir. I used a foot to nudge her feet slightly further apart, and pushed on her upper back, causing her ass to come up in the air.

I had wanted to go slow, but there was no way I could after all of the foreplay. Dropping my dress pants to my knees, I rubbed my cock along her pussy, causing her to push back and buck slightly. I knew she wasn't going to keep quiet. Lining myself up with her, I reached forward and covered her mouth with my hand, just as I slammed balls deep into her.

I had to pause, to give her time to adjust and also to catch onto my own pleasure. She was so tight and hot, I could barely control myself. Brooklyn had other plans though, as she began to rotate her hips against me.

"I need you to be quiet, love. I'm going to fuck you hard. Can you control yourself?" I asked.

"Yes. Jaxon, please," she whispered.

Pulling out, until just the tip was still inside her, I slammed back in without warning. I could hear her moan, but she kept her mouth clamped shut. I grabbed her hips as I pistoned my own, fucking her roughly.

I knew I couldn't hold much longer. Reaching around, I found her clit and put gentle pressure on it. That was all it took before I felt her pussy walls clamp down on my cock. Her orgasm practically strangled me, and I felt my balls tighten just seconds before I shot deeply into her.

She collapsed limply on her chest on her desk. Luck for us both, she was a very tidy business person and there wasn't anything to knock on the ground. That noise might bring someone to check on her. As it was, I hoped the walls had some decent sound proofing. Some of the sounds we made were pretty unmistakable.

Suddenly, her body began to shake and I carefully pulled from her. Panicking, I pulled her up to face me. Instead of the tears I was expecting, she was full on giggling. I let loose a relieved laugh, though I wasn't sure a woman laughing after I fucked her was a good thing or not.

"I literally just told you the worst things about me and you still made me feel like that. I swear, if I'm dreaming, I can die right now in my sleep," Brooklyn laughed.

Using tissues from her desk, I carefully cleaned her up and myself. I pulled my dress pants up and as I buckled my belt, Brooklyn was buttoning her dress shirt again. Mostly dressed, I pulled her into my arms, kissing the top of her head, her forehead, her nose and then her mouth.

"Nothing you told me was about you. It was about things done to you. And that doesn't change a damn thing in my eyes," I said.

"Thank you, Jaxon."

"Thank you for the sex or for being so wonderfully caring?" I joked.

"Hmmm, both? Do women usually thank you for sex?"

"Not recently. But we could start a trend if you'd like," I laughed.

Her face shuttered for a moment, but then she wiped it away and hid her thoughts with a smile.

"Well then, thank you. I'd be happy to be a reference for you, if needed," she said.

She turned away and went to her desk. Picking up the folder I brought for her, she stared at it for a moment.

"I don't want this. I know all of this already. You can take it," she said, holding the folder out to me.

I followed her, caging her between her desk and the wall.

"Hey, what just happened? I saw your mood shift. Why?" I asked.

"Nothing. It's nothing," she said, but her hands rung together and I knew she wasn't telling me the truth.

I just raised an eyebrow at her and she huffed a breath.

"It's really stupid. I just, for a moment, when I thought about you and other women. Well, I don't have any right," she said.

"Love, did you feel jealous?" I asked.

"Maybe. But how dumb is that. You, Oliver and I. Like, I have no idea how this even works. How am I allowed to have you both, but you only get me? I'm so confused," she said, covering her blushing face with her hands.

I pulled her hands down, so she had to look at me. Her utter embarrassment shouldn't have been adorable, but it made me smile. And a deep part of me really liked that she didn't want me with other women. Brooklyn was under my skin and I couldn't even imagine being with someone else.

"My brothers and I, we're not opposed to sharing. It might seem weird, but we've been family so long, it just comes naturally."

"Wait, all four of you…?" She asked, her voice trailing off.

"We have, yes. And if that was something you were interested in, we could talk about it. Oliver and I are obviously interested," I replied.

"Does Oliver know you're here?" She suddenly asked.

"He knew I was coming. He figured I would be good at talking to you about this," I said, tapping the folder on her desk.

"Will he be mad, that we, ya know, without him?" She asked.

It amazed me as her pink blush deepened further. This was the woman that just moments before was begging me to fuck her. But when we were in the heat of things, she had a hard time saying what was on her mind.

"Will he be mad that I bent you over your desk and fucked you?" I said, lowering my voice as I ran my mouth along her jaw. She didn't speak, just nodded her head.

"No. That's not how it works," I replied, placing a soft kiss below her ear.

"Can you teach me? How does it work?" She asked timidly.

"First rule, no other women for us. No men other than us for you. Can you do that?"

She laughed slightly. "Uh, that won't be a problem. It's been a while since I even thought about dating."

"Good. We don't like to share outside of our brothers. So, we can each spend alone time with you, as you or we wish.

Then we can always spend time as a group, if you want that. Did the other night feel weird to you?" I asked.

"Not at all. Which when I thought about it later, I thought maybe I just didn't know enough to understand how I should feel?"

"But you wanted it again?" I whispered near her ear.

She didn't speak again, just nodded.

"Going to need you to say it, love."

"Yes, I wanted it again. Want it again," she said breathlessly.

"You have no idea how happy I am to hear that," I said, stepping away from her.

I picked up the folder, already planning on shredding it to pieces the moment I got home. She walked me to the door and I saw her looking around the office strangely. She grabbed my hand before I got to the door.

"Uh, my panties. Do you know where they went?" She asked, nervously.

I realized she was probably picturing the cleaning crew or a co-worker walking in and finding her red thong somewhere on the floor. I patted my pocket and grinned at her, as her mouth dropped open.

"No more avoiding our calls, yeah?" I asked.

"No more. I'm sorry for that. I just, I was thrown off. But I'm glad it's all in the open. Will you, well, can you tell Oliver about everything. I'd like to not have to tell it again?" She asked.

"Absolutely, love. Whatever I can to do help."

I pulled her close for a sweet kiss, then kissed her knuckles before letting myself out of her office. The receptionist smiled nicely at me, and I waved before getting to the elevator. I smoothed my hair a bit, but I didn't even care. I couldn't wipe the smile from my face.

Taking the elevator down to the garage level, I was glad I had decided to drive myself. I took longer in Brooklyn's office than I had planned. The sex wasn't in the plan of today's visit, but it was a welcomed edition for sure.

As I drove, I let everything I learned today float around in my head. This Lyle guy was clearly a threat to Brooklyn. I knew Oliver would agree with me, that we needed to figure out how to handle the issue. Though, I could see that Brooklyn would likely not be excited about us getting involved.

When I walked into the house, Oliver was already coming down the stairs to meet me. When he saw how disheveled I was, he grinned.

"Oh, I see, the talk went well," he laughed.

"There's a lot to talk about. I need a damn drink if I'm going to go through this though. And we should bring Gideon and Aiden in on it. This is going to be a complication," I said.

My jovial mood dropped through the floor, knowing Aiden was going to be annoyed with the issues surrounding our relationship with Brooklyn. But I wasn't willing to just give her up because she had a past. We all had a past and ours wasn't any less dangerous than Brooklyn's. We just had the money to keep it at bay most of the time.

We had to wait for Aiden to get off a business call, but once he was done, I called everyone together in the family room. We had a small wet bar in the back and I poured a glass for my brothers. I poured one for myself, downed it, then poured another before I could tell them.

"That bad, brother?" Oliver asked.

My eyes cut to Aiden, who already look annoyed. I knew he had a heart, probably bigger than the rest of us. He was kind and warm. But work had been getting to him and he needed to get his mind out of it sometimes. A small thought popped up in my head, but I decided to think about that later. I had enough to face at the moment.

"Y'all are gonna want a few once you hear what I have to tell you," I said.

"More than what's in that file?" Gideon asked, his jaw tense.

He already saw some of the bad stuff. But he didn't know everything. And I knew it was going to send his protector mode into overdrive.

"So much more. And we assumed right. That delivery yesterday, was from him. And he shouldn't know where she lives. She also has a protection order," I said.

"That's just a shit piece of paper," Aiden said.

I nodded. Then I dove in. When I got to when he first raped her, Aiden shot to his feet and downed his drink before going for a refill. He didn't turn back to me right away. Gideon's knuckles were white around his glass and I hoped the big man realized it before he smashed it to pieces.

As I started to explain the last incident and how Lyle tried to kill her, Oliver had to practically put his head between his knees. Aiden had gone stark white and Gideon was pacing like a lion through the room. His drink was long forgotten and I knew it would take a lot to keep his rage at bay.

"She can't be alone," Aiden said.

I couldn't do anything but stare at him, surprised he even cared about her safety.

"Well, you said her roommate is out of town," he added, uneasily.

"Ash. Yeah, she's in Europe for a few months, I think," Oliver said.

"Maybe you guys should go over. Make sure she's not alone at night at least?" Gideon said.

Oliver looked over at me and I nodded.

"I actually have some work I put off today. Can you go over tonight? Make sure she freaking eats too. This is really messing her up," I said.

Oliver nodded and stood to walk out of the room. Aiden called to him to stop.

"This is going to be weird, because we're doing business. After the party, let's figure out a better solution. Gideon, find this guy," Aiden said.

Oliver and I exchanged a look, wondering what he meant about figuring out a better solution. It didn't really matter. I saw the determination in Oliver's face. We were in. And we weren't going to let anything happen to her.

CHAPTER
Sixteen

Brooklyn

I COULDN'T HELP but to float through the rest of the day in a sense of euphoria. I had worried about Jaxon or Oliver knowing the truth about my past. In reality, once I told Jaxon everything, a weight came off my chest. The fear was still there, but I no longer felt alone in this void.

When the end of the day came around, the euphoria faded and fear dominated everything again. I debated going to a hotel, somewhere Lyle wouldn't know. But, what if he was watching me and then I was in an unknown place without escape? Too many scenarios conjured in my mind, until eventually I knew I was just going to go home.

As I was saying goodnight to our receptionist and stalling my exit from the protected building, I saw her eyes move to the elevators and her face lit up with a smile. Turning to see what caught her attention, my own smile appeared, as a casually dressed Oliver stepped off the elevators. He was wearing glasses that he didn't normally wear, a v-neck t-shirt and perfect jeans. He immediately focused on me and strode forward.

"I didn't miss you," he said when he came through our glass doors.

"I was working late," I replied.

"Not surprising," he laughed.

He nodded to the receptionist, before taking my elbow and leading me to the elevator bank. There, he dropped his hand and for a second I started to doubt what Jaxon told me. Was he mad that I was with his brother without him? Did he know? Did Jaxon tell him all the horrific details that weren't in that police report and now Oliver didn't look at me the same?

The elevator dinged and I stepped in first, pulling my shirt collar closer to me. Once the doors closed, Oliver rounded on me and carefully grabbed me by the throat crashing his lips to mine. When I gasped, he invaded my mouth with his tongue. The sensual dance he did made me moan and pull him closer, but he ended the kiss just as we reached the parking garage level.

I was panting and blushing as he took my hand and led me to a black classic car. He opened the door for me and held my hand as I slid in. Pressing a kiss to my knuckles, he released me and closed the door. He then went to the driver's side door and smoothly got behind the wheel.

Even for a woman that had never known much about cars, seeing this beautiful man behind the wheel of this classic made my pulse race a little more. He caught me staring and his usual goofy grin popped up.

"What?" He asked.

"Uh, well hello to you. Are you always going to greet me like that?" I asked.

"Well, once we're away from prying eyes. I didn't want the receptionist to see me jump you," he laughed.

"You wear glasses?" I asked, smiling at how cute he looked with the round frames.

"Usually contacts. I can be blind as a bat without them. But I was in a hurry today," he replied.

He turned the key in the ignition and the rumble of the car vibrated my seat for a moment. I squirmed a little, remembering I wasn't wearing any panties. Oliver caught my movement and he slid a hand up my skirt slightly, so he could rest his palm on my bare thigh.

"What sounds good for dinner? I was thinking about ordering in," he said.

"You're coming over for dinner?" I asked, confused by the plans and distracted by his thumb making sweeps across my skin.

"Jaxon got his time with you. It's my turn," he said with a small chuckle.

"Ah, so it's a competition," I replied, crossing my arms across my chest.

"You shouldn't do that," Oliver said, glancing over at me a few times.

"Do what?"

"Cross your arms like that. It really makes me pay attention to your tits and I'm trying to drive," he said.

We sat at a red light and I watched him adjust himself in

his pants. My mouth dropped open, realizing it didn't take much to get this man revved up. It was an empowering feeling and I couldn't stop myself from taking advantage of the situation. I leaned over to slide my hand onto his leg, stopping short of the bulge he was struggling with.

"Did you miss the part about me driving?" He asked in a strangled voice.

"Of course not. I figured two can play. I don't live too far away," I replied.

The rest of the drive was quiet and thick with desire. I matched each sweep of his hand, with one of my own. His cock jumped when I allowed my knuckles to graze it during my movements. There was something fascinating in the way I could make Oliver feel.

My history left me with a feeling of inadequacy. I wasn't pretty enough, or sexually appealing. For a long time I believed I was only good enough for what Lyle would give me. My therapist took a lot of money from me, to explain why these thoughts weren't true, no matter how often I thought them. I hadn't taken the chance yet to really reflect on how different it could feel to not have that baggage.

When we pulled up outside my apartment building, Oliver threw the car into park and leaned toward me. I didn't wait, I met him in the middle, allowing him to devour my mouth. His hand went to the nape of my neck, tugging gently on my hair so he could get to my neck.

"I wasn't going to do this," he murmured.

"Do what?"

"Ravish you. I was going to drive you home. Order food. Relax. Maybe cuddle. But I can't keep my hands off of you," he said.

"We can do all of those things, just maybe not in that order," I replied with a giggle as he nipped my skin.

He finally pulled away and his eyes swept over me. I was sure I was blushing and a bit disheveled. But Oliver liked what he saw. He motioned for me to stay in my seat as he jumped out of the car. He rounded the front and I saw his eyes sweeping the street. It was a reminder that he probably knew everything I told Jaxon.

When he opened my door he took my hand to help me out. Together, we went into the building. Oliver checked the main door, ensuring it locked behind us. He had his arm around my waist as we climbed the stairs. If I hadn't told Jaxon everything I had earlier in the day, I would have known Oliver knew now.

I unlocked the front door and Oliver started flipping on lights when he entered. He tried to hide it, but he was definitely checking to make sure we were alone in the apartment. I slipped off my heels and checked the one window that worried me the most. I found it locked still and felt fairly secure once Oliver locked all of the locks on the front door.

"Do you want to talk about it?" I finally asked.

I didn't like how tense things were now, when everything was so hot in the car. I didn't want my past to ruin what was happening in my present. Just like I always expected it to. I tried to ignore it as I got my hopes up, because I normally would just shoot that hope in the foot. I didn't want to do that with Oliver and Jaxon.

"Didn't you talk enough today?" Oliver asked softly.

"I did. Honestly, I don't really want to go over it again. But you seem on edge. So if there's something you want to say, just say it," I said.

Oliver finally looked at me, and met my gaze. He walked to me and took both my hands in his. I waited for the let down I felt coming. Lifting my hand to his mouth, he kissed each knuckle. Then opened my hand and kissed my palm, then my wrist. Then he gathered me in his arms and hugged me to him.

"We don't need to talk about it. I just want you to know I'm here for you. That prick won't get near you with me around," he said, his voice taking on an hardness that told me to not doubt his words.

I just nodded into his chest. When he pulled away, he deftly pulled the pins from my hair and let it flow down my back. He ran his fingers along my scalp and my eyes rolled into the back of my head and I groaned.

"How about you get comfortable and I order in? What sounds good?" He asked as he massaged my neck.

"Mmmmm, pizza?" I asked, peeking one eye at him.

"Ok. I can do that," he replied.

"There's a menu on the fridge. They already know my favorite pizza," I said as I started for the bedroom.

"How often do you eat pizza?" He called after me.

Leaning around my doorframe, I shrugged my shoulders at him.

"We're two single chicks. Whenever we want?" I replied.

In my room I could hear his chuckle at my response. Oliver was about to see that I wasn't a woman to be shy about eating. Our first meal shared together had been fancy. I can do fancy and I can enjoy it. But I do love an evening in, where I'm wearing sweat shorts and demolishing pizza with all the toppings.

I quickly changed into house clothes and piled my hair back up on the top of my head. I took a quick glance in the mirror. I rarely was this relaxed around anyone other than Ash. Even my co-workers had never seen my scars because I had gotten really good at choosing outfits that hid it just perfectly.

Oliver already knew everything and when I was honest, he had seen everything too. I wanted to pull off relaxed, but also sexy. I adjusted my oversized sweater that came off one shoulder. I had ditched the bra on purpose, knowing he would notice. My shorts were quite short and hugged my ass and thighs. I nodded at my reflection, this would do.

When I entered the living room, I found Oliver sitting barefoot with his ankles crossed on the couch. It didn't particularly matter what he was wore, he was gorgeous. His pale gray v-neck t-shirt showed off his toned arms and wide shoulders. His distressed jeans hugged thighs that I knew were muscled and hot as hell.

He beckoned me forward, and held out an arm for me to curl under. I pulled up my feet and allowed myself to lean into him. He wrapped his arm around me and kissed my temple. He handed me the tv remote.

"I was thinking a movie while we ate dinner?" He asked.

I scrolled through the apps we had until I found one with a movie we could agree on. We were laughing as we went back and forth between action movies and romcoms. We agreed on a romantic comedy and I felt at complete ease with Oliver just sitting on my couch.

The buzzer sounding made me jump out of my skin. Oliver squeezed me for a second before getting up to go to the speaker by the door. He confirmed it was the pizza guy. When I stood to join him he shook his head at me.

"Why don't you get plates? I'll handle this," he said.

I didn't argue. I didn't particularly feel comfortable being at the door in the evening. I was thankful for our buzzer system, but there was no way to prevent someone from coming in behind someone else. That thought sends a shiver through me and I peer back around the kitchen wall so I can see as Oliver gets the pizza and waves goodbye at the delivery kid.

The door closed and I finally felt relief, not even realizing how stiff I was holding myself. I grabbed paper plates and two beers from the fridge. We settled on the floor on either side of the coffee table and I couldn't miss the domestic feeling of the situation. We chewed in silence just watching each other, which should have been weird. But I was obsessed with watching his jaw flex with each bite.

Finally, I decided I should break the silence and I had lots of questions.

"Tell me about you. Now, that you basically know every piece of my life, I feel like it's only fair I get to know something," I said between bites.

Oliver looked thoughtful for a moment.

"A lot of my history, isn't only mine to tell. The four of us have been together since we were preteens basically. Jaxon and I even longer, but not by much," he said.

"Ok. Where did you grow up?"

"Here, in the city. Well not in this nice of a neighborhood, or the neighborhood we live in now. If I could, I would have our old hood bulldozed to the ground."

He said the statement with such emotion, I knew there was something deeper there.

"Sounds like we could have been neighbors," I said, prying just a little.

"If we had been, I would hope I would have noticed you back then," he said with a little smile on his face.

"We were all just kids back then. Is that why you guys care so much about the kids my non-profit supports? Because you were those kids?" I asked.

Oliver nodded. "Something like that. We were raised in lives of crime. My dad was a dealer, who worked for Jaxon's dad. I never really knew what it meant to live in a crappy apartment, with a constant revolving door of people that were always bringing money to my dad. I got older and my dad didn't give me much of an option, so I was like a junior dealer before I had even graduated high school."

"Did you have your mom around?" I asked.

Oliver shrugged and looked down at his pizza.

"No. Never knew who she was. My dad used to just say she was a whore and wouldn't talk about it again. Sometimes I think he was so strung out, he didn't actually know who she was either," he said.

I reached for a third piece of pizza and I saw him grin.

"Yes, I enjoy eating. Which is why I run. I mean I really hate running, but I love pizza. So, I have to run," I said.

"Hey, I'm not saying a word about a woman that doesn't just sit there picking at a salad as if eating is the last thing she does in life," Oliver said, holding up his hands in defense.

We fell silent again as we ate. It was weird to think of Oliver or any of the Knights as kids, growing up in the slums, dealing drugs. But it did explain their need to support those kids that were now going through something similar.

"Do you still speak to your father?" I asked.

Oliver just shook his head before asking, "Do you talk to your mom?"

"She died. And no, you don't need to be sorry. That's what everyone always says. But according to my therapist, after everything she put me through it was normal that I didn't really feel anything when the police showed up on my doorstep to tell me she had OD'd."

"How long ago was that?"

"I was nineteen. Lyle just laughed, saying she got what she deserved. I didn't necessarily feel that way at the time. But therapy got me through," I said with a shrug.

With full bellies we got comfortable on the couch again. Oliver crossed his bare feet on the coffee table and I lounged into his side. It was all so normal and comfortable. I started yawning, dozing off in the middle of the movie. Oliver just pulled the couch blanket over me and let me use him as a pillow.

I woke up when Oliver shifted and picked me up. When I looked around, I realized he had straightened up the living room, putting away the leftover pizza. All of the lights except one were off and it was dark out. He carried me into my room and laid me in the middle of the bed. Without a word, he stripped out of his t-shirt and jeans, climbing into bed next to me in his boxer briefs.

Turning me to my side, he spooned behind me, wrapping an arm around my waist. He nuzzled my neck and kissed me softly.

Sleepily I asked, "Are you staying because you want to, or because you think you need to protect me?"

Oliver ground his hips into mine and I could feel his hardness. Even though I was almost asleep, the feel of him wanting me woke me up. I ground back against him, and he gripped my hip.

"You were sleeping," he growled.

"I'm not anymore," I replied.

I flipped myself, so I was facing him. He looked down at me with hooded eyes. Reaching down, I ran my hand over his thick length, stroking him outside his briefs. He closed his eyes briefly before looking at me again, his eyes bright with desire now.

His kiss started soft and exploratory, kissing each of my lips separately, before sucking my bottom lip into his mouth. I opened my mouth and slid my tongue along his in a heated dance. The kiss became more demanding as I reached up and gripped his curly hair, securing his mouth to mine.

He ran a hand to my knee, pulling my leg over his hip, so his cock was lined up with me, our clothes still separating us.

He rubbed against my heat and I moaned at the friction that was building my need, but just wasn't enough.

My hair fell around me, as Oliver found the tie and pulled it free. He fisted some of the strands and rolled me to my back.

"I love this. I love it when it's down and around you, like a halo," he said.

He reached a hand down between us, and found the bottom of my sweatshirt. Warmth shot through me as his palm skimmed up my ribs to my bare breasts. He palmed one and then tweaked the nipple of the other. Shoving the material out of his way, he leaned down and sucked the raised peak into his mouth, teasing it with his teeth.

I yanked the shirt off, tossing it across the room. He continued the explorations of my skin with his mouth, running his tongue along my scar and up my neck. There was something extremely erotic about him lavishing attention on the thing that until now always felt grotesque to me. Oliver found a way to make my imperfections feel beautiful.

He leaned his chest against mine and his light chest hair rubbed against my skin, making me shiver. He got up to go to his jeans and I knew he was prepared, but I knew I wanted to feel him just as I had felt every inch of Jaxon.

"No. I'm on birth control. Jaxon and I, well we didn't use protection today. We don't need it," I said quietly.

Oliver's eyes flashed back to me and he grabbed my shorts and panties and yanked them off in one quick movement. I was left giggling at his exuberance. The laugh died in my throat as he fit his shoulders between my thighs and his mouth found my core.

"Oh god, Oliver, yes," I cried out as he sucked my clit into his mouth, while sliding a finger into my channel.

"Babe, I could listen to you scream my name all night, don't stop," he moaned against my pussy.

I gasped a light laugh at his words as he dove back into me with his tongue, lapping at my juices. Whenever he circled my clit, I couldn't help myself, my hips would rise and grind against his face. It began to feel like too much and I started to thrash. I wanted more but couldn't seem to figure out what I needed.

When I tried to pull away, Oliver clamped an arm across my hips. Adding a second finger to my pussy, he continued to fuck me with his fingers while his teeth nipped at my overly excited bud. It was all that I needed and I was exploding against his mouth. Stars seemed to flash behind my eyelids.

I was just barely aware of Oliver sliding up my body and settling his hips between my thighs. When I opened my eyes, he was looking down at me, brushing strands of my hair from my face.

"So beautiful," he murmured.

He kissed me softly and then his tongue ran against mine. I could taste myself and for a moment I wondered why women didn't talk about this more often. His hand ran down my side and lifted my leg so it was around his hip. I followed with the other and I felt his cock nudging my entrance.

"I want this to be slow," he said.

I nodded my head. He held my gaze as he slowly pushed into me fully. He dropped his forehead to mine for a moment.

"You are so fucking tight, this feels too amazing. I gotta be careful or it's gonna be over way too soon," he chuckled.

I tilted my hips, trying to pull him in deeper and he groaned before kissing me deeply. He pulled back his hips and slowly sank into me again. The pace was killing me in all the best ways. I lifted my knees up further, crossing my ankles behind Oliver, causing him to hit even deeper inside me.

Oliver leaned up on his knees, taking my hips with him. He continued to slowly thrust, but reached down and pressed his thumb to my hood before slipped further down and rubbing against my clit.

"Oliver," I moaned.

"Tell me what you want babe."

"More. Faster," I begged.

"Come for me, once more baby," he said.

I could see sweat starting to create a sheen on his body. He was holding back, waiting for me to come again. Moments later I was shattering around his cock and he groaned as he began to pick up his pace. I watched as he bit his lip and groaned as he spilled hotly into me.

Instead of collapsing on me, he twisted and shifted us so I was laying across his chest. His heart was thundering under my ear and I smiled against his skin, knowing I did that to him. After cleaning us both up, Oliver pulled me back into him and pulled the blankets over us.

"I'm here, because I want to be."

CHAPTER
Seventeen

Oliver

BEING WOKEN BY A WARM, soft body, wasn't a typical morning for me. I stretched, and Brooklyn's arm tightened around my middle. Her head was on my chest and one of her legs was over mine.

"Not yet," she mumbled, more asleep than awake.

I realized what had woken me was a vibration on the nightstand. The sun was barely peaking in, but my phone was ringing. Blindly, I reached over until my hand smacked it. Lifting I hit the answer button without seeing who it was.

"What?" I asked.

"Brother, wake up," Gideon's voice came through the cell.

"What is it?" I felt a bit more awake, realizing it was Gideon calling so early. He wouldn't call unless there was a problem.

"Thought you should know, Lyle has already broken probation. He hasn't been showing up to the group transition home he was supposed to be staying in. And he hasn't reported to his probation officer like required. He's in the wind as far as the authorities are concerned. I'll keep looking," he explained.

"Shit. Ok. Thanks for letting me know."

After a pause he asked, "You with her?"

I looked down at the blonde hair that was across my body. Brooklyn picked up her head and squinted at me, before burrowing back into my body.

"Yeah," I said quietly.

"Good. We should stick with her as often as possible. She needs protection until someone can track down Lyle."

"Got it."

"Go back to sleep. Enjoy," Gideon said.

As we hung up, I noted the gruff sound of Gideon's voice. I wondered what he meant when he said we need to stick with her. Did he include himself in that? It could be an interesting turn of events.

I didn't have time to think about it, because Brooklyn's hands were wandering under the blanket. Her touch was delicate and exploratory. I tried to lay as still as possible and let her have the fun she wanted to have.

When her fingers ran the length of my cock, which was already semi hard, it jumped. That seemed to only encourage her and she wrapped her fingers around me and began to stoke. I couldn't stop myself from thrusting up into her hand when she stopped.

"I thought you were sleepy," I said, through gritted teeth.

"You woke me up. And now there's better things I can think be doing before getting ready for work," she said.

She threw off the blanket, baring both of our naked bodies. Before I could react, she straddled my waist. Her blonde hair was tangled and mussed and her eyes were still sleepy. But I could see the sexy glint in them so I laid back to let her have her way.

Rising up on her knees, she positioned my cock at her entrance and slowly slid down until she was fully seated in my lap. She moaned as she adjusted to the full feeling and I was glad she sat still for a moment so I could get control of myself. It took everything I had to not flip her over and fuck her senseless.

Slowly, she began to rotate her hips, sliding herself along my hardness. When she hit the right spots she would gasp and do the same movement again. Her pussy pulsated around me and I knew she was getting close. I slid a hand between us and let her use my fingers for her pleasure as well.

The friction caused her to lose a bit of her control and she started thrusting her hips harder against my hand and my cock. I gritted my teeth, holding my control in check until I felt her come, her walls squeezing me tight.

As she slowed through her orgasm, I sat up and grabbed her hips. Using her hips and thrusting mine up, I fucked her from below. She clung to my shoulders as her orgasm continued and I came harder than I had the night before. I fell back onto the bed and Brooklyn followed with her face in my neck.

"That's a nice way to wake up," she mumbled.

"Maybe it's time for a bit of a nap, then shower?" I suggested.

"Mmmmm…" she mumbled, as she snuggled into me and started to fall asleep again.

In the shower, my hands seemed to have minds of their own. Brooklyn's long blonde hair flowed down her back with the water and my cock immediately reacted at the beauty of her arching back under the spray. When she looked forward again, she smirked seeing my predicament.

I moved forward and cupped her breasts, sliding a thumb over the taunt peaks. She sighed happily and I captured her mouth in a long leisurely kiss.

"I do have to go to work," she murmured against my mouth.

"I'll make sure you're there on time," I replied.

Sliding a hand down her stomach, she spread her legs to give me access to her pretty pussy. Softly, I slid my finger through her lips and dipped shallowly into her. She gripped my arm, and moved her hips, asking for more.

I moved her back to the wall of the shower and lifted one of her legs to my hips. She looked up at me, surprised as my cock nudged her entrance.

"Standing?" She asked.

"I want you in every position possible," I said against her ear.

The shower sex was slow and seductive. I was finding that being with Brooklyn was addictive. After, I used a fluffy towel to dry her and kissed her nose. She laughed and swatted me away, swearing if I made her late to work that would be the last time she let me spend the night. I backed away with my hands up, swearing I'd behave.

In the kitchen I found coffee already brewed, set by a timer. I poured two mugs and realized I didn't know how she took her coffee. As I was going to ask, she came into the room in her robe. I watched as she drank the coffee black and filed the information away for later.

I insisted on driving her to work, after much disagreement. We walked down to the car and I helped her slide in. She was wearing one of her signature outfits with heels that did things to my insides. At her office, she turned to me with an eyebrow raised.

"Are you going to let me go to the office alone?" She asked.

"I can walk you up if you'd like," I offered.

"Go away Oliver," she laughed as she opened the door.

She waved before closing the door. She was practically glowing and I was happy to take the credit for that. I rolled down the window before she could get too far away.

"Never, babe," I called out.

Brooklyn shot a mock glare over her shoulder before laughing and pressing the button for the elevator. I waited until she disappeared through the doors. I felt fairly certain that she was safe in her office But it was still hard to leave without one of us with her.

When I got home, I barely made it to my room before Jaxon was at the door asking how Brooklyn was.

"I think she's doing alright. I didn't tell her what Gideon called about this morning. I don't want her worrying about more than she can do anything about," I said.

Jaxon nodded thoughtfully and I knew he was wondering if that was the right call. To be honest, I hadn't told Brooklyn because I hadn't wanted to spoil the morning we were having. It felt so good and strangely domestic to be with her as she got ready for the office. And the way she was so giving with her body was something I wanted to receive as often as possible.

"Did you happen to tell her about us heading out of town?" Jaxon asked.

"Shit, no. I completely forgot," I replied.

"Don't tell Aiden that," Jaxon said, laughing.

He was right. If Aiden knew I was distracted from work by Brooklyn, he would be livid. Oliver and I both had to travel to the newest 4K club to do a spot check of operations. Gideon had done his trip the week before, ensuring the security team that had been hired was handling things as expected.

We rarely traveled together as a team, because we found spot checks worked better when it was only one or two of us. Jaxon and I were the only two left to do our walk through. I rubbed at my chest, as a weird feeling crept up on me.

"I'm worried about leaving her too," Jaxon said from the doorway.

Was that what this feeing of pressure was? Worry? I wasn't sure. But I knew I hated the idea of being away from Brooklyn, especially with her ex stalking her.

"Do you think Gideon would watch out for her while we're gone?" I asked.

"You want me to do what?"

Speak of the devil, Gideon was walking by my open door just as I said his name. He looked like he was coming up from a workout. His hair was down and wild around his shoulders. He was breathing heavily still and dripping with sweat.

"Jaxon and I are on the way out of town tomorrow. Can you be available for Brooklyn, in case anything happens?" I asked.

"You want to just leave her alone? Even though Lyle knows where she lives?" Gideon asked.

"We don't have much of a choice. We gotta make this trip. Plus you're the one with security experience. Maybe there's a way to ensure her safety while one of us isn't with her," I said.

Gideon looked thoughtful for a moment, then nodded to us.

"I'll handle it," he said, with no further explanation before walking away.

Jaxon and I shared a look and I shrugged.

"She'll win him over. He can't be gruff all the time," I said.

"Is that what we want? It doesn't bother you, thinking about her with someone else?" He asked.

"Fuck yes it bothers me. But it's not the same when it's you or one of the other guys. We've done this before. Sharing with you guys doesn't feel the same as some other random dude getting with my girl."

"Your girl? Does she know that?" Jaxon asked with a grin.

"Not in so many words, but I'll make sure she does. What about you?" I asked.

"Same, brother. Same," he replied.

Jaxon clapped me on the shoulder before leaving my room. This trip was going to have to be quick. Aiden would expect us to be there for a few days, but I wasn't sure I could handle that. I knew Brooklyn was way too busy with her own work, so we couldn't just take her with us.

I changed my clothes and threw together what I would need for the trip. Next was having to tell Brooklyn we would be gone. I wasn't looking forward to dropping that bomb. I trusted Gideon with her safety, but would it be in time to ensure nothing further happened?

CHAPTER
Eighteen

Brooklyn

OLIVER AND JAXON were gone on a business trip, and it was a Friday night. I sat alone in my sweats, on the couch. Work had been extremely busy, so I hadn't been able to dwell on the idea of not having one of them at home with me. Sitting flipping through a magazine wasn't the distraction I was hoping it would be. I huffed out a sigh and threw my head back on my couch.

The night before they had to leave, they both came to stay

with me. I could feel my face heat and a shock at my core as I remembered how that night went. They had me in positions, I wasn't aware my body was capable of doing. It made me hot and horny to even think about it.

I stood and went to the kitchen. Opening my fridge, I stared in mindlessly, just looking for a distraction to my sex thoughts. I pulled out a chilled white wine and poured myself a glass. I hadn't needed my vibrator in days, but I was already planning on a session before I fell asleep.

Somehow, having two men had turned me into a complete sex monster. I wasn't sure if it was the whole new world of multiple partners or just the simple fact that I hadn't known what sex could really be until them. Whatever it was, I didn't want it to end anytime soon. I thought of them as my men, but I hadn't told them that. Oliver and Jaxon just didn't strike me as relationship types.

The buzzer at my door sounded and I almost dropped my wine glass. My throat went dry. I knew I wasn't expecting any deliveries. I was planning on making a small meal of spaghetti for dinner and hadn't ordered food. Slowly, I went to the buzzer and pressed the button.

"Yes?"

My voice came out in a squeak I wasn't proud of.

"Brooklyn? It's Gideon Knight. Are you alright?"

His voice sounded anxious on the other side. I recognized the deep roughness of his voice, just from the few times I've heard him on the phone. The man hadn't spoken directly to me on purpose since I met them.

"I'm fine. Can I help you Gideon?" I asked, trying to pull myself together.

"I told my brothers I'd check on you while they're gone. I also have some security upgrades I'd like to make to your place. Can you buzz me up?"

I took a shaky breath and laughed at myself. I should have expected Oliver and Jaxon to do something. They had been texting me constantly throughout the day and explained they would be working in the evening so might not be as reachable. Of course, I understood that, work still needed to be done.

I pressed the button to unlock the door and waited with my eye to the peephole of my apartment door. A few moments later, I saw the beast of a man coming across the landing. He must have taken the stairs two at a time to get to the door so fast. I watched in fascination as he ran a hand over his hair and then over his beard. A smile spread across my face, as I spotted what seemed like nerves.

He knocked on the door and I waited a beat, so it wouldn't be obvious I was spying on him. When I opened the door, I smiled brightly at him. He smiled slightly back at me, but was already looking around my door and glancing back on the landing.

"Are there no cameras on the landing?" He asked.

"No. I mean, some residents have those doorbell things, that record in front of their door. But Ash and I never had one installed," I explained.

I stepped aside and waved him in. Closing the door, I flipped all of the locks out of habit. Gideon watched me and nodded his head, approving of my vigilance.

"Well, I brought a camera. I think it would be good to see what happens at all times outside your door. Also, I just wanted to double check your locks. And I brought something to add to the window with the fire escape ladder," Gideon said, showing me the duffel bag he had.

"Oh wow, ok. Thank you. I appreciate that," I said.

I stood there awkwardly for a moment, having no idea what I was supposed to do now. And Gideon just stared at his feet. All of the self confidence I had around Oliver and Jaxon seemed to escape me around this big man. I snuck a look at him, when I didn't think he would catch me staring.

He towered over his brothers. I wanted him to take his hair out of the tie, so I could see how long it was. I imagined it was perfect on him He had a full beard, that was sleek and well taken care of. I could see the end of a black tattoo that came from his shoulder, up his neck. It made me wonder what the rest of it looked like. His chest was broad and his shirt was tight, as if it struggled to hold in the bulk of him.

Suddenly, his green eyes flashed up at me and I knew he was aware of my intense studying. I could feel the flush on my cheeks and to cover I held up the wine that was still in my hand.

"Would you like a drink?" I asked.

"Sure," he replied.

I rushed off to the kitchen. Once I was hidden from view I opened my fridge and stuck my face in it for a moment. Damn me and my need to blush at the drop of a hat. The guy probably thought I was a complete loon. When I stood up and had the bottle in my hand, I turned to find Gideon studying me. A squeak escaped my lips and the largest smile I've seen on the man appeared.

"Sorry, didn't mean to scare you. I wasn't sure if I was supposed to follow or not."

"Oh, no, it's ok. I'm sorry. I mean, you didn't scare me. Lord. I'm acting like a weirdo," I said, laughing at myself as I pulled a clean wine glass from the cabinet.

"Nah, it's cute," he chuckled.

I had to stop and look at him in shock. Had the big man actually joked with me? He raised an eyebrow at me, until I realized I was completely staring at him. I turned away to pour the wine and handed him the glass. I held up my glass in a mock toast.

"Here's to making sure I don't die," I said and then gulped the wine.

He set down the glass without drinking and walked closer to me. His big palms rested on my shoulders, and he looked me in the eye.

"Hey, no. That's not going to happen. We're going to do everything possible to keep Lyle away from you," he reassured.

Warmth spread through my body, from the wine and from Gideon's touch. I appreciated the comfort he was offering. I smiled at him and nodded my head, showing I understood. He stepped back and sipped his own wine for a second.

"You can do whatever it is you want. Just let me know what you need from me. I really appreciate it," I said.

"I think I have everything I need. Once it's all done, I'll show you how it works," he replied.

With that, he turned and left the kitchen. To distract myself, I started pulling out the supplies I need to make sauce and noodles. I pulled out a loaf of French bread to make garlic bread.

Once everything was on the counter, I realized I was easily making enough for two. I went back out to the living room to find Gideon. He was crouched by the front door, pulling out electronics from his duffel. His gaze came to me when I approached and he smiled softly.

"Would you like dinner? I'm making enough for two. Spaghetti?" I asked.

Gideon seemed to consider for a moment, before nodding.

"Sure, if it's no trouble."

"It's the least I could do for you installing all of this stuff. I wouldn't know how to go about any of this without your help," I replied.

Back in the kitchen I turned on my Bluetooth speaker. I

scrolled through my music lists until I found something smooth to listen to. "Tennessee Whiskey" by Chris Stapleton came on and I swung my hips slowly to the melody and gravelly voice. The music calmed my nerves and I got to making the meal.

I mixed the pasta and tasted the sauce. Cooking wasn't my strongest talent, but I could make a few basic meals. Enough to keep myself from starving over the years. Lost in my own world in the kitchen, I didn't realize Gideon had come to the entry.

I sipped my wine and sang quietly to myself. As I drained the noodles, "Pillowtalk" by Zayn had come on. As I sang along about fucking and fighting, I turned to find Gideon watching me with a sly grin on his face.

"Shit," I said, gripping my chest, "You need a bell or something."

"You aren't super aware of your surroundings are you?" He laughed.

"How long have you been standing there?"

"Long enough to know you enjoy music. And have quite the eclectic taste."

"I do. Music has been one thing I could say is constant in my life. No matter how bad things were, I could turn to music. It's reliable and doesn't abandon you," I said.

I busied myself with serving the meal and setting the table. I had to slide by Gideon's wide body to get to the table, but he didn't move to make it easier for me. He took up so much space and I felt like some of the air was sucked out of the room too.

Once I had the food on the table, I motioned for him to sit and he pulled out my chair first.

"Are you all so gentlemanly?" I asked with a smile.

"Probably one of the things we do have in common.

Treating women well, is something we all strive to do. And do well," he said, sitting across from me.

"I hope everything is ok. I'm not great at this, but who can mess up spaghetti?"

"You'd be surprised," he said with a knowing smile.

"Sounds like there's a story there," I replied.

We ate in silence for a few moments and I refilled our wine glasses. It was easier to study Gideon closer with him sitting across my small dining table. His knuckles were scarred, old wounds if I had to guess. His nose had been broken at least once and maybe not set correctly. The damage gave his handsome face a tougher look.

It was clear he took great care in his body and style. Though his hair was pulled back in a bun, it was slick and smooth. His beard was trimmed to perfection and I had to wonder if he did it himself or had a barber he saw regularly. I found myself fascinated with the flex of his forearms and the gentle way he handled the wine glass in hands that I knew could snap the stem in one motion.

Gideon cleared his throat and I realized I had stopped eating. And I was once again caught staring. I looked up to meet his gaze and then looked down at my plate again, busying myself with getting a bite ready. After I put it in my mouth and chewed, I decided I didn't like all the silence.

"So, you clearly know everything about me at this point. I knew it wouldn't be hard to pull up a lot of what happened to me," I said, gesturing to the scar on my neck that was exposed with my hair up on the top of my head.

Gideon didn't say anything, just nodded with a tight jaw.

"Tell me about you, Gideon. Why are you in charge of security?"

His eyes widened for a moment, as my question caught

him off guard. I smiled sweetly. It was only fair to dig a little into his past, since he knew all of my skeletons.

"It just was the natural progression I guess. I was always the rough one when we were kids. Always fighting, protecting everyone. When we got older and into business, I could read people, know who was good or not. So, I dove into it more, electronics, security systems and personal security."

"Why were you always fighting as a kid?" I asked, cocking my head to the side.

"I know the guys told you some of what life was like for us. One difference is, I grew up with both parents at home. But it didn't make things any better for me. It was like growing up training for a boxing match always," he said.

I grimaced, trying to picture a little Gideon defending himself against the people that should have loved and cared for him. The idea broke my heart a little and I could feel myself wanting to hug him and heal the little boy somehow.

"I survived. I don't think about it too much. My parents are long gone. It was always my dad who liked to be heavy handed. And I learned young that my mom was either too scared or didn't care. I was five when he broke my fingers the first time. He wouldn't take me to the hospital. I'm lucky he set them somewhat correct, or I might have more than just a few crooked ones. My mom didn't do anything when she came home from work," he explained, holding up one of his hands.

A few of the fingers didn't lay perfect, but I wouldn't have noticed if he hadn't pointed it out. Without thinking, I reached forward and pulling his hand toward me. I rubbed my thumb along the fingers that hadn't healed straight, feeling so sad at that moment.

"Hey, it's not something to feel bad for now. It was a long time ago," he said quietly.

"Right. Yeah, I know," I said, releasing his hand. "How did you meet your brothers?"

"Well, believe it or not, Aiden and I met when he used to get teased in elementary. He wasn't the tough guy he is now. And I could tell when he came to school sporting black eyes, that we had a lot in common. So, I took care of the kids that wouldn't leave him alone. I'll never forget that first lunch, Aiden tried to give me a fruit cup in payment. We've been family ever since."

I got myself lost in the idea of Gideon and Aiden as defenseless children, finding a way to handle the life the world handed them. I took a deep breath, realizing we were all so alike in our origins. In a way, it made me feel closer to all four of them. I could understand the life Gideon was describing.

"I envy what you guys have. It must be amazing to have three other people in this world you can rely on," I said. My voice came out a bit more wistful than I had planned.

Gideon looked at me seriously for a moment before saying, "Well, now you have four more people in the world for you."

I had no response to that. I just stared into his green eyes, wondering if that was the truth. Aiden hadn't spoken to me since the business meeting debacle. Did he actually care what happened to me. And this was the first time Gideon had spent time alone with me. Did these guys stick around because they pitied what I had been through.

That idea caused a lump to stick in my throat. I gave Gideon a polite smile, before standing and taking my plate to the kitchen. I leaned over the sink, hanging my head. I had worked so hard to not allow the people around me to know the truth of my past for this exact reason. I didn't want pity friends. I didn't want people watching and waiting for me to fall apart.

A warm hand landed on my back, and a plate was added to the sink in front of me.

"What is it?" He asked.

He rubbed my back, sliding his hand up to my shoulders where he could knead one and then the other. His hand on my neck, created a little bit of pressure, to encourage me to turn and look at him. He towered over me, but it didn't feel imposing. No, instead it felt normal and comfortable.

"I don't want people in my life because they feel bad for me. I've taken care of myself for a while now. I can keep doing that," I said.

"That's not what I meant, not at all," he said.

He yanked me into him then and wrapped his arms around me, hugging me to him. I slid my arms around his waist. He pulled away with a smile and left the room muttering something that sounded like "stellina".

CHAPTER

Nineteen

Gideon

BROOKLYN'S COUCH wasn't the most comfortable place to sleep. Not that I could even think to close my eyes with her in the room right next to me. I couldn't stop picturing what she slept in or how little she could be wearing. Fantasizing about Brooklyn had become my new favorite thing to do before bed.

Installing the camera and locks took longer than I had anticipated, especially with the break to eat dinner with her. If I was being honest, I hadn't rushed through the work. I enjoyed being around her and the conversation was easy and familiar. Answering her questions seemed only fair since we knew everything about her.

When I was finally done, she asked me to stay. She hadn't slept alone in her apartment since Lyle had shown that he knew where she lived. With her roommate out of town, she really just didn't want to be alone. I agreed to sleep on the couch, though she offered a side of her bed. I didn't want to feel like I was taking advantage of a woman that was scared, so I took the couch.

Now here I was, uncomfortable as hell. I took off my shirt, but left on my jeans to stay somewhat proper. Though I knew nothing my brothers did with her in this apartment was proper. And there went the fantasies again. Hugging her in the kitchen had been a big mistake. Feeling her body, all her perfect curves, pressed against me had set fire licking through my body.

I sighed and tried to adjust my large frame on the couch. That was half the problem, I was too damn big for the piece of furniture. I was longer than it by at least a foot and my shoulders didn't both fit if I laid on my back. The damn thing was made for little people and I was not that.

As I was starting to count sheep, a scream ripped through the apartment. I jumped to my feet, grabbing my small handgun that was hidden under my shirt on the floor and ran for Brooklyn's room. I flipped on the light, checking the entire room. It only took a moment to realize she was alone and having a nightmare.

In the middle of her king size bed, she was clawing at her neck, her eyes wide open and wildly looking around the room. I put the gun down on her desk and rushed to her side. When I got to the bed, she held out her arms and I gathered her close.

Sitting on the bed, I pulled her into my lap and squeezed her tight.

"I'm sorry," she said through her tears.

"No, Stellina, don't be sorry," I whispered.

For a long moment, she just clung to me, her face pressed to my chest. I could feel the wetness where her tears slid along my skin.

"Stellina?" She asked.

"Oh, uh, it's Italian. It kinda just felt like it fit," I muttered.

I hadn't meant to call her that to her face. Since the night I saw her dancing with Oliver and Jaxon in Club 4, I had one thought about her. She reminded me of a star, the way Oliver and Jaxon seemed to gravitate toward her. If I hadn't been with Aiden, she may have pulled me in too that night. She had a way about her that made you want to be close.

"What does it mean?" She asked.

"Uh, well, it means little star."

"Is this a comment about my height," she said with a watery laugh.

"I mean, next to me, it makes sense, doesn't it?" I replied with my own small laugh.

She pulled back from me and rubbed at her face. I reached up and wiped away some stray tears. I moved her hair away from her neck and saw a few places where she had scratched her skin. Nothing was bleeding, but it would probably leave a mark for a day or two. I set her back on the bed and went to ensuite.

I returned to her with a cool washcloth. She watched me as I carefully wiped at her scratches, just to cool the skin and make sure nothing was too badly injured. Once I was done, I put the cloth back and went back to her bedroom door. I motioned for the light and she nodded. Her voice came through the darkness after I flipped the switch.

"Gideon?"

"Hmmm?"

"Please stay in here with me. I feel safer with you here," she said quietly.

I hesitated for a moment. Being in bed with her was something I wanted and badly. But that wasn't what she was asking me. I took a deep breath and grabbed my gun. I set it on the bedside table and it was light enough that she saw it. She looked up at me and then back at the weapon.

"I guess I shouldn't be surprised. You're the security guy," she said.

"I have a permit and all that fun stuff. I don't carry it all the time. But I just thought, in case, ya know?" I replied.

She nodded. I stepped to the side of the bed and she slid over to one side. I climbed on top of her blanket and laid back on the pillows. She slid close to me, but with her under the blanket and me on top, she couldn't get close like she wanted. I felt her hand tug on my jeans.

"This can't be great to sleep in."

"It's ok. I don't want to make you uncomfortable."

"You won't make me uncomfortable, Gideon. You are clearly the picture of respect and chivalry," she said.

I slid back out of bed and took off my jeans. In just my boxer briefs, I got back into the bed, under her blanket this time. Immediately I felt her soft leg slide along mine as she settled against my chest. I wrapped an arm around her shoulders, letting her know she was welcome however she wanted to be.

I had thought the couch was the worst place to fall asleep. I was wrong. Laying in Brooklyn's bed, with her soft leg across one of mine and her arm wrapped low on my waist, I thought I was going to die. Her lavender scent permeated everything around me and it went straight to my head.

Eventually, I nodded off to the sound of Brooklyn breathing evenly on my chest. My dreams were a mix of hot bodies and cold showers. Even my subconscious wasn't sure what my body should be feeling so everything was at odds in my mind.

It was mid morning when I finally cracked an eye open. Sleeping in was one of my favorite things to do on the weekends. As lazy as it sounded, I had grown up in a way where I could never sleep regularly without being worried about being beaten for sleeping too long. Now, my brothers knew not to wake me on a weekend morning unless someone was on fire or dying.

As I became aware of my surroundings, I realized I was curled around Brooklyn's body. In our sleep, we had changed positions. Brooklyn's ass was cradled against my thighs and my arms were wrapped around her. Our fingers were intertwined at her waist. Brooklyn's face was still soft in sleep, but her hips moved and pushed back against me.

My cock didn't seem to know that we were supposed to be keeping control of ourselves. I tried to pull back and put space between us, but Brooklyn stirred and I froze. When she turned her head to look at me, I pulled back.

"Er, sorry. I didn't mean to, uh, wake you," I said.

"It's ok. I rarely sleep in, so this is late for me. I must have needed the sleep," she replied.

She began to stretch, but that rubbed her along my hard cock and I knew the moment she felt it. She froze and looked down and then slowly up my body. I was waiting for her to jump out of bed, but instead I felt her fingers tracing the tattoo on my arm, that led up to my neck.

"I had wondered," she said softly.

"What?" I asked, as her hand continued its trail over the black ink.

"What the rest of this tattoo looked like. It's beautiful the way it seems to hug your muscles," she replied.

Brooklyn completely turned so she was facing me. I looked down at her and she played with the ends of my hair.

"This too. I wanted to see it down. I like it."

Instinctively, I lifted my hand to smooth down the strands and Brooklyn pushed away my hand. Instead, she ran her fingers through the length and smiled up at me.

"Thank you for sleeping in my bed. I didn't have any nightmares with you here."

"I'm glad to be of assistance, stellina," I said.

She smiled shyly at the nickname and I decided to call her that as often as possible, just to see the pink rise in her cheeks. I watched as her eyes dropped to my mouth and then looked back up into my eyes.

"Gideon, could I ask you for one more thing?"

I nodded, waiting to see what else she could need.

"Kiss me," she whispered.

I stared at her for a long moment. Questions ran through my head. My brothers hadn't expressly given their permission for this. It wouldn't be the first time we'd all been with the same woman. But I thought a conversation would be appropriate before. Then again, where I was, almost naked, next to her and she was asking me for this one thing.

Wiping away my reservations, I knew I really wanted to know what kissing Brooklyn felt like. Her mouth, with her full pouty lips, looked made to be kissed. I told myself that Oliver and Jaxon would forgive me.

Lowering my face to hers, I softly pressed my lips to hers. I kissed her top lip first, then her bottom. I pulled back and she looked up at me with a smirk.

"That wasn't exactly what I meant."

Her hand that was still in my hair, gripped it and pulled

me back down to her. This time, the kiss was fused with heat as she licked at my lips until I opened for her. When I licked into her mouth, she moaned and moved closer to me, throwing a leg over my hips. My hands went to her ass, pulling her core against my cock and she moaned again as she gyrated her hips against me.

She pulled back to catch her breath and looked into my eyes again.

"Much better. I knew that was in you," she whispered.

I went to move my hands off her, but she reached back and stopped me. She rolled her hips against me again and I had to close my eyes to control my response. I started to count backwards from ten, trying to make my body relax. Her phone ringing on the nightstand made both of us jump and Brooklyn giggled at us.

She went to roll toward the phone and I released her. She held up the screen for me to see Jaxon's name. I nodded and started to roll from the bed, but she grabbed my arm to stop me. She slid her finger across the phone and put it on speaker.

"Hiya, Jaxon," she purred.

"Hey, love. Did I wake you?" Jaxon's voice came through the speaker.

"No. Gideon and I were just waking up. We slept in," she said with a smirk.

There was a short pause, then Jaxon barked out a laugh. I then heard him click his phone onto speaker and speak to Oliver on the other end.

"Oliver, our brother is keeping our girl nice and warm apparently," he joked.

"Oh shit, Gideon!" Oliver exclaimed from further away from the phone.

Brooklyn laughed at their antics and I just shook my head. Sometimes Jaxon and Oliver could act like teenagers.

"Well, he did help keep the nightmares at bay, but he was trying to leave me in bed this morning. Not nice," she said, pouting in my direction.

"Baby, you just tell him what you want. Gideon is just a big softy," Oliver said, his voice closer to the phone now.

"I miss you guys," she said.

"We miss you. We'll be home by Monday, no later," Jaxon promised.

"Tell Gideon he has to stay with me while you're gone," Brooklyn said.

Both of the guys laughed on the other end.

"All I have to say is, good luck telling her no to whatever she wants, brother," Oliver said.

"Buh bye, guys," Brooklyn said.

The guys chorused their goodbye and Brooklyn hit the end button. She then turned to me and propped her head up on her hand. Her beautiful mouth was turned up in a grin and I knew I was completely done for.

CHAPTER
Twenty

Brooklyn

"YOU HEARD THEM," I said.

Oliver, Jaxon and I had talked at length about the expectations of our relationship. They had been clear that the four brothers were a package deal. Until I had Gideon to myself, I hadn't realized that wanting him would hit me like a freight train. It had been a slow sizzle all day while he worked around my apartment and we sat to eat dinner together.

Having him in bed with me was originally about comfort.

The dream I had was so vivid, it was as if Lyle was slicing my throat again. I knew the mix of his threat over my head, missing my men and restless sleep caused the nightmare. It had been a long time since I had one that bad.

When Gideon came rushing into my room, shirtless, and pulled me into his lap, I was immediately surrounded by his comfort. Once we were curled up together for sleep, I fell asleep better than I had in days. He just brought that calmness to me and it was like a weighted blanket across me.

Waking up with his spooning behind me, I quickly realized he was large all over as his hardness rubbed against my ass. I felt myself go wet just with the idea of him fucking me. Jaxon calling was actually perfect timing, because it was clear that Gideon was holding back. And if his brothers were the reason, they just made sure that wasn't an excuse.

I could see the wheels turning in Gideon's mind as he looked at me. His hand came up to caress my cheek and I leaned into him. He pulled me close to him again, with a hand on my jaw, he tilted my head up so he could drop his mouth to mine. This time, the kiss was all his lead, without me needing to prompt him. He seductively rubbed his tongue against mine, before nipping at my bottom lip.

"What do you want, Brooklyn?" He asked, his voice low and gravely.

"You. However you want me," I said.

His hand snaked down and lifted my nightgown over my head. The garment was tossed across the room, before his fingers found the edge of my panties and he slid those down my thighs. Those joined my nightgown on the floor. Now that I was completely bared to him, he laid back on the pillows.

"Come sit, right here," he said.

I looked at him, confused as he pointed to his mouth. When it occurred to me what he wanted me to do, I shook my head.

It felt too personal, too forward. However, Gideon wasn't going to allow me to back out now. With a growl, he reached down and grabbed me by my thighs. Without much effort, he lifted me until I was above his head, my knees on either side.

"I want to taste you, but I want you to have control," he said.

I shivered at his words. Though he wanted to give me control over some of the situation, he didn't let me hesitate. With my hips gripped in his hands, he pulled me down to his mouth. With the first sweep of his tongue along my core, I cried out and grabbed my headboard. Gideon moaned and the vibration caused me to clench and roll my hips against his mouth.

Before I knew it, I was thrusting against his face and he was forcefully holding my hips down so I couldn't buck away. His tongue fucked me slowly before circling my clit and sucking it into his mouth. I didn't have any warning as an orgasm crashed over me and was a shaking mess on him.

He slowly licked me through my pleasure and when I was ready to collapse, he finally released me and allowed me to slide down. His face and beard were soaked with my juices and I had to look away, feeling embarrassed. Gideon grabbed a Kleenex and wipes his face, before pulling me back to him.

"You are fucking delicious. Don't ever think differently," he said.

His dirty words made me groan and I slid my core along his hardness, causing him to grit out a curse. I reached between my legs and slid my hand into his briefs. I could barely circle his cock with my hand, telling me what I already knew. He was huge. My hips were stretched to the max while I straddled him. I felt a tremor of anticipation shudder through me and I wanted him inside me badly.

As I stroked him, I pushed his briefs down, until he used

his feet to get rid of them completely. He flipped us suddenly, and I gasped. Leaning down, he took one of my nipples in his mouth and sucked harshly, causing me to cry out and grip his hair at the same time. I could feel the tug low in my belly and I knew I was dripping wet for him again.

Leaning back, Gideon grabbed my thighs and flipped me onto my stomach. He pushed one of my knees forward, until he could wedge himself behind me. I could feel his pulsing head at my entrance.

"I don't know if I can go slow," Gideon said, his grip practically bruising on my hip.

"Then don't. I want all of it, all of you," I moaned.

His cock slipped through my wetness, hitting my clit before he pulled back again and found my entrance. He was slow when he first slid into me and thank god he was. His thick length stretched me beyond what I thought possible. Once he was completely sheathed, he made small motions, helping me stretch and fit him even deeper.

"Ready, stellina?"

I nodded. A tug on my hair had my head turning to the side where Gideon was able to capture my mouth in a punishing kiss. His hand slid under me, until he found my hard nipples and he pinched one, causing me to spasm around his cock. He groaned into my hair and pulled out until just the tip was left. When he slammed back into me, I couldn't stay quiet.

"Fuck! Gideon!" I screamed out.

He leaned up so he was on his knees, pulling my hips to the position he wanted and he started fucking me roughly. I started to come before he even reached around to touch my clit. Once he did, I ignited for a third time. Using my hips to anchor me, he swung into me, plunging his cock into me, until he cried out with his own release.

Falling together on the bed, I needed a moment to catch my breath. Gideon pulled me into him, and I laid across his tight chest. I ran my hand over his muscles and over his six pack. I studied the way he flexed and moved with my touch.

"This wasn't my intention when I came here," he said gruffly.

I laughed lightly. "Trust me, I don't mind."

His grip tightened on me and I felt him inhale near my hair. Shifting, I reached up, stretching so I could wrap my arm around his neck. I buried my face in his throat and fell into a snooze again. One of his rough hands, ran down my back to my hip and up again, soothing me and making my body melt into his.

The rest of the day was lounging in bed. Once I got Gideon to relax, he was funny and personable. I got him to tell me more stories of the Knights as children. We stayed away from anything to heavy, keeping the mood light and happy. We ate breakfast and lunch in bed, with me on his lap and him lovingly feeding me.

We made love twice more, once so tender it made tears pop into my eyes. The big man had a lot of facets hidden behind his gruff exterior. But in all his ways, he made me feel precious and delicate. I loved every moment of it.

Showers were taken separately, because Gideon said there was no way he could handle himself if we were together. I laughed and tried to convince him there was nothing wrong with that. But he shook his head, insisting we leave the apartment to get dinner at least.

"Fresh air, we need fresh air," he said, shaking his head from the bathroom door

I giggled and stepped under the spray. When I peaked out again, he was gone, clearly serious about not being able to control himself. I loved the power that gave me. I felt myself move with more confidence. I picked out short shorts and a v-neck t-shirt for dinner, since I made him promise something casual. It was more revealing than I normally wore on a normal day. But something about being around my men, was making me feel less self conscious about my scars.

We walked out of the apartment building hand in hand, with Gideon walking on the outside of the sidewalk. I noticed the moment he changed, as his eyes started to narrow and he looked around each corner, as if waiting for something to jump out. I knew his gun was tucked safely at his waist band, just in case. Some of the ease of the day seeped out of me, as I was reminded I wasn't completely safe.

I took him to a small bistro that was a few blocks from home. It was one of the best places to order in from, but Ash and I sometimes came here after work to unwind. It was a brick front building with wide windows, giving a perfect view to people watch the people of the city as they bustled by.

As we stood in front of it, Gideon studying the menu on the glass, I caught my reflection. My hair was wild around my shoulders. My cheeks were pink and my eyes were wide. I looked happy. Something that I wasn't very accustomed to. As I studied it, movement behind me caught my attention. My stomach flipped as I was positive I saw Lyle standing across the street.

I cried out, and swung around so I could see with my own eyes and not in the window reflection. Gideon immediately picked up on my energy and grabbed me, tugging me to behind him.

"What is it, stellina?" He asked, his eyes sharp as he looked up and down the street.

I peered around him, looking to where I thought I saw Lyle. There was only people strolling along the sidewalk, families with strollers, people on bikes. Not one person stood still, looking across the street. I let my forehead fall against Gideon's arm as I shook my head.

"Sorry. I thought I saw... him. But I think my mind is playing tricks on me," I said.

Gideon slid a hand along my jaw, pulling my face up so I was looking at him. His thumb rubbed at my cheek and I closed my eyes a little before smiling up at him.

"Quite the reaction, big man," I said.

"Habit. Never be sorry for being cautious. Always tell me what you're seeing or if something feels off. I want to keep you safe," he said.

I nodded and pressed my hand against his on my face. His stern look calmed and he smiled a little at me. He gestured to the restaurant and I nodded. Intertwining our fingers together again, Gideon led the way into the building.

The hostesses recognized me and greeted me by name. I couldn't miss the way her eyes widened as she took in Gideon next to me. Her gaze slid down to where our hands were connected and I saw a look of disappointment flash before she shut it down. I looked over to Gideon to find him studying me and a flutter passed through my heart, realizing he didn't even notice the pretty hostess checking him out.

The girl cleared her throat, breaking our gaze. She waved us to a table in a back corner, as requested by Gideon. I knew he didn't like the look of the big windows. Ash and I would have immediately asked for a window seat, so we could laugh and make up stories about people walking by. Gideon thought about things from a security point of view, a way I never needed to think about until now.

Eating with Gideon made me feel more normal. We both seemed to have a love for food. I didn't feel even a little bit bad for demolishing a plate of fettuccine alfredo and a side of breadsticks. The man put away a huge portion of lasagna and even had side salad. We both had a glass of wine with our meal and I was just feeling warmly happy with the entire day.

As we waited for our check, Gideon's phone rang. He frowned for a second before answering it. I could only hear his side of the conversation, but I got the feeling it was Aiden calling about work. Gideon grunted or gave one word answers, until he told Aiden not to stress that he would handle it and said goodbye.

"How do you feel about going out tonight?" He asked.

"Well, it is Saturday. I'm not opposed to it," I said with a smile.

"Tonight is ladies night at Club 4. That was Aiden on the phone. I had a security guy call in sick. We usually need extra security on ladies night. Too many dudes thinking that means it's an easier playing field for them. So, I'm gonna need to cover."

"Do you think it's safe, ya know, with everything going on?" I asked.

"I'll take you to our private VIP level. I'll make sure all of my guys know who you are and that they are to keep an eye on you. And I won't be far. I can keep you safe, Brooklyn," he said.

I looked at him and knew he really meant that. He held out his hand and I placed my palm in his. He tightened his fingers around my hand, squeezing with reassurance. I did feel safe, with Gideon. I felt safe with all of my men. They would look out for me.

"Sounds like fun!" I said, throwing some excitement into my voice.

Gideon walked me home. As we walked, he explained he needed to go home for clothes, but he would be picking me up in an hour. After making sure I was inside, he kissed me thoroughly goodbye, with instructions to keep the door locked and not to buzz anyone up that wasn't him. I nodded obediently with a small tug on his beard that got a smile from him.

As soon as he was gone, I flipped the locks and looked through the peephole. I saw him nod his head to himself once he heard the deadbolt turn, before going down the stairs. The feeling of unease tried to rise in me again. I pulled up the camera app on my phone that Gideon had installed. I could see clearly that no one was outside my place.

In the bathroom, I propped the phone up so I could watch the door the whole time. In the back of mind I knew it was a bit obsessive to watch it constantly. I rationalized that if it helped me feel more secure, it didn't hurt anything.

Quickly I washed my face and decided to curl my hair, feeling glad I took a shower before dinner. With the long blonde strands in ringlets down my back, I applied a smokey eye and deep red smudge proof lipstick.

At my closet, I stood and considered. Normally, I would disregard anything that I owned that showed my chest, cleavage or neck. But my Knights wanted me, no matter my marks. I didn't want to hide anymore.

Twenty~One

Brooklyn

I WAS PACING the living room waiting for the buzzer, but the noise still caused me to jump slightly. I could see no one at my door, as I went to the buzzer to answer.

"Stellina, let me up," Gideon's voice came through.

I immediately pressed the button to unlock the security door for him. My heart did a dance every time he used his pet name for me. A little star was not something I pictured myself as, but it felt warm and sweet that Gideon felt the word applied to me.

This time I didn't wait when he knocked. As soon as he lifted his hand, I threw open the door. I stood there, staring, taking in all the deliciousness that was Gideon. I once again found myself thinking it was completely sinful that these men looked so damn good in suits.

Gideon was wearing black on black. His suit was tailored for his broad shoulders and thick arms. Under he wore a skin tight black shirt. His hair was slicked back in his normal man bun. He looked all security, which I was sure was the exact point. But to me, I just wanted to lick him.

I realized after a moment of my staring, that Gideon was doing a slow sweep up my body as well. I chose a silver spaghetti strapped skin tight dress that ended just above my knees. I was braless again, and it was instantly apparent as the heat of seeing Gideon passed through my body.

"When I kill someone tonight, you have to bail me out," he said.

I started to laugh as he came closer. He kicked the door shut behind him, before wrapping an arm around my waist. He lifted me to my toes so he could bury his mouth in my cleavage. He kissed and nipped along the top of my dress before making his way to my mouth.

After he kissed me hard, he pulled away. I glanced down and saw I was having the same effect on him and I put a hand on my hip and grinned at him.

"Maybe we should just say we are sick and you call in too," I said.

"Aiden would hunt me down and murder me in my sleep," he replied. But then he looked down my body again and added, "It could be worth it."

"This will be here for you later tonight. Take me out, big guy," I said, grabbing my small clutch and keys.

At the curb, I stopped and stared. Gideon grinned at me as I took in the Harley Davidson motorcycle he was standing next to. He held out a helmet and I timidly took it. When I couldn't figure out the straps, he carefully tightened it under my chin before he swung his leg over the seat of the bike.

"Never been on a bike before?" He asked, looking over at me.

I shook my head and wondered how I was going to do this in the dress I was wearing.

"Just slide on, stellina. Sit close to me, so everything will be hidden by my body," he said with a wink that had my toes curling.

I do as he instructed and slide my arms around his waist. He patted my hands, indicating that I was doing the right thing and then fired up the beast. The bike was loud and vibrated underneath my ass. It was a weird, sensual feeling to have that vibration while I was glued to the back of Gideon.

He used his foot to kick up the stand and took off from the curb. I squealed as the air lifted my hair, making it fly behind me. I could feel Gideon's body shake with his laughter. I started to slide my hands around his chest and abs and he stiffened. I laughed then, glad I could make my point.

When we got to the club, he pulled the bike toward the back of the building. A black town car was parked in a spot that said 4K parking only. Three more spots were lined up with the same signage. Gideon pulled the bike up next to the town car and dismounted. He turned and lifted me by the hips off the bike and held me until I became steady on the ground.

"That was crazy," I said breathlessly, as he helped me remove the helmet.

I tried to straighten what I know was wild hair, but Gideon stopped me.

"You look beautiful. I look forward to rumpling you more later," he said in my ear.

"Promise?" I asked.

"Abso-fuckin-lutely," he replied with a sexy grin.

Gideon led us to a back door that he explained was a private staircase for the Knights. No one else used it and guests didn't even know about it. It made it easy for them to move between floors of the club without being stopped. And if they wanted to leave without attention, they could easily duck out.

"Before we go in, I just wanted to let you know the precautions we've taken. Lyle's picture is at the front door and every security person has been told he's on the banned list. They don't know the details, but he won't be getting into the club tonight," Gideon explained.

I looked at him, feeling a bit of surprise at the lengths he'd gone to keep me safe. Knowing that there would be multiple sets of eyes keeping an eye out for Lyle, if he were to somehow have followed me here, made me feel much better about the night. I nodded to Gideon, to show him I understood and we continued.

At the top, Gideon opened a door into the darkness of the club. He held my hand as he led me through dark curtains and to an area that held two large u-shaped booths with two tables in the center of each. No one was on this level and he took me to one booth and indicated with his hand.

"This is all yours tonight. Aiden will be here at some point, but he's harmless. There's a guy on the stairs and no one will be allowed beyond that point. I will be back to check on you. I need to do a round and make sure everything is covered before things get really busy. Are you ok up here?"

I nodded and used my finger to indicate he needed to come closer. I tugged on his beard until he was close enough for me to kiss.

"Be careful, big guy. I'll be fine," I said.

He smiled and swatted my ass before walking away. I squeaked and looked at him in shock. He just threw back his head and laughed before heading to the interior stairs. I watched him as he spoke with the man at the stairs and they shared an handshake before Gideon went down a level.

I couldn't stop myself from watching him go, his big body moving smoothly through crowds. Mostly it was like they moved out of his way without him saying a word. Once he reached the main floor, he looked up my direction and I was caught staring. His face was serious now, but I knew I would see the smile and affection later tonight when we were alone.

Sitting alone in the big booth, felt immediately lonely. As soon as I sat down an extremely beautiful woman approached me. Her smile was wide and genuine. She slid into the booth next to me and I realized she was carrying a tray.

"Hiya. I don't see women up here often. I'm Vivian. You can call me Viv though. What can I get ya from the bar?"

I couldn't help but smiling back, her voice was so friendly and her demeanor relaxed.

"I'm Brooklyn. Uh, from the bar? Something fruity?" I asked.

Vivian looked me over once and nodded her head before standing up.

"I got the perfect thing. Be right back," she said

She walked away and I had to admire how fast she moved in her heels. I loved my shoes, but even I knew I had to be careful in certain circumstances. Vivian looked like she was born in them.

As promised, she was back with a drink faster than I'd ever

been served at a bar. I figured being in the owners VIP section had its perks. She smiled and said she'd be back to check on me often, so don't worry about going to the bars below. I nodded, though I had no intention of leaving the floor without Gideon.

Below, the dance floor erupted in cheers as Jason Derulo's song "Want to Want Me" came on. I stood and went to the railing again to watch the crowd dancing to the upbeat song. Even though I was alone, I couldn't help but swaying to the song. Gideon was right, ladies' night really packed the club with women. As I watched the dance floor, it seemed there was three or four ladies to one man. It was no surprise that they needed extra security.

I sipped my drink and looked around to see if I could catch a glimpse of Gideon. When I didn't see him, I turned back to the booth and froze when I found someone sitting behind me. Aiden eyed me with little emotion on his face. Of course, I knew I'd see him, but I hadn't been sure how to deal with the hostility I was expecting from him.

Compared to my men, Aiden just seemed darker. His hair was pitch black and he seemed to always gravitate to black suits with dark shirts. However, it wasn't just his physical characteristics. I wasn't one that believe in seeing auras, but if I did, I felt like Aiden's was black, hanging around him like a cloud.

I sucked in a breath and stopped standing like a statue. Sliding into the opposite side of the booth, I smiled when Aiden looked my way.

"Nice to see you again," I said, slipping into business mode.

Though there had been little said about Aiden to me from any of the guys, I had the distinct impression he wasn't pleased about our relationship. It wasn't the sharing that bothered him, the four of them had been there done that. However, Jaxon and Oliver had given me little information on their previous relationship and Gideon shut down questions pretty quickly on the subject. There was something they all wanted to forget.

"Miss Reeves. You look, well… Different outside of the office," he said slowly.

I couldn't help but fidget with my dress, wishing I had worn something longer, something less revealing.

"Yes, well. Typically a woman doesn't wear a business suit to a club, does she?" I said, digging up some courage.

"I suppose not," he said with a nod.

He lifted a tumbler with dark liquor toward me before sipping. He made me feel like I was under a microscope. I knew he and his brothers were as close as people could be and his sense of protectiveness would likely extend to me. But I had no idea how I was supposed to broach the conversation, to show that I wasn't playing with his brothers heads or hearts.

Vivian floated in and dropped two more drinks, a tumbler for Aiden and another tall red drink for me. She flashed me a wink and smiled politely at Aiden. I downed the last of my first drink, not the most ladylike move, but I couldn't control the nerves buzzing in my gut.

"How are things coming along for the gala?" Aiden asked.

I looked at him for a moment, my mouth hanging open slightly. Business it was.

"Very well. I'm looking forward to seeing it all coming together. I think it's going to be a beautifully successful event. The RSVP list is completely full. Thanks to your brothers pulling strings with everyone they know."

Aiden nodded and looked away. He stood and went to the railing of the VIP section. I sagged a bit in my seat, relieved to no longer being under his watchful gaze. Gideon suddenly appeared at the top of the stairs and met with Aiden at the railing. They looked over the crowd together and discussed something that I couldn't hear. Aiden nodded and Gideon turned toward me.

He bent near my ear to talk so I could hear him.

"Doing ok, Stellina?" He asked.

"I'm fine! You don't have to check on me. I'm a big girl," I replied.

Leaning back to look him in the face, I ran my hand along his beard and tugged it slightly. He leaned down and pressed a rough kiss to my mouth before standing back up with a smile. I waved him away and turned back to my second drink.

"Hands Free" by Keke Palmer came on below and I heard another rise of cheers. It made me smile, thinking about the people feeling the music as they moved their bodies to it. When I looked up, the smile fell from my face when I realized Aiden was studying me again from where he was standing. I knew I needed to say something, figure out how to put him at ease with the closeness that was developing between his brothers and I. In the end, I didn't want Aiden to create a fracture we couldn't overcome down the road.

I stood and went to stand at the railing to watch the crowd as well. I turned and leaned my hip at the rail so I could face Aiden.

"You don't like me, do you?" I asked, leaning forward a bit so he could hear me.

"I don't really know you, to not like you," he replied.

"I'm not messing with them, you know. I'm not playing games and planning on screwing them over down the road," I said.

Aiden raised his eyebrow at me, clearly surprised by the direction of conversation.

"I didn't say that," he started to say.

"You didn't need to. You assumed the worst about me at our first meeting. I cleared that misunderstanding up with Oliver and Jaxon, I'm sure they told you. So you know I'm not some club bunny, chasing down the owners to get in tight. Hell, I had no idea 4K was you guys or that you were as successful as you are. I just want to clear the air," I finished.

He considered me for a moment and I didn't miss the sweep of his eyes along my body, but I decided to ignore it.

"Consider it cleared," he finally replied.

I smiled politely and turned to look into the club again. Part of me really wanted to be dancing. I wouldn't even mind dancing alone, but it wouldn't feel alone if I was on the dance floor. I turned to set my drink down and looked at Aiden.

"If Gideon comes looking for me, let him know I went down there to dance," I said.

"I'm not sure he'll be thrilled with that," Aiden said.

And for the first time a small smile appeared on his face. For that brief moment, he wasn't as dark as I originally thought. It was something for me to think about later.

"He'll be able to find me. I have no doubt," I replied with a smile.

Carefully I made my way down the two flights of stairs that took me to the main dance floor. The club was hopping and was still heavily women, which I sort of loved. The vibe was wild when "Hypnotize" by The Notorious B.I.G. came on. I carefully worked my way into the crowd, moving with the beat and flowing with the bodies around me.

As I got into the song, I closed my eyes and raised my hands above my head. Suddenly a hand slid down my back and I shifted to look behind me. A sweaty man gave me a look that I think was an attempt at sultry. It didn't work and I just smiled and shook my head no. The guys shrugged but took the hint and moved onto to another woman dancing alone.

The songs flowed from one to another and I could feel sweat beginning to drip down my back and between my breasts. A shiver ran through me and it reminded me of the first time I had been to Club 4. It made me immediately look around, because I knew Gideon was close. My body recognized his and suddenly, he was there, on the dance floor with me.

He shook his head at me, admonishing me for leaving the safety of the VIP section. But instead of acting like I was sorry, I turned and slid my ass along his crotch and thighs. His hands immediately came to grip my hips and his fingers dug in deliciously. His mouth landed on my neck and I felt his teeth graze along my skin. I felt my nipples pucker against the material of my dress and I wasn't sure how long I could behave in public.

Suddenly, Gideon froze and I turned to look at him. He was touching the ear piece that he had. At his height he could see over most of the dance floor and he held up a mic that was clipped on the inside of his jacket sleeve. I couldn't hear his words but he looked down at me with a hard look.

"Don't go anywhere other than the dance floor or back upstairs, ok?" He said.

I nodded and watched him rush away. He got to the stairs that lead to the VIP sections and he climbed the first set two at a time. When he got to the main VIP section, he was met by two additional security officers. My eyes followed him as he got to a crowd that had gathered inside one VIP booth.

Before anyone had a warning, a fist snapped out and slammed into Gideon's face. His head snapped to the side. I wasn't sure, but I thought I screamed his name, though it was drowned out by the crowd and music pumping through the club. Gideon slowly looked back at his attacker and I could see how he squared up. The security officers around him all jumped into action and suddenly there was a brawl happening in the VIP section.

Afraid for Gideon's safety, I made my way to the stairs. By the time I was able to get free of the dance floor, the security officer at the bottom of the stairs, was talking into his radio as well. He looked at my face and waved me through without a word. I climbed the stairs as fast as I dared with my heels on.

At the second floor, the security guard of the section was blocking any foot traffic from going further. I tried to go around him, but he put out an arm to stop me.

"I need to see Gideon," I called out.

"The incident is under control. Mr. Knight will come find you when he's available," the man said to me.

I shot him a dirty look, not liking being kept away from Gideon. Instead of fighting, I took the second set of stairs and made my way back to the booth Aiden was in. He was casually sitting with his drink and his phone in hand.

"Someone punched Gideon," I exclaimed as soon as I walked up.

Aiden looked up for a moment and then looked back to his phone. He nodded his head absentmindedly.

I sat down next to him and poked him in the shoulder, which got his attention.

"Did you hear me? Some guy sucker punched Gideon in the face," I said.

"And you're worried about Gideon? Sweetheart, you should be more worried for the man that hit him," Aiden said, the word sweetheart coming out in a sarcastic tone I didn't appreciate.

I jumped up and began to pace, watching the stairs with each pass. Aiden finally looked up and watched me moving. When I caught him grinning, I stopped and put my hands on my hips.

"I don't know what the fuck you think is so funny. But Gideon, ya know one of the guys you claim is a brother, got punched in the face. And we have no idea what else is happening down there," I yelled.

Aiden stood up and walked over to the rail. He sipped his drink and I thought he was completely ignoring me. I turned, ready to start yelling some more, when he pointed down. Irritation dripping off of me, I followed his hand. I immediately locked onto Gideon's form moving around the dance floor.

My grip on the rail became a vice as I watched across the dark room. I saw he was manhandling someone in front of him, toward the door. Behind him two more men were being shoved by other security guards. When they exited through the door, I let out a sigh of relief.

"You don't know everything about my brothers yet, Sweetheart," Aiden said, his voice snarky near my ear.

Suddenly incredibly irate with him and his smug attitude, I shoved him away from me and sat back down in the booth. My heart was still thudding in my chest and I thought about the fist Gideon took. I evaluated the way I was feeling and I had to admit to myself, seeing him in that element was a huge turn on. The combination of worry and lust were mingled, causing me to break out in a cold sweat.

CHAPTER
Twenty-Two

Gideon

AT THE DOOR, I turned just in time to see Brooklyn shove Aiden away from her. I almost stopped and went back inside, wondering what was happening between them. But the douche I had in custody, wouldn't stop fighting me through every step. I had to keep him under control until the cops arrived to take him and two of his buddies into custody.

As anticipated, at least one group of men would get too overzealous and women would complain. This trio had gotten into the VIP section with one woman. But when they got too handsy, the ladies of the group asked for help. By the time I was called into the situation, the three guys were getting heated with my guys.

The sneaky bastard caught me good in the face when I first walked up. It was the biggest mistake he could make, as the pain only fueled my desire to pummel him into the ground. I was in control enough to not break any bones, though the guy's nose had been bleeding like a fountain with no stopping in sight. They would definitely need a stop at the emergency room on the way to the station.

Thirty minutes later and I had finally handed off the trouble trio and was heading back inside. I could feel the slight swelling on my cheek, but it didn't bother me. My blood was boiling, but not in anger. Fighting, that moment of heightened adrenaline and focus, always bled into me and I had two options. Sex, or more fighting.

At that moment, there was only thing on my mind. I needed to check on Brooklyn and then I was dragging her away somewhere private. A few of my guys stopped me on my way back to the third floor. I gave quick instructions and then informed them I was going off radio for a little while.

When I reached our VIP area, Aiden was standing off to the side, staring out into the club. I approached him first to give him the update on the situation. He nodded through the story, then turned to study my face.

"You good?"

"Yeah, man. Always," I replied.

"Well, she was pissed at me for not being more worried. She's got quite the fight in her, huh?" He asked.

"I guess she can, when it's something she cares about," I replied, thoughtfully.

I thought about her pushing Aiden and being angry with

him. In Aiden's defense, he had seen me in tough places and I had always fought my way out. We had been together long enough that he knew a bar brawl was just a normal weekend night for me. However, for Brooklyn, it seemed violent and unexpected.

"I'm going home. I assume you'll be staying with her?" Aiden asked.

I nodded and we shook hands really quick. Aiden made his way to our back stairs, without a word to Brooklyn. I made my way to the booth, only to find her staring into an empty glass.

"Hey," I said, loud enough to catch her attention.

Her eyes snapped up and she immediately stood up and rushed to me. Her hand came up to my face and she grimaced.

"It's already bruising," she said.

"I'm fine," I said.

Before she could say another word, I started pulling her to the private stairway. I couldn't keep my hands off of her and I didn't want witnesses. In the stairs, I looked down the stairwell, ensuring Aiden had already exited. Then I took her down to a middle landing.

"Gideon, are you ok? I'm sorry if you're mad I was dancing. I just loved the music," she was stammering behind me.

When we got to the landing, I spun her and pushed her up against the wall. My mouth came down roughly on her lips and she moaned at the contact. I immediately licked into her mouth and she raised up on her toes to meet me with her tongue.

"I need to be inside you, now," I growled.

Her eyes went wide, but her hands went to my pants immediately. She had my belt undone and was working on the button as I reached under her dress, ripping her thong from her body. I pocketed the material as she pushed my briefs down. My cock fell into her hand and I groaned at the contact as her soft hand rotated around and then circled my weeping tip.

I grabbed her hips and lifted her against the wall. Her legs wrapped around my waist and I lined myself up with her. Without warning, I slammed balls deep into her and her cries echoed throughout the stairwell.

"Fuck, you are so wet. All for me, stellina?" I asked against her neck.

She nodded and I pulled out and slammed into her again. She gripped my shoulders, holding on as I fucked her roughly against the wall. I pulled the front of her dress down, so her tits popped out. She arched into me as I pulled one of the pebbled peaks into my mouth. I sunk my teeth into the flesh and she began to come.

Her hot channel clamped down on my cock and I had no idea how much longer I could last. My mind was foggy with wanting her and the adrenaline in my system that needed an outlet, I couldn't think of anything but fucking her. She cried out my name, spurring me on as I thrust until I was exploding into her.

Our breathing was loud and erratic. My fingers were digging into her thighs, keeping her impaled on my cock. I could feel the little spasms of her pussy, as her orgasm slowly ended. Carefully, I withdrew from her, but I didn't put her on her feet. Instead, I gathered her into my arms, supporting her ass in my hands.

She brought her mouth to mine and the kiss was slow and calming. Then she slid her mouth along my jaw and placed soft kisses near the bruising that was starting on my cheekbone. She pulled back for a moment, to get a better look of the damage and just shook her head.

"I should have known. I really got mad at Aiden. But this is just who you are, isn't it?"

"It's just a part of who I am. I've just always been the fighter," I said.

"Is it real inappropriate for me to say that it was a huge turn on too?" She said softly.

I ran one of my hands closer to her core and she trembled against me.

"So, I guess that explains why you were dripping wet when I got you in here," I said.

She nodded and kissed me again.

"When can we go home?" She asked.

"Give me five minutes," I said.

We straightened our clothing and I walked her to the bathrooms on the third floor. After leaving her there, I found my shift manager and had a quick meeting with him. I reminded him to load the trouble trio into the banned list and to call me if there were any further issues before closing.

I rushed back to meet Brooklyn on the third floor. She was flushed and smiling when I pulled her into my arms for a quick kiss. She waved goodbye to Vivian and we made our way down the exit stairs.

"Never going to look at these stairs the same," she quipped.

My laugh reverberated around us. I wanted to tell her I'd never done that with any other woman. I wanted her to know she was special. I also didn't want to scare her off after only being with her a total of one night and two days. So I didn't say anything that would be hard to explain.

Placing the helmet on her head, I let my knuckles slide along her neck before securing the strap. She turned her head, giving me more access to her skin. I leaned down and pressed a kiss to her mouth. Mounting my bike, I held out a hand to help her climb behind me. Her arms came around me, one around my waist and the other hand resting over my heart.

I pulled one of her hands to my mouth and pressed a kiss to her palm before putting it back on my chest. She wiggled closer and though I was just inside her earlier, I wanted her again. I pulled out of the parking lot and picked up speed when we hit the main road. I knew she was enjoying the ride as her arms tightened around me.

The ride felt entirely too short when we arrived at her apartment building. I promised myself that I would take us somewhere further away, just so I could have her on my bike and curled around me longer. I helped her off the bike and she did a little hop step before turning to me to get the helmet off.

"I can't believe you get to ride that bike all the time. It's so much fun!" She exclaimed.

"It was one of the things I wanted from the time I was young. My first big purchase when we became successful. The guys all have cars. I ride my bike. If I need a car, I order a service," I said with a smile.

She grabbed onto my arm as we walked through the security door of her building and walked up the stairs. Once inside the apartment, I did a quick walk through, ensuring all of the windows were locked still. I also glanced into Ash's room to make sure I wasn't missing anything. When I was sure we were alone, I came back to find Brooklyn in her room.

She was slipping off her shoes and I just leaned against the doorframe to watch her. She reached behind her for the zipper on her dress. She slowly pulled it down and I remembered she was completely naked underneath. With her entire body bared, she turned to look at me.

"You're wearing too much clothing, babe," she said.

Slowly she came to me, her hips swaying seductively. She pushed my jacket off my shoulders and discarded my shirt across the room. With her hand in my waistband she led me over to the bed. She tried to push me down, but when I didn't budge she just glared at me playfully, until I sat down.

On her knees she unlaced my boots and removed them and my socks. She leaned up and undid my belt and with my help, pulled my pants and boxer briefs to the ground. Staring at her naked, on her knees in front of me was doing things to my body. Her soft hand circled my hard cock and stroked it a few times before she looked up at me.

"There's something I want to do. I've only done it a few times and I might be bad at it. But I so badly want to try," she said quietly.

"Anything," I replied.

She propped herself up high on her knees and as she leaned forward, my life seemed to flash before my eyes. Her beautiful mouth parted and she ran her tongue along the underside of my cock, before circling the tip and sucking the head into her mouth. My hips jerked off the bed and she smiled up at me.

"On the bed, stellina," I ordered.

She pouted and sat back on her heels.

"I wasn't done," she said.

"You don't have to be done. But we're going to get more comfortable for this."

She quickly got up on the bed and waited for me to get into position. I laid back against the pillows and she kneeled between my legs.

"I don't want you to stop me. I want to make you come with my mouth," she said.

I groaned and just nodded my head, not trusting myself to say real words at the moment. She smiled happily and leaned down, wrapping her hand around my cock before lowering her mouth over the head again. As she hollowed her cheeks and swirled her tongue around me, I fought the urge to thrust into her mouth.

Reaching down, I moved her hair, so I could see her mouth as it stretched over my thickness. I knew my size would make it impossible for her in some ways, but she enthusiastically moved her hand with her mouth and the sensation was amazing. Her eyes flicked up to mine and she watched me through her eyelashes.

It didn't take long for me to get close. She pulled back again, running her tongue along the sensitive area under my head and I groaned, fisting the comforter in my hand. Brooklyn caught sight of my hand and I saw her smile wickedly, before taking even more of my cock into her mouth. I knew I couldn't hold back any longer.

"Brooklyn, I'm going to come, stellina," I muttered.

She continued her movements, twisting her hand as she rose. My balls tightened and then I was shooting into her mouth. She gentled her movements, lovingly licking the last of my release off my cock, before sitting up with a triumphant look on her face.

"Who told you that you weren't good at that?" I said, my voice strained.

"Well, no one really. I just never got this type of reaction. And I didn't enjoy it nearly as much as I enjoyed this."

She crawled up the bed to lay next to me and I cuddled her to my body. I kissed her hard, before sliding my mouth along her jaw and nipped her ear. I flipped her so she was below me and she gasped.

"My turn," I said.

Taking my time, I used my mouth and tongue along the skin of her neck. I ran kisses between her breasts before lavishing one and then the other with my tongue. Her hands went to my hair and pulled the elastic band from my bun, causing the strands to fall over her chest.

I ran my hands over her nipples, tweaking both as I continued to kiss down her stomach. I ran my mouth over her burn scar and I could feel her jump. When I made my way back up to the center of her, I spread her thighs and settled my shoulders between them.

Clamping my hands around her hips, I kept her still. I looked up her body and found her watching me intently. Keeping eye contact, I flattened my tongue, running it between her outer lips. Her taste was intoxicating and I had to remind myself to take my time before diving straight in.

Her little moan and arched back, was all the encouragement I needed. I spread her for my mouth and slid my tongue along her hood, uncovering her clit. When I pressed my tongue there, circling it, she cried out and threw her head back. I retreated and circled her entrance before shallowly fucking her with my tongue.

When I looked up at her again, her chest heaved with her breathing and she was fighting against my hands on her hips. I slid one hand down between her legs and slid a finger into her soaking wet channel. My cock was hardening under me, just at the idea of sliding into her again.

I added a second finger and began to finger fuck her, curling my fingers in the place that made her cry out the loudest. When I sucked her clit into my mouth, she came apart on my fingers, squeezing them and shaking. I let her come down slowly, before sliding up her body again.

Brooklyn gave me a surprised look when my hardness bumped her hip. But she didn't speak, just grabbed my face and pulled me to kiss her. The kiss was messy and charged. I slowed her down. After the stairwell sex, I wanted to take her slowly. She smiled sweetly at me and spread her legs for my hips.

I stared into her ice blue eyes as I slowly pressed into her wet pussy. She moaned and arched against me, but didn't break our connection. I didn't know what to call it, but I could feel something passing between us as I moved. She lifted her hips, meeting my thrusts and her fingers dug into my back.

Her orgasm built and I could feel the small spasms right before she clamped down on my hardness. I bottomed out into her and thrust in small movements, fucking her through her orgasm. Her eyes were glassy and her pupils blown from the pleasure.

I pulled out and thrust into her fully, causing her to lock her legs around my hips. Reaching down, I gripped her hip as I increased my speed, chasing my second orgasm. She gripped my ass and pulled me into her harder. Her nails scratched at my skin as I changed my angle.

As I exploded into her, her walls squeezed down on me again and she cried out my name. I was sure to not completely crush her under me, but I pressed my body against her and buried my face in her neck. She wrapped her arms around me and held me close to her.

I didn't know how long we laid like that. We didn't leave bed to clean up, choosing to use the Kleenex on the nightstand. I pulled her into the crook of my arm and she automatically twined a leg through mine. I fell asleep thinking about how fantastic her naked body felt against my skin.

CHAPTER
Twenty-Three

Brooklyn

MONDAY CAME FASTER than I had wanted. The alone time with Gideon had been so hot. And if I was honest with myself, it meant a lot more than the sex. The big guy was a big softy, just as Oliver had told me. For the entire weekend he spent his time ensuring my safety, but also attending to my every need.

When he dropped me off at work, he helped me off his bike

and pulled my skirt into place for me. He hugged me tightly, holding me longer than necessary. I wanted to climb into his leather jacket and make him take me with him wherever he was going. But I knew it was time to get back to real life.

When I pulled back I felt a slight panic hit me. We hadn't talked about the future. We hadn't made plans to see each other again. He knew Oliver and Jaxon were headed home and would want time with me. And I missed them, a lot more than I realized I would. But that didn't change the fact that I was afraid Gideon was walking away from me.

I grabbed his hand before he got back on his bike. He looked back with a question on his face.

"I'll see you soon, right?" I asked.

He studied my face for a moment, before smiling slightly and stepping back onto the sidewalk with me. His hand cupped my jaw and tilted my face up to him. He crashed his mouth to mine and I gripped his shoulders, pulling myself up on my toes to better reach him.

"Definitely soon, stellina," he breathed against my lips.

My heart did a little flip, getting the exact answer I wanted. I nodded and reluctantly released him. I watched him speed away on his Harley, loving the deep noise that vibrated between the buildings as he left. It was actually hard to walk into the office and not just calling him back to take me back to bed.

Focusing on work was more difficult than I had anticipated. We were busy with the last minute plans for the gala. We'd hit a snag with the fundraiser and the auctioning of dances with people. Turned out, we were missing a headliner, the one that would bring in the most money.

"I have an out of box idea, Brooklyn," The event manager said.

"Better than having nothing right now, let's hear it," I said.

"The headliner of the auction, should be you," she said.

I laughed, but stopped short when I realized no one around me was laughing.

"Why would anyone bid to dance with me?"

"You're young, beautiful and your heart is with the kids we provide for. I think that would catch the attention of bidders," the event manager said.

"I'm not so sure..." I said at the same time as the President said, "That's a fantastic idea!"

I looked around the table and gulped. In my head, I reminded myself that it was one dance. And if I could raise enough funds, it would be worth, no matter who I'd have to dance with. It was better than us having no top dance for the auction.

Eventually, I reluctantly agreed. Back in my office I started sorting through emails to distract myself from the idea. The gala was just a few days away and everything was falling into place nicely. To get into the gala a person had to pay for a spot at a table. Companies could sponsor an entire table and send whoever they wanted to fill the seats. All of the tables were sold out and already we were looking at a very successful event. The auction would be the icing on the proverbial fundraising cake.

My phone vibrated on my desk and I turned to see a text message from Gideon. A smile appeared on my face and everything else just faded away.

Gideon: Stellina, caught up at work today. I'm sorry. Oliver and Jaxon will be there to pick you up after work.

Me: I can always get myself home, on my own.

Gideon: Not right now. Plus, good luck keeping them away. Haha

Me: I wouldn't even dare to try. ;-)

Gideon: It'll be hard sleeping alone tonight, if I'm honest.

Me: I'm sorry. I need a bigger bed I think.

Gideon: I'll work on that. Talk soon.

Me: xoxo

I SAT LOOKING at the conversation longer than necessary. Butterflies fluttered in my chest as I reread Gideon saying it would be hard for him to sleep alone. I wished I could split myself to be with all of them at once. I didn't think Gideon told me that to make me feel bad, it was his way of letting me know how he felt. And I appreciated that from the big man.

In my mind, I still struggled with understanding how this all worked. How to make sure I didn't make anyone feel left out. How to make sure I could show each of them what they meant to me. It was clear the guys already knew the dynamics for them. Not having to deal with typical male jealousy or dominance displays, did make the relationships much easier.

I was caught daydreaming by my assistant when she poked her head in. A last minute meeting request had come in, so we sat and worked through my schedule to see if I could make it fit. All it meant was I would be working late for sure. I shot off a message to Oliver and Jaxon in our group chat, to warn them about the delay. Almost immediately I received responses of not to worry and that they would wait downstairs for me.

While on my last meeting of the day, my assistant, Pam, quietly popped in again and left a beautiful, wrapped box on my coffee table. I nodded to her and continued with my call. The gentleman on the call was the owner of a construction company, donating time and supplies to building a new group home we were funding. We had previously worked out logistics, but supplies had been delayed so we had to hash out the new expected due dates for points of the project.

I rubbed under my eyes, being sure not to smear makeup all over my face. I was exhausted. I'd remind Gideon to make sure I got more sleep the night before work. That thought made me smile and I started to pack up. The package on the table caught my eye and I went over to it.

There was a simple cream colored card on the outside. I opened it, but there was no signature. Just a simple "To show you how much I care" computer printed inside. I sat on the loveseat and carefully undid the ribbon. The scent of the contents hit me before I realized what I was even looking at. When it all registered, I covered my mouth to keep myself from crying out.

Immediately, I shoved the lid back on the box and pushed it away from me. I started to think about who was still in the office. I didn't want any of my co-workers to have any idea what had been delivered here. I texted Oliver and Jaxon, asking them to come up to my office instead, the idea of riding alone down to the parking level felt impossible.

Neither of them answered, but a few minutes later, my door opened, and their anxious faces appeared. Oliver came through the door first and I all but threw myself into his arms.

He wrapped himself around me and lifted me slightly off my heels. He kissed my temple and moved to the side so Jaxon could come in and close the door. Jaxon kissed my cheek as he walked by.

I didn't say anything, just pointed at the box. Jaxon sat and I hid my face in Oliver's neck, so not to see it again. I could picture it fine in my mind. Oliver watched over my head as Jaxon read the card aloud and then opened the box.

"What the fuck!" Jaxon exclaimed, before closing it again.

I knew what he had seen. A box full of dead roses, perfectly cut and placed to create a bed for the dead rat in the middle. The rat, with its throat sliced, blood dried along the dead rose petals. It didn't take me long to understand, I was the rat. I was the one that told the truth and Lyle went to jail. I was the one with the sliced throat. But I didn't die.

"Where did it come from, babe?" Oliver asked.

"I have no idea. The card doesn't say. My assistant dropped it off before she left for the day. I was on a call and just now opened it," I said.

"We need to have Gideon look into this," Jaxon said.

He came to us and Oliver released me into Jaxon's arms. I allowed his comforting scent to surround me and tried to calm myself. I wasn't alone. I wasn't vulnerable. Jaxon rubbed my back and massaged at my shoulders and neck. My hair was up in a bun that felt entirely too tight now.

"Can we just get rid of it, on the way home? I'll send a message to my assistant to ask if she knows what service brought it," I said.

The guys exchanged a look, before Oliver tightly nodded. He placed the cover on the box again and picked it up. Jaxon took my briefcase and I grabbed my purse. I didn't bother shutting down my computer. I just wanted out of the building as fast as possible.

This delivery meant not only did Lyle know where I lived, he knew where I worked. I thought back to when I thought I saw his reflection during dinner with Gideon. Was he out there, following us as we drove out of the parking garage? Did he know my every move? I shuddered and leaned into Oliver as we drove toward my apartment. Jaxon had one of my hands and Oliver had an arm around my shoulders.

Jaxon was on the phone with Gideon, but I wasn't listening to their words. I stared out the window, until I couldn't handle all of the faceless people. Each time someone was the same height, or had the same color hair as Lyle, my eyes would snap to them. Finally, I just shut my eyes and moved so my face was in Oliver's throat.

"Love, Gideon wants to talk to you. Just for a second?" Jaxon said, holding his phone toward me.

Without opening my eyes, I held out my hand for the phone. Bringing it to my ear I mumbled into the speaker.

"I'm here, big man."

"Stellina, are you ok?" He asked.

His voice was tight with anxiety, and I knew he was likely already at his computer looking up what he could find on the delivery service my assistant thought the box came from. She couldn't be sure, but it was definitely a service, and it was a woman that delivered it, so not Lyle himself.

"I'll be alright, don't worry," I replied.

"Stay with Oliver and Jaxon, no matter what. When they aren't with you, I will be. Ok? I'm going to find this guy, I promise you," he said.

"I'm going home and not leaving until I absolutely have to. I'll be careful. I'll talk to you soon," I replied.

"Ok. Brooklyn?" His voice stopped me from handing the phone back to Jaxon.

"Yes, Gideon?"

"I'll, uh, see you soon, ok?" He said.

"Sounds perfect," I replied and handed the phone to Jaxon.

At home, Oliver took my keys and went up to the apartment first. I stared out the window after him, counting in my head the amount of time he was gone. It felt like a lifetime before his face showed again. When he opened the town car door, he was breathing hard from running up and down the flights of stairs.

"The apartment is clear. No unusual movement from the cameras that we saw. Let's get you upstairs," he said.

I could feel the tension in the guys as we made our way up the stairs. When we got the apartment door, Oliver unlocked it again before ushering me inside. He dropped my keys in the bowl by the door as I hung up my purse and Jaxon placed my briefcase on the ground.

Everything was feeling overwhelmingly domestic and I just stared at them for a moment before turning toward my room.

"Uh, I'm going to get comfortable. You guys are welcome to anything in the kitchen," I said, walking away quickly and shutting the door before either of them said a word.

I tossed my shoes to the side and sank to the floor against the wall. Everything that had been happening around me, started to crash down and I suddenly didn't think I could breathe. As I tried to take in deep breaths, I realized I could smell Gideon in my room as if he were standing next to me and that didn't help my panic.

Meeting the Knights wasn't a bad thing, it was the most exciting and sexy thing to happen to me in my life. But now here I was, with three men, that thought they needed to take care of me, protect me, because my past was coming to finish what had been started. It wasn't the way I wanted to start a relationship, let alone three. I wanted to feel happy and giddy with new romance. Instead, I was scared and feeling over-whelmed.

I ran my fingers along the scar at my neck, thinking about the rat and if Lyle had been more accurate the first time he cut me. I would be no different than the animal in the box. And that was Lyle's message, he wasn't finished with me.

CHAPTER
Twenty~Four

Jaxon

WHEN BROOKLYN CLOSED HER DOOR, Oliver and I just stood in the middle of the room staring at it. Rushing home, we didn't need to compare our thoughts, to know we both just wanted to spend time with her.

Entering her office, I couldn't help but remember bending her over the desk. However, the box of dead roses and sliced up rat, changed the atmosphere completely. Brooklyn had been ghost white and her color hadn't improved on the drive home or after she spoke with Gideon.

I looked over at Oliver, my worried expression mirrored on his face.

"How long do we let her do that?" He asked.

"As long as she needs, I guess. But if she doesn't come out, we're going in," I said.

Oliver got to ordering pizza from Brooklyn's favorite place and I opened a bottle of wine. When all of this was done, Brooklyn still hadn't come out and I wasn't waiting any longer.

"Brooklyn? Can I come in?" I called through the door, while knocking lightly.

"Yeah," she called softly.

The bedroom was dark except for the sliver of light that snuck in around her dark curtains. I looked around, squinting, until I found her against the wall getting to her feet. She looked rumpled and mascara had smeared beneath her eyes.

"Love, what is it? The box?" I asked.

I stood in front of her and pushed a strand of hair from her face. Her hair was still up in a bun, so I reached up and pulled the pins from it, rubbing her head as the hair came free and flowed around her shoulders. She looked up at me, her eyes shining with unshed tears.

"Yeah. The box is part of it. Lyle. Everything. I just wish I had met you guys at a different time," she said.

"Hey, why would you say that?" I asked.

She sighed and hung her head, her hair shielding her face from me.

"All of this, my ex coming after me, you guys feeling obligated to protect me, is really not the way to start a relationship," she said quietly.

"Ah, so you admit it, we are in a relationship," Oliver quipped from the doorway.

Brooklyn looked over at him with a small smile on her face.

"I had hoped it was leading there. As unconventional as this is, I'm growing attached to you guys," she said.

I reached out then, pulling her into me, wrapping my arms around her. Oliver came to join us, hugging her from behind, until we were effectively cradling her body.

"We're right there with you, babe. All this other stuff, it doesn't matter," Oliver said.

"And we don't feel obligated. It's simple. We want you. And for us to have you, you have to be safe. Plus, we're not fans of men that abuse women," I added.

"I wish I was more experienced in all of this," she said, circling her finger in the air to indicate everything.

"You've been doing perfectly fine," Oliver said, placing a kiss on her neck.

"I don't know how to manage the feelings I'm having," she admitted.

I slid my hand to her jaw, and pulled her face up to look at me. I placed soft kisses on her lips, the corner of her mouth, her jaw and neck, before pulling back to look her in the eyes again.

"Manage them with us, love. We're here. You aren't alone."

She looked at me and then turned so she could look into Oliver's face. He pressed a rough kiss to her lips, before she turned back to me and nodded her agreement.

"Can we show you how we're feeling?" I asked quietly.

Her eyes widened slightly and she licked her lips before nodding her head. I ran my finger along the high collar of her shirt, letting my skin slide along hers. She leaned her head so I could access her neck better. I began to unbutton the shirt, while Oliver found the zipper on her skirt.

It only took a moment to have her in her bra and thong. I pressed her against Oliver's body, while I let my mouth slide along her skin, down the middle of her breasts, over her flat stomach, to the edge of her lace panties. I got on my knees in front of her and she watched with her eyes wide.

Oliver slid her bra straps off her shoulders, reaching around her body to pull the lacy material down. He cupped both of her breasts and she arched into his hands while watching me on the ground. I leaned forward and kissed her lace covered pussy and smiled when I heard a small gasp come from her.

"Don't let her fall, brother," I said with a small chuckle.

Lifting one of her legs, I slid my shoulder under her thigh, leaving her off balance on one foot. Oliver gripped one of her hips, pulling her ass against him. She turned her face toward him and he plundered her mouth with his. Her hand was in his hair, pulling him closer to her.

With her distracted by Oliver, I slid her panties to the side and softly kissed her bare skin. She moaned as I slid my tongue along her folds. Her free hand came to the top of my head, trying to control my movements. Instead, I pulled back, to look up at her again. She immediately looked down at me, desire tight across her face.

"Did we mention how much we missed you?" I asked.

She nodded without breaking eye contact with me.

"I'm going to show you just how much, love," I said.

Leaning forward again, I pressed my tongue against her clit, circling it before closing my lips around it. She bucked against my mouth, but Oliver anchored her back against him. I then let my tongue wander along her entrance, before slowly fucking her with my tongue. Her hips gyrated, trying to get more of what she wanted.

I had to smile against her core, my girl was so needy, and I loved every minute of it. She had alluded to the fact that sex hadn't been enjoyable for her, like ever, in her life. I was going to make it my mission that sex was the most enjoyable thing in her life going forward. And if that meant I licked her tight pussy every night, that was a sacrifice I could make.

Not wanting to drag it out too long for her, wanting to give her the release her body and mind both needed, I went back to her clit, sucking on it and flicking it with my tongue. She cried out and thrust against my face as her orgasm hit her. Oliver's arm had wound around her waist, keeping her from sinking to the ground.

Slowly, I licked her until she stopped shaking. I set her leg down and made my way back up her body, sucking one of her nipples into my mouth as I passed. When I stood up, her eyes weren't as shadowed and sad as when we first came into the room. I kissed her nose and smiled.

"Pizza should be here any minute," I said.

This caused her to giggle and lay her head on my chest. Oliver looked at me over her head and nodded with a big smile on his face. I kissed the top of Brooklyn's head and just let her lean into me until she was ready to stand up straight. When the buzzer at the door sounded, Oliver kissed her shoulder and went to get the food.

I stood with Brooklyn in my arms for a while longer. Her arms eventually came around my waist, just holding herself to my chest. I rubbed her bare back and tried not to focus on her naked breasts that were pressed against me. My cock was already straining after getting a taste of her. But right now, it was about her. Her pleasure, releasing her stress, making sure she was happy.

Oliver called from the living room, reminding us the food had arrived. I released Brooklyn and pulled her robe from the bathroom hook she kept it on. She slid her arms into the garment as I held it up for her and then from behind I wrapped the material around her and tied the belt. She leaned back against me for a moment.

"Thanks. I feel better," she whispered.

"Never have to thank me for a chance to get my hands, or mouth, on your body," I replied.

With a smile on her face we met Oliver in the living room where he'd opened the pizza and grabbed paper plates from the kitchen. The bottle of wine was there with three glasses. Brooklyn's face lit up when she saw her favorite pizza in the box. She snuggled into the couch and Oliver handed her a plate with food.

"Wine and pizza?" She asked.

"Seemed appropriate," I shrugged.

She smiled again and Oliver and I sat on either side of her. We ate in silence and Brooklyn didn't finish her piece of pizza. I knew that wasn't normal for her, my girl loved to eat. She sat back on the couch, her glass of wine in her hands, staring off into space.

"Babe, you wanna talk about it?" Oliver asked.

Brooklyn just sighed and took a sip of wine.

"I'm not really sure what to say," she replied.

"Whatever you want. Whatever is on your mind," he replied.

"It's hard to even organize my thoughts, everything is really muddled in my head. There's a lot happening all at once. And I wasn't really prepared for any of it."

I wasn't liking the sound of this. This wasn't just about Lyle and his gifts he'd had delivered to her. There was more she was struggling with and I had a feeling it was about my brothers and I.

"Tell us what you need, love. We're here for you," I said.

She didn't look at either of us, just kept her eyes straight forward.

"I think, I need some time to myself," she said quietly.

Oliver's eyes met mine over her head and I could see the same sadness I was feeling. All of our desire to see her as soon as we got back to the city, the excitement and happiness we had been feeling, deflated all in once moment. I tried to push my feelings away, tried to see where she was coming from.

"You guys are fantastic, all of you. I've really enjoyed this time together. But I'm feeling really overwhelmed with every-thing happening and the gala coming up. Sometimes, things don't happen at the right times. Maybe it's just bad timing, right?" She continued.

Now that she was on a roll, she stood and started cleaning up the food and dishes. She walked to the kitchen and neither Oliver or I said a word. I wasn't sure what to say. Less than an hour ago I had her leg over my shoulder, my tongue on her pussy and now she was telling me it wasn't the right time for us. To say that was a hit to my ego, was an under-statement.

When she came back in, she had her arms wrapped around her and her robe had been tightened so it covered all of her exposed skin. She was pushing us away, with her words and physically. Everything in me wanted to fight back, but I couldn't. I understood what she was saying. We came into her life just as Lyle showed up again, a surprise that shouldn't have happened. And not only that, there was more than one of us that wanted her and she wasn't even sure how that was supposed to work.

Oliver was running his hands through his hair, looking frustrated. Before he could say something dumb, I decided to take control of what I could.

"Ok. We hear you. And I do understand where you're

coming from. But this, isn't something I'm willing to just chalk up to bad timing," I said, motioning between the three of us.

"We searched for you. Did we ever tell you that?" Oliver asked.

Brooklyn just shook her head, looking confused.

"That first night, at the club, when you took off. We watched the security video over and over. Trying to figure out a way to find you. We knew that night, we wanted you. You drew us to you," he continued.

Her face softened for a moment and I thought maybe Oliver was going to get through to her. But she just shook her head softly.

"I'm sorry. I know this isn't exactly what you want to hear. I just need some time to sort things out in my head. And honestly, when you're around, all I can think about is sex. It's hot as hell and god knows I enjoy it. But it makes it impossible for me to think straight," she stammered.

I looked over to Oliver and nodded. It pained me to stand up and walk toward the door. Oliver followed suit, his head hung down, like the world was completely lost to him. As I unlocked the door, I looked back to Brooklyn. Her face was sad and I could see tears that were about to spill. But our girl was strong and when she decided on something, that was it.

Last minute, I turned and went to her and just kissed her forehead. I looked down into her eyes and one of those tears slipped down her cheek. I wiped it away with my thumb.

"I understand why you think you need to do this. And we'll go. But know something. We won't give you up this easily. All those emotions about this relationship, we feel them too. And when you're ready to talk about them, we'll be there," I said.

She took in a shuttering breath and nodded her head. With that, I went back to the door which Oliver had opened.

"Brooklyn, beyond all of this with us. Please be careful. Stay aware of your surroundings. Use the cameras Gideon installed. And we're only a call away," I said.

I pulled the door shut after us and waited for the locks to turn. I knew it was time to turn away and walk down the stairs, but I just stared at the door, my head spinning from how fast everything turned.

"Are we really going to let this happen, brother?" Oliver asked.

"I don't think we have a choice."

"You're telling Gideon," Oliver said as he walked down the stairs.

CHAPTER
Twenty-Five

Brooklyn

THE DOOR DIDN'T OPEN. I stared and waited for them to open it, to knock, to buzz from the bottom security door. When I was met with nothing but silence, a desperation hit me. I began to cry, really sob, while I stumbled into my room and fell onto my bed. What had I done?

I laid awake in my bed for hours, staring at the ceiling, going over everything in my mind. I slept fitfully for a while and was awake before my alarm went off. I was dragging and decided a quick run was what I needed to get myself moving. I quickly got myself dressed in leggings and a hoodie.

Pulling my hoodie over my head, I stepped out into the crisp morning air. It felt fantastic to get a deep lung full of the fresh air after the long night. I took off at a slow pace for a warm up, before pouring on speed to push my body. The physical exertion helped keep my mind clear of any confusion I was having.

During my shower, I convinced myself that putting distance between myself and the guys was the right decision. I couldn't focus. I didn't know what was really happening with us. Everything felt real and serious, but it had only been a short time. I hadn't even been on the market, looking for a boyfriend. Suddenly, I had three men in my life. It was a lot to handle.

Even believing I had made the right choice, the look of hurt on Oliver and Jaxon's faces haunted me. My phone vibrated throughout the night with text messages from Gideon, once he realized I wouldn't be answering his phone calls. I could tell he was confused and hurt as well, just from the words in the messages.

I didn't have the words to clearly explain my decision. I needed to wrap my mind around what was happening with the threats from Lyle. I needed to call the police. The gala was looming and I needed to focus to make sure the event went off without a hitch. I didn't need to be getting into intense relationships, with three men.

Feeling more resolved, I hailed a cab for a quick ride to my office. As soon as I walked into the building, anxiety rose as I remembered the box that showed up the evening before. I started looking around at every person walking near me, afraid I would suddenly see Lyle. However, I got to my office without incident.

I threw myself into the gala planning, ignoring the gnawing pain in my heart. Typically, the guys would be texting me all day, but all three had gone silent. I knew I'd asked for it, but getting what I wanted didn't feel fantastic. I needed someone to talk to.

Looking at the time, I figured it was evening overseas and Ash would likely answer her phone. We hadn't talked much in the weeks since she'd been gone, beyond me texting her updates about the Knights. I didn't want her to know about the Lyle threats. But I definitely needed her opinion on the situation with the Knights. I was so thankful when she answered the phone on the third ring.

"Brooklyn! I miss you, girl!"

"I miss you too! How much fun is your life right now?" I asked.

Ash launched into how training had been amazing and she was learning so much. She then talked about how everyone drank wine at lunch and they didn't just go for an hour on lunch. They took their breaks seriously. She laughed about trying to order food when all she spoke was English. I laughed along, though it felt hollow.

"So what about you? How are things back home?" She finally asked.

"Well, not great, I guess," I replied.

"What? Did something happen with the guys? Is it work? The gala is coming up right?" Ash asked, firing off questions one after another.

"Yes, the gala is coming. Everything is going really well and work is fine. I sort of, I guess broke up with the guys last night?"

"Uh, ok. Why did you do that?" She asked, her voice laced with uncertainty.

"It was just too much. Like who has three boyfriends? Who am I to hold the attention of these men? It all was happening so fast and does anything real just happen like that? I don't think so. I was fooling myself, into believing it was something. And honestly, I couldn't think with them around me. I always felt foggy in some sex daze."

Ash's laugh rang through the line loudly.

"How is a sex daze a bad thing? I want to meet the person that wouldn't want to feel that way everyday."

"I'm serious, Ash," I groaned.

"Oh I realize you're serious. I also know, you run from anything that threatens the wall you've set up around you. And honestly, hon', who can blame you for having that jerk reaction? You've lived in hell, like lived in it, before getting out. So the idea of something that could really mean something in your life, scares the hell out of you," she said.

"I don't have a wall set up," I mumbled.

"Brooklyn Reeves, seriously? We've been friends long enough that I'm well aware of how you avoid any sort of situation where you just might meet a man that catches your attention. It's not even about saying no to a date offer, it's about making sure that offer never happens," she said, her voice taking on a soft tone.

"I don't really know how to be any different. I've only had one relationship and it wasn't healthy. I don't know how a healthy one works. And three men, well that's not normal," I said.

"Who cares? Seriously? If three men want you, are willing to share, each of them fulfill your needs, so what? Enjoy your life. Find love, if that's what this is meant to be. Do not shut yourself off. How have you felt since you told them to go?" She asked.

I didn't say anything. Did I really want to admit that I felt horrible? That I couldn't sleep, because I knew I turned away two men that would have slept in my bed with me. That I wanted to delete Gideon's contact badly, so I didn't have to see his words, but I kept reading the messages over and over.

"That's what I thought. Don't make yourself miserable, Brooklyn. Allow good things into your life, into your heart," Ash said.

"Thanks, girl. This is why I called you," I replied.

"You called me cause I'm cheaper than a therapist," she said, laughing.

"That too. Have a ton of fun. I'll let you know how the gala goes," I said.

We exchanged goodbyes before hanging up. I looked at my phone for a long moment, wondering if Ash was right. Had I just created a wall around myself, preventing anyone from coming in and finding me?

That question ran through my mind the rest of the day. I picked apart everything I had done in the time since Lyle had been sent away to prison. I figured out my life. I picked up and worked hard for the job I have. A job I cared about and felt good about doing.

That was my entire life. Between work and Ash, I had no one else. If I wasn't going out with Ash for dinner or drinks, I didn't have a social circle. I even avoided drinks with co-workers after hours.

After work, I rushed home, looking over my shoulder constantly. When I got inside, I locked the door immediately. Thinking about what Gideon would do, I checked the entire apartment before I allowed myself to get comfortable. I also checked the history on my camera and only saw my neighbors moving on the floor.

I took a deep breath and let myself relax. Kicking off my heels I went to the kitchen and pulled out the cold pizza. I stood next to the counter, eating the pizza without warming it up. Because that's what lonely women, that push everyone away, do. Eat cold pizza, alone, in their work clothes.

Brooklyn

CLUB 4 HAD BEEN COMPLETELY TRANSFORMED. I
walked onto the main floor, looking around at the room. It was
still slightly dim, but not as dark as on a regular night. There
were large chandeliers hanging over the dance floor. A stage
had been erected in front of the DJ stand.

The DJ was already playing music as the attendees began
to arrive. "Leave the Door Open" by Silk Sonic came across the
speakers and I smiled, happy with the mood of the music. I

stood near the President, as he greeted the arrivals. I smiled, but took a backseat so he could take the accolades for the success.

My assistant came to me, a clipboard in her hand. There was a seating fire that needed to be handled so I walked with her to behind one of the bars that wasn't being used for the event. We discussed the situation and I glanced at the seating chart, showing where to switch people before it became a bigger issue. She rushed off to do that and I took a moment to settle my nerves.

I was standing in Club 4 and I hadn't talked to the guys in days. My stomach was a whirlwind, knowing they would be here somewhere. I would be lying if I said I didn't dress with them in mind. My dress was black, sleeveless where the bottom hugged me like a pencil skirt. The top had a high lace neck, to hide my scar, but the modesty stopped there. The back was a wide cut out that stopped just above my ass.

My mask was simple black lace as well that just went around my eyes. My hair was down, curled in ringlets down my back, a look my co-workers very rarely saw. My assistant was surprised when she saw me, not even recognizing me at first. Once she did she smiled brightly and gushed on about how good I looked.

I was ready for the gala. However, I wasn't prepared to see the guys. My heart ached in my chest, for just the chance to see them at a distance. But I was scared. They had given me the space I wanted, but part of me wondered if they just weren't worried about seeing me. Maybe I had given them the out they were looking for. No longer being strapped with the damaged girl that didn't know what in the hell she wanted in life.

A clearing of a throat on the microphone caught my attention and I saw that my company President had made his way to the stage. He had a speech written to kick off the event before dinner was served. He started with thanking the donors for attending. He then thanked 4K corporation for the donation of the beautiful venue and meal we would be serving. Lastly, he called my name and I waved from the back as well as the rest of my team to give us credit for all the hard work we'd done.

Even though faces turned to look at me and a polite applause was given, my eyes searched for the guys. As the meal began, I had to stop my search as I was pulled into the kitchen to discuss a few diet restriction issues. We easily managed the requests and the catering company had everything running smoothly.

Back in the main room, I picked up a glass of champagne and sipped, trying to take the edge off. The event was going off without a hitch and I knew a lot of that was thanks to the Knights and the vendors they work with. Everyone was super professional and even the waiters and bartenders were wearing masks to go along with the masquerade theme. I couldn't have been more pleased.

I moved around the room, speaking with someone at each table. Smiling and ensuring they were enjoying themselves. It was really a beautiful crowd. Women were wearing stunning ballgowns and ornate pieces of jewelry, while the men wore well cut suits. Masks were worn by almost everyone, as they enjoyed being part of the fun in the theme. I told myself that if I talked to Oliver and Jaxon, I would thank them for coming up with such a great idea.

Not seeing the Knights was putting me on edge. Part of me wanted to just pull off the bandaid and see them. I wanted to quickly assess the situation I was in and then handle it. The other part of me was completely terrified that they would dismiss me as no one and the heartbreak I had caused myself, would explode inside my chest.

Myself and my team hid in the kitchen area to grab a few bites to eat before the auction started. The butterflies were flying in my stomach again. I was to be the last person auctioned off for a dance. I knew a lot of the donors that were in attendance, so I hoped it wouldn't be a very awkward moment. I couldn't decide what would be worse, having no one bid on me, or having to dance with some old man that didn't know how to keep his hands to himself.

Standing on the edge of the dining area, as people began to make their way to the dance floor, I felt like I was being watched. It wasn't the same feeling I normally felt if one of the guys was watching me. This was an unease that made the hair on my neck stand up. I looked around the room and didn't see anyone specifically looking my way.

My eyes floated up a few floors, expecting to see the Knights on their balcony. But it was dark and empty. I frowned, wondering what was giving me the creeps. The crowd on the dance floor was now facing the stage, where the DJ was standing. He would be running the auction and he called the first person up.

The line up of dance partners before me were local business owners, a clothes designer, a social media influencer and a local fitness coach. Each was dressed to impress and I suddenly wondered if I didn't plan my outfit accordingly. The bids were going up quickly on the first dancer and I smiled and clapped when the highest bidder finally won.

Out of those to come before me, the highest bid was seven thousand dollars. I was extremely pleased with the amount of money we were raising with this auction. And also I was astounded with the disposable income some of the attendees seemed to have. I'm sure a tax break didn't hurt for them either.

My introduction was starting, so I began to walk forward

toward the stage. My nerves were through the roof and I still had a creepy feeling. But now so many eyes were on me, I couldn't be sure what was bothering me. I forced a smile on my face as the DJ pointed me out to the crowd.

Suddenly, a brown suit caught my attention at the edge of the dance floor. It stood out because it was a dirt color that most of the elite in the room wouldn't wear. When I turned my head to focus, I tripped on my own feet and barely caught myself from falling. The mask less face looked at me and a greasy smile spread across his mouth. His too long dull brown hair was slicked too far back, only making his forehead look larger than it was.

Lyle.

Lyle was in the club, in my event. I stopped moving for a moment, staring at him. He raised an eyebrow at me and slowly brought his hand up to his throat, making a slashing motion with his thumb. My mouth went dry as sand and I looked around for security, for one of the guys, for anyone that would be able to protect me.

But as I looked around wildly, I realized the crowd was cheering and chanting my name. Everyone around me thought I was having stage fright, not real fear for my life. In a split second decision, I knew I was safer on the stage, then going anywhere else in the room. Somehow Lyle had gotten in and if I wasn't surrounded by this crowd, I would be vulnerable.

When I got to the stage steps, the DJ held out his hand to help me up. I carefully took the stairs and stood next to him. My eyes immediately went back to where Lyle was standing. I watched as a masked woman leaned over and say something to him. He nodded, but his eyes never left mine.

I barely heard as the bidding started. Laughter rose around me and applause as each new bid was called out. The DJ next to me worked to hype up the men, talking about my successes with KidsUpFirst and how powerful women were all the rage these days. I heard only snippets of what he was saying, but it seemed like the crowd was eating it up.

Suddenly my mental fog was broken by someone calling out from the crowd.

"Fifty thousand dollars!"

CHAPTER
Twenty~Seven

Aiden

A SENSE of pride filled me as I watched all of the city's upper class file into my club and enjoy a meal. The club looked fantastic with a mix of my team and Brooklyn's team, working together to come up with the perfect atmosphere for the masquerade.

My brothers were floating around the outside of the event, avoiding being seen by Brooklyn. The three of them had been so ridiculous since Brooklyn sent them away, I could barely live with them. They didn't come down to socialize in the house at all. At work they were strictly business and then they were either in their rooms or in the gym.

It wasn't that I didn't see the temptation with the woman. She was absolutely gorgeous. And the bit of fire I saw from her the night she was in our section, it was a turn on. I just didn't have the time or space for that in my head right now. I could see that my brothers had tumbled for her quick and now they were suffering for it.

The gala was moving along at the scheduled pace. I heard from my staff that the few issues that popped up were handled directly by Brooklyn. I admired her hands on approach to something as large as this. She had a good team as well, who respected her and worked hard. But when it came to the details, she had her hands in things. I liked that.

When the auction for the dances started, I made my way into the crowd to watch and ensure bidding was handled appropriately. I had seen events devolve into fist fights before, though I doubted a dance was enough to get people worked up. When Brooklyn's name was called, I was surprised. I hadn't seen the list of people, but Oliver had mentioned he had helped with some contacts for the auction.

My head swiveled around, looking for her. When I saw her, I took her in slowly. She was in all black, her hair down and flowing around her. The delicate mask didn't hide her identity as much as accentuate her beauty. Her eyes were locked on something in the crowd, and she tripped for a moment. I started to make my way over to her, but she was on her feet and beginning to move again.

As she made her way onto the stage, I knew immediately something was wrong. In the interactions I'd experienced with

Brooklyn, I'd never seen her uncertain. Right now, she looked scared. I studied her posture and the way she gripped her hands in front of her. Everything felt wrong, not just stage fright, but real fear.

I listened as men yelled out bids around me. The noise was grating on my nerves as I watched Brooklyn pale even further. Something wasn't right and I wasn't going to allow her to just stand there looking so miserable.

"Fifty thousand dollars!" I called out, before I even knew what I was doing.

Brooklyn's eyes immediately snapped over to mine and she looked shocked. Everyone around me erupted in applause and the DJ had to call over the chaos that the bidding was over and I had won the dance with Brooklyn. I went to the stage to help her down the stairs, but she was already down and she was walking quickly toward the hall that held the bathrooms.

I stood at the end of the hall, watching the door, ensuring that if something happened, I was close enough to help. Time ticked by and I felt my phone vibrating in my pocket. I pulled it out and read the group chat messages flowing into my text messages.

Oliver: Aiden, did you really just bid on Brooklyn?

Jaxon: I'm not sure she's going to be happy with this.

Gideon: WTF Aiden?

Oliver: Where is she?

I SIGHED and typed out a response to calm them all down.

> Aiden: Something is wrong, I didn't want her to have to deal with all the chaos. She's in the bathroom. And it's not me that she broke it off with.

I KNEW it wasn't a nice response, but it was the truth. Brooklyn and I weren't involved and it wasn't me she was avoiding. And I really was just trying to help. As I tried to figure out what must be bothering her, the bathroom door opened and she came striding out. She had put on her business mask again by the time she reached me.

"Aiden, you really shouldn't have done that. You already donated your space and money for this event. I'm sure you could cancel the bid," she said.

"Why would I do that?" I asked.

"You just bid fifty grand for one dance with me. That's, well, absurd," she stammered.

"It's money well spent. I get a dance with the most beautiful woman in the room and the money goes to a good cause. Will one dance be so bad with me?" I asked.

"Of course not, I'm sure I can manage," she replied, trying to be cool, though a pink flush had come to her cheeks.

Brooklyn's name was called by the DJ and she was asked to make her way to the dance floor, along with her winner. I offered her my arm and we walked toward the center of the circle of spectators. Brooklyn's eyes were flying around the room and again she seemed to be on edge.

Sia's voice came across the speakers, singing the song

"Helium" and I pulled Brooklyn into my arms. Her left hand rested on my shoulder and she allowed me to take her right in my hand. I began to guide her around the room and I watched her eyes never stop moving.

I pulled her closer, so my mouth was near her ear. My hand on her waist found the skin of her back, exposed by her dress design. I allowed my thumb to sweep along her skin.

"What is it? Something's wrong," I said.

I felt Brooklyn shiver in my arms and I tightened my hold a bit, trying to give comfort. Her hand on my shoulder moved to the back of my neck, where she played with the short hair on my neck.

"He's here," she said in a small voice.

"Who?" I asked.

"Don't react. Lyle was here," she said.

Her hand on my neck locked me from moving, because I was about to react and she knew it. Her hand that I held, squeezed, until I stopped trying to pull away. As soon as I could act normal, I pulled back slightly, until I caught sight of Gideon. I jerked my head, calling him to us.

Gideon's long legs ate the space between us and Brooklyn's eyes widened as she saw him coming toward us. When he got close enough to quietly talk, I leaned away from Brooklyn to act as if it was a business matter I need to discuss.

"Lyle was in here. Find him," I said.

His eyes widened for a moment, before sharpening in anger. Brooklyn looked toward him, as if she wanted to speak. But Gideon just ran a finger down her cheek before turning away. She continued to stare after him for longer than necessary, before I pulled her back into dance with me.

"This song is ironic," she whispered.

"Why?" I asked.

"It's all about asking for strength, when the world becomes too much. Seems like I'm having to do that," she said.

"It's ok to ask for help once in a while," I replied.

I allowed my hand to slide along her back, until I splayed my fingers across her skin. She pressed her forehead against my jaw. I could feel her breath on my neck. Her lavender scent flowed around me as we moved. Her body seemed to melt into mine, seeking the comfort I was offering. I held her tightly as we danced. In the back of my mind, I was sure that would cause gossip around the socialites, but at the moment, I didn't care.

"Are you going to continue to torture my brothers?" I asked.

"Torture? I'm not torturing them," she said, but her voice faded off at the end.

"You're only hurting all of you by pushing them away. They've been unbearable. Fix it, please. I beg of you," I said, with a small chuckle.

She pulled back to look up at me and a small smile was on her mouth. When the song came to an end, we slowly stopped and stepped apart. The attendees all applauded and I smiled at Brooklyn, trying to help her keep up the appearance. The next dancer was announced and I took Brooklyn's hand to lead her off the dance floor. She didn't resist and allowed me to hold onto her.

Oliver met us with a grave look on his face. I held her hand as the two of them studied each other from a distance.

"Gideon has his men searching every inch of the club. We don't know how he got in. The only guess is he came as a guest and used a fake name. We didn't think to check every-one's faces against our banned list. We never found a connec-tion between him and anyone influential," Oliver explained.

"I'll find Gideon to get an update," I said.

Leaning over, I kissed Brooklyn on the cheek and then released her hand and watched as the two of them just stared at each other. I walked away, trusting the two of them would figure it out, that they all would. I had a feeling Brooklyn was going to be a fixture in our world, and I didn't feel as much frustration around that as I should have.

CHAPTER
Twenty~Eight

Oliver

SHE WAS GORGEOUS. My fingers flexed at my side as I fought the urge to reach out for her. I knew I had to wait, wait and see what she wanted.

"Hi," she said.

"You're beautiful," I blurted out.

A soft smile came across her face that gave me a thrill of hope. She stepped forward and then paused before she was within arm's reach. Indecision crossed her face and I almost grabbed her, before we were interrupted by her assistant.

"Brooklyn, I'm sorry, but we need you over by the bar. There's a question about the provided alcohol, and I'm not sure how to answer it," she rambled.

"I'll be there in one moment," Brooklyn responded, without taking her eyes off of me.

Her assistant nodded, clearly realizing there was something she was interrupting. She rushed off and neither of us paid any attention.

"I've missed you," she said.

"Missed, doesn't really cover it," I replied.

She quickly closed the distance and threw herself into my arms. Her arms wrapped around my shoulders, burying her face in my neck. I lifted her off her feet, gripping her to me. There were so many things I had replayed in my mind, obsessed over and tried to not forget. The smell of her, the feel of her, were two things that memories didn't do justice.

"I'm sorry. I'm not sure what I'm doing," she said.

"I hope you're not saying sorry for letting me hold you," I replied.

"No, I mean, pushing you away. And now pulling you back in. I'm a damn yo-yo. I don't mean to be."

"Baby, just don't make me leave you again, and you can do whatever you want," I whispered into her hair.

She pulled back and flashed me a smile, that didn't quite reach her eyes. I knew she was still worried about Lyle. But Gideon's team would have worked fast. My guess was once she saw him and he caused her fear, he ditched the party to ensure he wasn't caught by anyone looking for him.

"I have to go handle the bar situation. I'll see you later though, right?" She asked.

"How about I come with you?" I asked.

I lifted her hand to my mouth, pressing a kiss to her knuckles. She smiled and I could tell she felt relieved by my offer. Even if she had said no, I was going to follow at a distance to ensure she was safe. I placed my hand on the small of her back, which was bare and I felt her shiver at my touch.

"Did I mention how beautiful you looked?" I whispered near her ear.

"You did sort of blurt it out," she laughed.

"This dress, really perfect," I added.

"I guess I was right when I picked this dress for you guys," she said.

"Babe, it doesn't matter what you wear. I'm gonna think you're the hottest thing in the room," I said.

She flashed me a smile as we arrived at the bar. I stood back and watched her handle the small issue with finesse and business. She was impressive when it came to work, her confidence made her shine. So much of her life had caused her to not have that same confidence when it came to personal relationships. As I watched her, so much came into focus at that moment.

Jaxon walked up and joined me. His eyes were glued to Brooklyn as well.

"Gideon and his guys haven't found anything. They finished the search. How is she doing?" He asked.

"Keeping it together, at least here. I can imagine she's freaking out on the inside," I replied.

"Think she'll let us help?"

"Yeah. And I think she's coming around," I said, with a smile.

As if on cue, Brooklyn turned. Her eyes widened when she saw Jaxon standing with me. He shifted uncomfortably and I clapped my hand on his shoulder to keep him from running. As she walked toward us, he shoved his hands in his pockets. I knew he was having the same reaction I had, wanting to reach out to her just because she was nearby.

"Hey," Jaxon said when she stopped in front of him.

She looked between us with indecision. Her assistant walked by and patted her arm as she walked toward the dancing. Brooklyn watched her go, but then turned back to us.

"Can we, go somewhere, private?" She asked.

I nodded and took her hand to lead her to the hallway that led to our offices. I brought her into my office with Jaxon following. As soon as the door was closed, Brooklyn spun to Jaxon. He didn't have any warning as she crashed into him. He was knocked back a step, but he recovered quickly and wrapped his arms around her.

"Sorry. I just didn't want everyone out there see me all over the two of you, especially after dancing with Aiden," she muttered.

I laughed out loud and she shot me a playful glare.

"You men don't have to worry about your reputation with all these richie riches. I have to be on my best behavior!" She exclaimed.

"I'm not complaining, love. But can I ask, what's going on?" Jaxon asked.

She pulled back and looked at us both.

"I'm sorry. I'm still, a mess. Damaged and clearly can't even go out in public without being in danger," she said.

As she spoke, she began to pace the office. Her hands getting more animated the more that poured out from her. I pulled out my phone and texted Gideon to meet us in my office. If she was going to let this all go, he should hear it too.

"That's not your fault, love," Jaxon said.

Just as Brooklyn opened her mouth to speak again, Gideon walked in. She froze in her tracks and he immediately shut the door behind him.

"That was quick," I muttered.

"Was already on my way here," he replied.

"I, shit, what was I saying?" She asked.

"You're damaged, a mess and you're being stalked," I replied.

"Nice, dude," Jaxon said.

"She asked," I shrugged.

Brooklyn started her pacing again, her eyes flashing to each of us as she walked.

"Right. The three of you, have literally seen my scars. All of them. I don't have to hide from you, like I do everyone else. But that means you also know that I'm a wreck, a total nut job. And frankly, I keep waiting for you to figure this all out. That I'm too much work. That I'm not worth the time and effort. So I guess, when I thought about that, I figured I'd do us all a favor and put an end to it," she said.

She stopped in the middle of the office and turned and looked at the three of us.

"But, honestly, the last few days, have felt horrible. I'm literally the idiot that shot myself in the foot and made myself miserable, on my own. And now I'm standing here, ranting, only proving the point. You three may want to just turn and run now. But I kinda hope you don't. Because really, it's sinful how good you three look in tuxedos and I'm really just rambling now," she finished, with a huff and her hands on her hips.

We all just stood and stared at her. She was adorable when she got all worked up. Her face was flushed, she fidgeted and despite the words she was saying, her confidence was up. Before any of us could say anything, Gideon pushed through Jaxon and I, until he was standing in front of her.

"Gideon, I'm sorry," she whispered.

Reaching down, Gideon lifted her clear off her feet so he

could hug her. She laughed and hugged him around his neck. When he put her down, he touched her face and smiled down at her. Aiden chose that moment to walk into the office as well, interrupting our moment. I rolled my eyes at Jaxon, figuring Aiden was messing with things on purpose.

"Sorry guys. Brooklyn, you are being looked for. I didn't think you'd want your boss coming back here," he said, with a smirk on his face.

"He's probably trying to duck out, which is his normal agenda. He does all the flashy speeches and such and then goes home for a quiet evening. I'll catch up with you later?" She said, pointing at Jaxon, Gideon and I.

She rushed out of the office, looking a lot happier than she had when we first walked in. Aiden's gaze passed over all of us and he nodded.

"Thank god. I couldn't handle you all pouting anymore," he said.

"Don't be jealous," I joked.

"I definitely don't need this complication in my life right now," he replied, looking toward the door Brooklyn just exited.

"Keep telling yourself that, brother," I said.

The four of us joined the party again. It was starting to slow down a bit, this crowd not being a typical all night club crowd. That didn't matter, the event had succeeded where it needed to. Especially with Aiden's bid on Brooklyn. It was easy to find Brooklyn, near the stage talking with her boss. The man was talking animatedly and had a huge smile on his face.

"Aiden's donation probably pushed the fundraiser well over the goal," Jaxon said quietly.

"Why do you think he did it?" Gideon asked.

"Bid on her? Not sure. But our girl has a pull to her. Aiden would have to be dead to not notice it," I said.

"She was super uncomfortable up there. I think Aiden noticed and wanted to end the whole bidding thing before she had a complete freak out," Jaxon said.

I thought about it and realized Jaxon was right. I was so lost in seeing her, I wasn't noticing her behaviors. Now I realized I missed what was happening. I was glad it was Aiden that won the bid. Some of the elite at the party were dirty scumbags and I didn't want their hands anywhere near my girl.

After Brooklyn walked her boss to the door and bid him goodbye, she wound her way through the crowd to us. She slipped her mask off and we got the first good look at her face. She smiled, but there was stress behind her eyes too.

"When can you take me home?" She asked.

No asking if we were coming with her, just an assumption. An assumption that was correct. I wasn't letting her go tonight. I looked at Jaxon and Gideon before answering.

"I can go anytime you want, babe," I said.

"I have work to wrap up first, but I can be to your place in a bit," Jaxon said.

"Yeah, I can meet you there too. I have to finish up the updates with everything that happened tonight," Gideon said.

He didn't directly address or say Lyle's name. But we all knew what he meant. Brooklyn's smile tightened as she nodded up at him. Gideon stepped forward and cupped her jaw. He leaned down and kissed her on the edge of her mouth. As he moved away, Jaxon took his place and he hugged Brooklyn and pressed a kiss to her neck.

After both of my brothers were gone, Brooklyn turned to me and nodded toward the backdoor. I took her hand in mine and led her through the crowd, to the private exit we had. In the back, my GTO was parked in its usual spot, and I opened the passenger side door for her.

As we drove to her apartment, she held my hand in her lap. I focused on driving, even though I wanted to pull over and dive into her. I reminded myself she had experienced quite a scary evening, and I needed to comfort her in the way she was needing from me. That calmed my desire down to a low burn instead of the inferno that was threatening to burn me up from the inside.

At her building, I parked and quickly rounded the car to help her out. She shimmied a bit, pulling her dress down where it had ridden up her legs. Once she was all straightened, we headed up the stairs. I was lost in the feel of her hand in mine, the warmth of her body close to me. I couldn't stop picturing all of the things I wanted to do with her once we got inside.

All of that flew out of my head as we got to her door. The wood was splintered at the jam and the door was ajar. She froze and I pulled her behind my body. I looked up and down the stairwell and then the hallway, nothing moved. I pushed her back toward the stairs.

"Call Gideon. Tell him to get here now," I said.

I started toward the door and she grabbed my suit jacket.

"Where are you going?"

"I'm checking the apartment. Stay here, until I come get you or Gideon gets here," I said.

"Oliver…" she started.

"No. If there's someone in there, they aren't getting away," I said.

I pushed the apartment door open with my foot, waiting to see if anyone attacked. The inside of the apartment was dark, except the splinter of light coming from Brooklyn's bedroom door. It was almost completely closed, only letting out a thin line of light.

Using that, I looked around the living room and didn't see

anything out of place. I could see Ash's door from the front door and it was closed. I backed slowly toward it, keeping Brooklyn's door in my view. Ash's room was empty and all in order.

I glanced in the kitchen as I made my way by and nothing moved there either. I started to think Brooklyn may have accidentally left her light on and someone broke in and thought again. The moment I thought that, I knew it was ridiculous. She was being stalked by a man that tried to kill her the last time they were alone together.

At her door, I pushed it open, and stood to the side to make sure I wasn't open to an easy attack. The breath rushed out of my lungs when I saw the absolute carnage that was in Brooklyn's room. I quickly checked her bathroom and knew the apartment was empty.

"Oh my god."

CHAPTER
Twenty~Nine

Brooklyn

I COULDN'T UNDERSTAND what I was seeing. Oliver stood in the middle of the room, looking around for the intruder, but I knew, the damage was the point. He was already gone. I slowly came into the room and my feet crunched on glass. I looked down and found pieces of the full length mirror that was on the back of my door on the ground.

"Be careful," Oliver exclaimed, coming over to me and taking my arms.

"What, I don't understand," I muttered.

"I told you to wait," he said.

"You didn't come back. I didn't know what was happening," I said.

I looked at him, clearly for the first time since I walked in. Looking him over, I knew he was ok. It was his safety that made me barge into the apartment. Gideon had also told me to stay outside, but I couldn't do it. The idea someone had gotten Oliver, wasn't something I could handle.

Oliver held onto me, trying to stop me from looking. But I gently moved him to the side and took in the destruction that was my room. In my bathroom, the light fixture was hanging by wires and all of my makeup was pulled out. It was either smashed into pieces or soaked in the sink that was full of water.

I moved beyond the bathroom to my closet, where the doors were almost ripped from the hinges. Not one piece of clothing was hanging in the closet, confirming what the material strewn all over the room was. I reached down to pick up a shirt at my feet and found that it had been slashed into pieces. I let it slide from my fingertips.

My bookshelf contents were thrown everywhere, some books looking to be torn apart. Turning toward the bed, I just stared at the wall behind my headboard. The words "rat whore" had been spray painted in black. My stomach twisted, knowing without a doubt it was Lyle that had been in the apartment.

Something caught my attention under the ripped comforter on my bed. When I pulled it back, my hand flew to my mouth. Oliver came to stand next to me, just as Gideon came tearing into the apartment yelling my name. I didn't turn to look at him, though, I was too horrified by what I was seeing.

With shaking hands, I picked up one of the photographs

that was laid out. It was Gideon and I on his bike. From my outfit, I knew it was the night we went out to dinner and I was sure I saw Lyle in the reflection of the restaurant window. I dropped that one and picked up another, one of Jaxon and I leaving my office hand in hand. I sifted through them, finding some of Oliver, Jaxon and I together.

"He, he, he's been...oh god, he's been following me this whole time," I croaked.

I tossed photos around, finding ones of me through the apartment windows. Everything felt incredibly violated. Photos of intimate ways my guys touched my back or held my hand. Me getting on the back of Gideon's bike, was zoomed in close enough that I could see the look in his eyes as he helped me climb on.

My stomach turned as I focused on a photo of Gideon and I in the back alley of Club 4. There wasn't one place I had been that Lyle hadn't followed to take photos. I threw myself toward the bathroom, barely making it to the toilet before bile began to come up my throat.

Hands came to my head, pulling back my hair, holding it and saying soothing words. I wasn't hearing anything. I hadn't been safe. I hadn't even been alone and I still hadn't been safe. Lyle had gone from sending packages to tracking my every move. How could he possibly do all of this on his own? I started to ask myself what the end game was for him, but I knew the answer. Me. Alive or dead, I wasn't sure. But he wanted to get me.

I stopped vomiting and someone flushed the toilet and put down the lid, so my face wasn't completely in the bowl. I leaned against the cool porcelain for a moment, trying to wrap my head around how much worse this was. I had been living in a fantasy, to believe that Lyle would just stop with deliveries or idle threats.

Gideon's big arms came around me, pulling me back against him. His big body curled around me as he dropped his mouth near my ear.

"Stellina, come away from here. You can't stay here," he said softly.

"I, can't leave. I need to call the police," I said.

"I already did. I have some friends in the force coming to handle it. But you can't stay here," he said again.

"I, don't have anywhere to go," I whispered at first.

My mind was racing, trying to put together the pieces of what had been ripped away from me. Get it together, Brooklyn, I said in my head.

"Ok, no, ok. I'll get a hotel. I just need to see if there's any usable clothing in here. And I'll need to get the door fixed. This is Ash's home. I can't leave it violated like that," I said, pulling from strength I didn't really have.

"Babe, you aren't going to a hotel. You'll come home with us," Oliver said.

The two of them were both on the bathroom floor with me. Oliver had a washcloth and he carefully wiped under my eyes and my mouth. I looked at them both, in confusion.

"What? No, of course not. I can get a room."

"Well, Jaxon is already at the house, getting a room ready for you," Gideon said.

I looked down Gideon's hands that were splayed across my stomach. He was the definition of strength and protection, it was just what he did. Decisions warred inside my mind. I knew we all expected the night to go differently. Digging deep, I tried to think about what a normal woman would do, that didn't have an obsessive need to stand on her own, or hide away. She'd probably go home with her super sexy boyfriends and let them take care of her.

"Ok," I said, leaning into Gideon.

The big man didn't wait for me to say another word. He stood and then bent down and swept me up into his arms.

"Oliver, see if there's any usable clothing left. If so, bring it. I'll tell the detectives they need to come to our house for her statement," he said as he began to stride out of the apartment.

I wrapped one of my arms around his neck and laid my head on his shoulder. Without strain, Gideon went down the stairs with me in his arms. Just as we got to the town car he had waiting for him, a plain dressed officer, with a badge around his neck, came walking up to us.

Gideon nodded to him and carefully placed me into the car. The man approached Gideon and the two shook hands. I could hear Gideon telling him there was a lot more to the story and that he would send all the files to them as soon as he got back to his desk. He also told the detective that he was fairly sure that this was Lyle coming after me and that he had been at the fundraiser, stalking me and breaking the protection order I had against him.

Eventually, I accepted that Gideon had everything handled and I leaned back into the car seat and waited. The detective disappeared into the apartment building and Gideon climbed into the car next to me. He nodded to the driver and pulled me sideways into his lap. I curled into him, trying to lose myself in all the comfort he was offering.

"Who was that?" I asked, gesturing toward the way the detective went.

"Lee. Detective Anderson. He's a friend, so he'll keep us in the loop on the investigation. I'm so glad you weren't there. I don't want to think about what that son of a bitch would have done to you," he said, his voice gravely and quiet.

I nodded into his chest and he wrapped his arms around my shoulders, pulling me tightly into him.

"I'm sorry, for being such a hassle," I said.

"Stellina, this isn't your fault. None of it. You can't be sorry for something you didn't even cause," he said.

"In the practical sense, I know that, of course. But I hate that you have to come to my rescue. I should be able to take care of myself," I said.

"We aren't running. It doesn't matter what this asshole does. We aren't going to run from you," he said.

His words held such conviction, I allowed my heart to soak them up and add it to the file of hope I had been feeling earlier in the evening. Before my home had been ruined. Everything I had worked so hard to build, my business clothes, my expensive shoes, my name brand makeup. All things I never could have had with Lyle. He took it all away from me again.

The car slowed and I realized we had driven out of the city and were at a large black gate. The driver leaned out of the window and put a number into a pin pad before the gate swung in and allowed us to drive up a long driveway. I pulled away from Gideon so I could see better.

The guys had called this a house. Their home was no version of a home I'd ever seen in person. The beautifully modern designed mansion loomed over us. I leaned closer to the window to see and Gideon rubbed my back.

"You'll get a tour, you don't need to hurt yourself," he said.

I pulled back, with a blush, snapping my mouth closed when I realized it was hanging open. As soon as the town car stopped, Jaxon was coming out of the front door and Aiden was just inside. Gideon popped open the door and helped me plant my feet on the gravel driveway. Jaxon collided with me, squeezing me tightly to him.

"God, I'm so glad you're ok," he said.

Then he pulled back and started looking me over, as if he wasn't sure he believed Gideon that I hadn't been hurt. When his eyes settled on mine, his face softened. I knew he could see the devastation painted in my look. He gently took my face in his hands and kissed my forehead. Then, with his arm around my shoulders he led me toward the front door.

"Welcome to our home," Aiden said, with less sarcasm than he usually had with me.

"Thank you, for letting me come here, with everything going on," I said.

It felt slightly weird to be in Aiden's home, when we had nothing but a business relationship. But it wasn't just his home, I reminded myself. Neither Aiden or Jaxon had changed out of their tuxedos from the gala. It was clear that as soon as the call was made that my house had been vandalized, they all went into action to get things handled.

"You're welcome here, as long as my brothers want you here. Don't worry about it," Aiden said.

He turned and went down a hallway off the entry. He disappeared into a room and the door shut with a quiet click. I stared after him for a moment, thinking back to our dance and how he had comforted me after I told him about Lyle being in the club. He came to my aid and protected me from making a complete fool of myself. I would have to tell him how much I appreciated that later.

I turned to Jaxon and Gideon. I tried to smile, but I was pretty sure it came out as a grimace.

"Let's do a quick tour. I'll show you to the guest room. And we'll get you something comfortable to wear," Jaxon said.

I nodded slowly, looking around the entry. They had so many windows, it made me feel uncomfortable at first. The front door was just one large piece of glass that swung open. But when I looked out, I couldn't see anything but the lawn and trees. The floor was a light hardwood, but the hallway Aiden walked down was carpeted in a light gray.

"That way is Aiden's office. Oliver and I also share a home

office in that hall. Though we don't work from home as often as Aiden does," Jaxon explained.

He took my hand and walked forward. He pointed out a bathroom downstairs and closet, before turning a corner that led into a huge kitchen. The counters were a white marble with light gray streaks through it. The center was dominated by an island that looked like it could double as a casual eating area, with stools on three sides.

The appliances were all stainless steel with black accents. There was a huge French door fridge off to one side. A stove with six burners was next to a double oven set. I found myself wondering if any of them actually cooked meals in the room.

Gideon went to the fridge and pulled out a bottle of water. He opened it and handed it to me. I looked at it dumbly for a moment, before he motioned for me to drink. I took a sip and the cool liquid felt good going down my raw throw and settling in my upset stomach. I smiled at him, appreciative of him recognizing I still wasn't feeling well.

Jaxon pointed out the mudroom that led to the garage before leaving the kitchen. Directly connected to the kitchen was a formal dining room. It was impeccably decorated, but for some reason, I didn't see the guys sitting around the large wood table for their meals.

Leaving the dining room, across a hall was a living room with large flat screen tv on one wall. There was a wet bar in the corner and a huge L shaped couch in the center of the room.

"When we get a chance to relax, sometimes it's here to watch movies or whatever," Jaxon explained.

I nodded my head. Next was pointing out the stairs that led into the basement, where the gym was housed.

"Do you have a treadmill?" I asked.

"Yes, why?" Jaxon asked.

"I like to run. I can't run outside right now I guess. It would be nice to get exercise once in a while," I said.

Jaxon nodded and continued to the stairs. The landing for the stairs was wide open air, where you could look down to the first floor if you wanted. Two hallways led off either side. Jaxon pointed down one.

"My room and Oliver's are down that way. There's also a study with a small library, in case you're ever wanting to read or anything like that. It's quiet," he said, before turning toward the other hall.

"Aiden and Gideon are down that way. And the guest room, is here right in the center," he said, opening a door right in front of us.

The room was large and simply decorated. One wall was covered by a shade, that told me there was a wall length window on that side. There was a small desk on one wall and a loveseat against the opposite, creating a sitting area on the one side of the room. On the other side a large bed, on an ornate black four poster frame.

Jaxon walked to a door and opened it and flipped on the light. The ensuite bathroom was white marble, with a large glass walled shower and clawfoot tub. Normally I would be exploring the bathroom, but it was hard to feel excited about anything.

Gideon entered the room and set clothes on the bed.

"I grabbed one of my shirts and a pair of boxers from Jaxon's room. Just for tonight. Tomorrow we'll figure out your wardrobe," he said.

I nodded, not really able to think about plans for the next day. I picked up the clothes and walked over to the bathroom.

"I'm going to shower," I said over my shoulder, before closing the door.

I turned on the water, allowing it to get scalding hot. I

stood with the water spraying down on me and felt the sting on my skin. Though I hadn't been in the apartment when it had been ransacked, I felt dirty and violated. Scrubbing at my skin, it began to turn pink as I tried to get rid of the invisible stains that were all over me.

Brooklyn

I DRIED my hair with a towel and fingered through it, since I didn't have any products or brush. I pulled Gideon's shirt over my head and looked at myself in the mirror. The shirt engulfed my body, almost as long as the dress I had been wearing. Jaxon's boxers would work for sleep.

When I went out into the bedroom, I found Oliver waiting with two boxes and a suitcase at his feet. He stood when I came out and he fished around in the suitcase and pulled out a brush. I smiled and took it from him.

"What's all this?" I asked.

"After the detectives let me back in, I packed up some of the things I thought you might want. There weren't really any clothes that hadn't been wrecked, so we'll have to handle that tomorrow. But make yourself comfortable, unpack what you might want and we'll figure out how to replace what else you need," he said.

"Did you see any more of the photos?" I asked.

"The detectives collected them all for evidence," he replied.

I nodded and turned back to the bathroom to brush my hair. Oliver followed and leaned against the doorframe.

"I know you're not ok, so I'm not going to ask. What can I do?" He asked.

I sighed. I didn't really know what I needed. The feelings of being overwhelmed and unprepared were raging back. But this time, I couldn't run away from the guys, I was under their roof.

"Nothing. You guys have done enough. I think I just need to sleep," I said.

Oliver came to me, put his hands on my shoulders and looked at me in the bathroom mirror reflection.

"Want to be alone?" He asked quietly.

That was really the elephant in the room. We were on the road to reconcile before everything blew up again. But I couldn't focus on those feelings and just wanted to hide from it all for a little while.

I nodded to him and he gave me a small smile. He leaned in and placed a kiss on my neck before turning and leaving. I heard the quiet click of the bedroom door and was engulfed in silence. I reminded myself that not only was it quiet, but I was safe and that was most important.

In the bedroom I popped open the boxes Oliver brought. There were odds and ends packed up, as well as my briefcase and my day to day purse. There were some photo albums of Ash and I from college on, the good memories I'd had in my life. I was surprised that Lyle hadn't destroyed those as well.

I pulled out my earbuds and climbed into bed with my phone. I switched on music and laid in the middle of the huge mattress. It was late and exhaustion was pulling me down. I fell asleep quickly, whether from exhaustion or fear, I had no idea. The music slowly dimmed in my ears as I got deeper into sleep.

Later, I shot straight up in bed, a cold sweat beaded on my skin. For a moment, I forgot where I was and panic clawed at me as I looked around the room. I had left the bathroom light on and the door partially closed, because I was too afraid to sleep in the dark. My eyes adjusted and I took deep breaths until my heart calmed down slightly.

Looking at the clock, I realized I had only been asleep for about an hour. I tried to bring back the nightmare so I could figure out what had scared me. But my life was a nightmare, it didn't really matter what I saw in my dreams. I could easily guess it was about my apartment or Lyle or thinking about how he was going to come after me next.

I quietly crept out of the guest room. I knew I couldn't sleep alone. I didn't want to admit to being scared or feeling a weakness, but if I was going to really give the relationship with the guys a chance, I needed to start being honest about a lot of things.

The house was dark and silent, all of the guys in bed trying to sleep off all the insanity of the night. I found myself at Gideon's door. Silently, I opened the door and slipped in before closing it behind me. I could hear the sounds of his deep breathing and it almost immediately made me feel more comfortable. I could just make out his sleeping form, on his back, his hair around his head, an arm under his pillow.

I lifted his blanket and slid next to his warm body. I laid with my back to him, not wanting to wake him, but just close enough I could feel he was there. His breathing changed and his arm came around me, pulling me closer.

"Stellina? You ok?" He asked.

"Nightmare," I replied.

He nodded and he curled his body around my back, pulling me into his embrace. His hand rested over my shirt on my stomach and his thumb lazily stroked me. I threaded my fingers through his and held tight.

"I'm sorry for pushing you away. I don't like to admit when I can't just do something on my own. And I don't want to become too complicated for you," I said.

Gideon's lips pressed against the top of my head.

"Brooklyn, stop with all the worrying. Sleep, you're safe. I'll keep the demons at bay," he said.

When I awoke again, the room was lightened only by a sliver of sunlight escaping the dark curtains over the windows. As promised, Gideon had kept the nightmares at bay, just by being there. His heavy arm still anchored me to him, so I just relaxed deeper into the embrace. His hand had slid under my shirt and his warm palm now laid on my bare stomach. I had no idea what time it was, but I knew Gideon liked to sleep in on the weekends and I didn't want to ruin that for him.

My eyes moved around the room. Compared to what I had seen in the rest of the house, Gideon's room was darker, with one accent wall that was distressed wood planks. His bed was also a large four-poster, except the frame was a dark hardwood and had a rail on the top that could hold a canopy.

I remembered that Jaxon hadn't pointed out an office for Gideon and now I saw why. The corner of his room was turned into a large work station, with multiple computer screens mounted on the wall. The desk was tidy, with only a few folders on top of it.

I wanted to turn over so I could look at the rest of the room, but Gideon's arm had tightened around me so I froze to ensure he was still sleeping.

"I know you're awake. The wheels in your head make noise," he grumbled.

"Sorry," I muttered.

His fingers flexed against my skin and he nuzzled closer to me.

"I could stay here all day, sound good?" He asked.

I laughed lightly. As hard as Gideon worked, the man loved to be in bed. I couldn't blame him, his bed was comfortable and his room was so dark you'd never be woken up by the sun. It was as if he had created a cave for himself, to hide in when things were too much.

I stretched and turned so I could face him. His hair was across his face, so I pushed it back, running my fingers through the long strands. He sighed as I scraped my nails lightly along his scalp.

"I really do love your hair," I said.

He bent slightly, to kiss my cheek, then near my ear, then my neck. We snuggled down into bed, Gideon on his back and me laying across his chest. I listened to his heartbeat and slowly my eyes closed. I wasn't one for naps, but laying with Gideon made it easy to just relax.

A knock at the door woke us both and Gideon called out for the knocker to come in. Oliver poked his head into the room and I could see relief flood his face.

"There you are. I got worried for a minute," he said.

"Think I ran away? Wearing nothing but a t-shirt and boxer briefs?" I asked.

"Something like that. I had a few things brought for you. I looked at your sizes at the apartment. It's all in the dresser and closet in your room," he replied with a grin.

My room. That was a weird way of saying the guest room I was staying in. But I let the thought float away, instead of stressing on it. Oliver leaned against the doorframe studying us. He smiled again before turning and closing the door.

"Am I going to have a lot of random clothes in the room?" I asked.

"Lucky for you, Oliver has pretty decent fashion sense. I'm sure he just got you the basics," Gideon said.

Gideon started to roll out of bed and I whined. He kissed my head and laughed.

"If I'm going to be awake, I need coffee. Come down to the kitchen when you're ready."

I watched as Gideon walked around the room. When he slipped on a pair of gray sweat pants, I thought I might need to wipe drool from my mouth. His wide shoulders and cut abs were on display as he left the room barefoot and shirtless. He left his hair down, a wave around the top of his shoulders. Just as he was about to be out of sight, he ran his hand through it and I sighed dreamily.

Back in my room, I stared at the almost full closet. Oliver said he had a few things brought. This was a larger wardrobe than what I had lost at home. The dresser had a drawer full of panties, all different colors, all different styles and a lot of lace. In the next drawer there were bras for every color of the panties and I realized Oliver got matching sets.

I found casual clothes in the bottom drawers and pulled out a v-neck t-shirt and a pair of shorts. I changed out of the borrowed clothes, but I put Gideon's shirt in the dresser with mine, I wanted to wear it later. In the bathroom I did my business and quickly ran my brush through my tangle of hair.

Tiptoeing, I made my way downstairs. I wasn't sure who else was awake and I didn't want to ruin my welcome on the first morning. However, when I got to the kitchen, I froze. All four Knights were in the room. Aiden was reading a newspaper, while Gideon did something at the stove. Oliver and Jaxon were both looking at their phones with mugs of coffee in front of them.

I fidgeted with my shirt, suddenly feeling very self-conscience.

"Uh, good morning," I said quietly.

Four sets of eyes snapped to me. I didn't miss the way Aiden took in my bare legs and how his gaze swept my entire body. His eyes rested on my face, as if he were studying me for any long last effects from the night before. He snapped the newspaper shut and stood up. He went to the coffee maker and turned to me.

"Good morning, Brooklyn. How do you take your coffee?" He asked.

"Black is fine," I replied with a smile.

He poured a mug and gestured for me to take a seat at the island. I slid onto a stool and blew on the hot coffee for a moment. I looked across and found Jaxon and Oliver looking at Aiden curiously, but no one said anything as he sat back on his own stool and watched me drink coffee.

Gideon turned away from the stove long enough to drop a kiss on the top of my head. Jaxon and Oliver both came to me, Jaxon squeezing me into his chest as he kissed my cheek and Oliver kissed my shoulder from behind. I closed my eyes for a moment and let the affection just sink into me. When they sat back down, I cleared my throat, trying to get the emotional feeling to pass.

"Oliver, you said there were a few things in the room. There are many more than a few. Let me know what I owe you and also, how did you get that all here that fast?" I asked.

Oliver turned his gaze to mine and he smiled.

"Being successful has its perks. One of those perks is connections in various places. I called the owner of a boutique I know of. I gave her your sizes and she sent everything over. It's my pleasure," he said.

I blanched, knowing the clothes were likely more than I could afford, but I wasn't sure I was comfortable with Oliver buying it all for me. The man watched me for a moment, picking up on my unease.

"If you want, payment could be you modeling a few things for me...in private," he said with a sexy grin.

The look on his face sent a shock directly to my core and I blushed into my cup of coffee. A plate was set in front of me with eggs, bacon and toast. I gaped at it for a moment and then turned to look at Gideon.

"You cook?" I asked.

"Sometimes," he said, shrugging.

I dug in and everything was cooked deliciously. I was impressed with Gideon's hidden talent and I decided I needed to find out what else he could cook. The thought that I could get used to this floated through my mind, but I pushed it away, reminding myself this was temporary.

"When will I speak with the police?" I asked.

"I spoke with them last night and again this morning. They will likely need a statement from you, but I've provided everything they need, including the video from the camera last night," Gideon said, all business.

"I didn't even think to look, was it Lyle on the camera?" I asked.

"It's not clear. Whoever it was, anticipated there being a camera. They were wearing a hoodie over their face. I've been running some applications to compare the person's height to Lyle's, but I'm not done yet."

I nodded and popped a piece of bacon into my mouth. I chewed thoughtfully, again wondering what Lyle's long game was. He clearly knew I was with the guys in a romantic way. So, was his goal to get me alone at some point? He wouldn't have taken that chance at the gala unless there was something more. I was so busy and always with someone. Even when I went to the bathroom, Aiden was standing guard in the hallway, without even knowing he was.

"What's going on in that head of yours?" Jaxon asked.

"I'm just stressed out, thinking about what Lyle's long plan is. I never knew him to be someone that liked to play with his prey. Seeing him last night was shocking, but that was his whole plan, to shock me. He didn't even try to get at me. Then the apartment. He would have known I wasn't there yet, so the whole goal was to ruin my home, but not get me yet."

The guys all exchanged looks, that told me they were all wondering the same thing. Gideon served food to everyone else and sat down next to me with his own. I looked around and realized it was like a family meal and it felt super natural to just be with them.

"I can't let him scare me from my life. I have to keep going," I said.

"Well, some adjustments should be made, to ensure your safety," Jaxon replied.

"I don't really need to go anywhere, but work. I'll use your treadmill for my runs, though it won't be as nice as running through the park. I think my runs could be a weak spot," I said.

"Can't you work remotely? We could get you a decent set up here," Jaxon asked.

"I could. But I don't want to hide. I need to go to the office tomorrow," I said.

"I don't think that's a smart idea," Aiden cut in.

I looked over at him, an eyebrow raised. This coming from the one man in the room I wasn't dating.

"I'm safe inside the building with my co-workers," I argued.

"Maybe. But there's the travel to and from the office. That parking level could be an easy place to snatch you or hurt you," Aiden said, not backing down.

"I'll take her," Gideon said.

Jaxon and Oliver both began to argue about the safety and likelihood that something would happen. I could tell they were reacting out of emotions, while Gideon knew security and he knew how to protect people. I held up a hand to stop the tirade.

"Gideon will take me. I'm going to work tomorrow."

Brooklyn

THE DAY WAS moments of sexually charged touches, looks and words. My mind was overwhelmed with feeling turned on, but the guys all played the respectful gentleman and didn't throw me over their shoulders and drag me to the nearest flat surface. By the evening, I was ready to do whatever necessary to get them to stop the games and fuck me. The break I forced for us had been wearing on me and I was a sexually frustrated mess.

Dinner was eaten together, again at the large island in the kitchen. This meal was cooked by a personal chef they employed. I tried to not let my mouth hang open when I realized they had a number of household employees. They didn't live at the house, but came and went on a set schedule.

I was pleasantly surprised with dinner. The food was of course delicious. However, the best part was the easy conversation between the guys and how they quickly included me in everything. Instead of feeling like an outsider visiting, they treated me like part of the household.

Even Aiden seemed to be relaxed and accepting of my presence. I had picked up things about each of the guys over the time we had spent together. But it was fun to see how those personalities worked together.

Jaxon was the calming presence who brought everyone around when they were debating. Oliver was a joker and he had everyone cracking up multiple times. Gideon was the strength, but was quiet in his way of speaking. His brothers gave him the chance to have his say, even when he wasn't forceful.

Aiden was harder to pin. He was clearly the alpha of the group. But he wasn't the asshole I had been assuming from the few interactions we had. The dance at the gala seemed to force us to turn a corner and he was more personable with me now. I couldn't help but stare during the moments he laughed. It was such a free sound and he was beautiful when he was just enjoying his time.

After dinner it was just me and my three guys lounging in front of the big screen. Aiden had excused himself, with work as his reason. I felt a certain disappointment, but I didn't want to think about what that meant.

We had closed the blinds, settled in, and debated movies. We finally agreed to a trilogy, figuring we had all evening after our fairly early dinner. By the looks the guys were sharing and the way their eyes were on me, I doubted we'd make it through all three movies.

As the first movie started, I was between Oliver and Jaxon on the couch. Gideon had stretched out on the other side. Oliver pulled my legs into his lap, causing me to lay across Jaxon. Both of them insisted they were comfortable so I snuggled in. It was difficult to focus on the movie with Oliver's hand on my thigh, making small circles until he was under my shorts and dangerously close to my center.

Jaxon had a hand under my breast and his thumb would swipe up and near my budding nipple, but never actually make contact. I had to fight my body, to not arch into his palm and force the contact I was desiring.

The game with the two guys went on, until the credits rolled on the first movie. I knew I was wet and if Oliver's fingers made contact with my panties, he would know too. But when the movie ended, he pulled away and stood to get drinks for everyone. I sat up and tried to breathe through the lust rolling through me.

Gideon called me to him and he pulled me down on his side of the couch, having me layout in front of him, with my ass nestled against his hips. Just like when we were sleeping, he slipped a hand under my shirt, so it was resting on my stomach. I snuggled into him and tried to focus on the movie.

During the second movie, Gideon's thumb brushed under my bra, touching my bare breast, but never going up further. I decided I was done with the games and ground my ass against him. His hand went to my hip, to grip me and try to keep me still, which only made me increase the torture. I would show them that two could play these games.

"Do you want me to fuck you, in front of my brothers?" Gideon whisper growled into my ear.

I just nodded my head. I could feel his thick hardness in his sweats and as I ground myself against him, his cock twitched. It made me want him inside me more than anything at the moment. I looked over at Jaxon and Oliver. Their eyes were on the screen, but I knew by the way they shifted and shot looks over at me, they knew what was happening on the couch.

Instead of giving me exactly what I wanted at the moment, Gideon slid his hand down the front of my shorts. His fingers grazed over my panties, barely touching my core. I gasped at the light touch and tried to move my hips to increase the pressure. He chuckled darkly, pulling his hand back, not giving me what I wanted.

His hand moved back to my stomach, wandering up to my bra covered breast. His circled my nipple before squeezing my breast in his large hand. I arched into the caress and he moved to the other. When he pinched my nipple through the fabric a small moan left my mouth.

I could see Jaxon shifting on his side of the couch, now watching me instead of the movie.

"Tell him to come touch you," Gideon said in my ear.

I held out my hand and Jaxon immediately came to me, sitting on his knees next to the couch, taking my hand and kissing the inside of my wrist. He dove for my mouth and I clutched at his hair as his tongue invaded me. With Gideon's hand on my breast, Jaxon's hand went under my shorts. Unlike Gideon, Jaxon didn't play around. His fingers moved my panties to the side and he slid through my wetness, causing me to moan loudly.

"You're soaked," Jaxon mumbled.

"Too much playing around today," I replied.

"Too much, Love? I think it was just the right amount," he said.

He slowly slid one finger into my core and Gideon pulled

one of my legs back over his, giving Jaxon better access to me. Suddenly, Oliver was between my legs, watching Jaxon's fingers on me. He leaned down and his tongue circled my clit, sucking it into his mouth. I cried out and I reached down to grip his hair. He moaned and the vibration went straight to my clit, pushing me right over the edge.

As I came, I could feel Gideon grinding against my ass, Jaxon slowed his fingers and Oliver just lapped at my clit softly. I looked over at Gideon and pulled his mouth to mine. When I pulled away I looked him in the eyes.

"It's not enough," I whined.

"Need something else in you, stellina?" He asked.

I nodded and Jaxon worked my shorts and panties off my hips. Gideon had me sit up slightly, so he could slip off my shirt and unclasp my bra. When my breasts fell free, Jaxon leaned over and captured a nipple in his mouth. Oliver moved up my body and ran his tongue around the other nipple.

Behind me, Gideon slipped his sweats down and I could feel the hard steel of his cock against my ass. He shifted me slightly, until his cock was sliding along my wetness. Overwhelmed with need, I rotated my hips, trying to push myself down on his length. He grabbed my hips to settle me and reached down to enter me from behind in one hard thrust.

"Oh god, Gideon!" I cried out.

While buried inside me, Gideon shifted, so he was under me and I was facing away from his face. Oliver and Jaxon both had their cocks out and were stroking themselves, only making me feel hotter. I wrapped my hand around Jaxon's cock and with a hand on his hip, and had him stand next to me. I circled his head with my tongue and he moaned, putting his hand in my hair.

Opening my mouth, I slid his cock as far as I could into my mouth, meeting my hand with my lips. I sucked him and slid my hand up and down with my mouth. Carefully, he began to thrust his hips and his cock moved in and out of my mouth at the pace he wanted. I loved the feeling of his length, thick veins and plush head against my tongue. When he pulled out, I leaned forward to suck just the head.

"If you don't stop I'm going to come," he moaned.

Gideon thrust into me from below and I ground down on his cock, so turned on and climbing to another orgasm. I dove back down on Jaxon's cock, wanting him to come in my mouth. I felt fingers against me and saw Oliver's hand stroking my clit. As I came a second time, I groaned on Jaxon's cock, causing him to swell and begin to spurt into my mouth.

My walls clamped down on Gideon and he groaned as he thrust up once more, filling me with his cum. He slipped from me and slid backward, until I was on my back on his chest. Oliver climbed between my legs, looking deep into my eyes.

"Can you handle it?" He asked.

"God, yes please," I moaned.

My wetness mixed with Gideon's cum made it slick and easy to Oliver to slam into me balls deep in one thrust. He lifted my hips off of Gideon, giving him the leverage to get deeper. He wasn't going to take his time. I saw the wild look in his eyes, a desire held back for too long. He began long hard strokes and I pushed my hips to meet his thrusts.

I felt Gideon's fingers sliding around in my wetness and then sliding toward my ass.

"Ok?" Gideon whispered into my ear.

I nodded, not sure what exactly I was agreeing to. But I wanted my men to own my body however they wanted to. My pleasure was starting to climb again and I suddenly felt pressure against my puckered hole.

"Relax, stellina," Gideon whispered.

I tried to do what he was asking, though I wasn't sure how.

Carefully, he rubbed my wetness along the entrance. Oliver slowed down, prolonging his own orgasm as Gideon started to work the tip of his finger into my back entrance. When he slipped through the tight entrance and worked out again, a shiver ran through my body.

"Good?" He asked.

"Yes, so good," I moaned.

Oliver took that as a signal and he started to fuck me roughly again. Gideon thrust his finger into my ass at a similar pace and when my orgasm crested over me, it was harder than anything I had ever experienced before. I threw my head back on Gideon's shoulder and he kissed and sucked the skin on my neck. Jaxon's hands were playing with my nipples, causing my pleasure to continue coursing through me.

As Oliver thrust into my tight channel, I saw the lust on his face. I watched him as he began to come into me and the pleasure was written across his features. It was amazing to watch and feel at the same time. He slowly lowered my hips so I was laying entirely on Gideon again, and slipped from my body.

"Oh my god, I missed you," I groaned.

That caused my men to laugh. Oliver leaned over and kissed me passionately. When he pulled back, he ran a finger down my cheek and looked in my eyes. There was some connection forged now, that I couldn't just turn off and push away. I could feel it with each of them.

Gideon shifted, pulling his sweats up under me. He then stood and lifted me into his arms.

"Grab her clothes. Let's get her cleaned up," he said.

In my room, Gideon took me into the bathroom and turned on the shower. He cradled my body against him while he waited for the spray to warm. He carefully stood me up under the water, holding me for a moment to make sure my legs didn't give out. Then he kicked off his own sweats and climbed in with me.

The shower was large enough for five people, though Gideon took up a good amount of space on his own. He started to lather my hair and massage my scalp. I leaned into his chest and just closed my eyes, letting everything that just happened flow over me.

As my hair rinsed, Gideon began to wash my body. When his hand swept between my legs, though he was trying to be methodical with cleaning, I felt my core tighten and I wanted more. He noticed my body shift and I could see him smiling behind the veil of his wet hair. The man knew exactly what he was doing to me under the guise of taking care of cleaning me up.

After he finished his process, he stepped out of the shower to wrap a towel around his hips. I couldn't help myself from drooling over the perfect v that showed above the towel. It made me want to lick the water drops from the area, one by one. Gideon just raised an eyebrow at me and smiled as he held out a fluffy towel for me.

I stepped out of the shower and he rubbed the soft material down my body. He kneeled down to dry my legs down to my feet and then back up to softly dry my stomach, my sides and my breasts. He handed me a second towel, so I could wrap my hair up to keep the water from dripping all over my dried body.

On the counter, were products all lined up. I realized they were all the things I used at home. I picked up my lotion which had a light lavender scent and looked over at Gideon.

"Oliver, of course. He's pretty good at thinking of every-thing," Gideon said.

I smiled and rubbed a bit of lotion over my arms and then each of my legs. Gideon just stood and watched the process. I followed him into the bedroom, where both Oliver and Jaxon were waiting. Gideon pulled me into his arms and hugged me tight.

"I'll leave you with these two. We need to think about a bigger bed in the house," he said with a chuckle.

I nodded into his chest and he pulled my face up to his so he could kiss me goodnight. He rubbed his nose against mine before smiling. He turned me and had me climb up into the bed. Oliver and Jaxon slid under the blankets with me, both of them wearing nothing but their boxers. I was blissfully naked as I stretched and curled up against Oliver's chest. Jaxon spooned me from behind, his hand snaking between mine and Oliver's bodies to palm one of my breasts.

Gideon went to the door and flicked of the light. It was way later than I would ever normally stay up on a work night. But relaxation washed over me and a yawn escaped me. Oliver squeezed me, encouraging me to sleep. I looked over at Gideon and flashed him a smile.

"Goodnight, stellina. Any nightmares, you know where to find me."

CHAPTER
Thirty-Two

Gideon

MY BED WAS cold compared to how hot I was on the couch and in the shower. Leaving Brooklyn with my brothers didn't make me jealous, we all had a place with her. I just always wanted to be with her. I shifted in my bed, trying to find a comfortable position, only being made harder by being able to smell her on the pillow next to me.

I badly wanted to ask her what she was feeling. The way she gave herself over to us, felt deeper than anything had been between us before. She didn't act intimidated or overwhelmed and the smile on her face after was clearly bliss. But she pushed us away before and I had a hard time not worrying about it happening again.

Thinking about her, riding me backward, made my cock harden again and I sighed, trying to will it to control the urges. I closed my eyes and tried to focus on anything else that would make sleep come. Protecting Brooklyn until Lyle was caught, was going to take all of my attention, so I couldn't be sleep deprived.

Halfway through the night, I felt a warm body settling next to me. Lavender flowed over me and soft curves molded to my side. I put my arm out and Brooklyn laid on my shoulder, sighing.

"Nightmare?" I asked.

She just nodded her head.

"I didn't want to wake both Oliver and Jaxon with my tossing and turning. We had just gotten to sleep. I think I tired them out. I just, feel safe when I'm with you," she said quietly.

"It's ok. They'll understand," I replied.

She nodded again and nestled into me. Her leg went across mine and her knee went up a little high, where she found a surprise.

"Well, you were having a good dream," she said with a quiet giggle.

"I am a man. These things tend to happen," I replied.

"I can help," she whispered.

Her hand ran down my chest to my stomach. She found the waist of my briefs and pulled them down, until I could help by kicked them off. Then, she straddled me, her long hair falling around her shoulders and over her breasts. She leaned down and pressed soft kisses to my lips. I threaded my fingers through her hair and pulled her down to kiss her hard, our tongues tangling.

Reaching between us, I found her already wet and ready. She lifted up so my cock could be positioned at her entrance. Using my hand as balance, she slowly lowered herself on my length, a moan escaping her lips once she was fully seated. She was burning hot and tight on me. I had to breathe deeply to not lose control and flip her over.

She thrust her hips, rubbing herself in all the right places. Leaning down she propped herself up on her hands and began to ride me faster. I captured one of her nipples in my mouth and she cried out as I sucked hard on the nub. My hand found her other breast and I pulled her nipple slightly, causing her to jump.

"Oh god Gideon, I'm going to come. I'm so close," she groaned.

"Come for me, stellina," I growled, biting down on her nipple.

She threw her body back, taking my whole cock into her as she came, squeezing like a vice on me. Her hips continued to buck and rotate as she road out her orgasm. When her eyes opened, she looked down at me with a little smile. I was gritting my teeth, making sure I didn't come too soon, but I couldn't hold back any longer.

I flipped us in one motion, without losing connection. Propping her legs on my arms, I began to swing my hips slowly. She gripped my forearms, her nails digging in slightly. At that moment, I couldn't have cared if she drew blood.

"Gideon, stop holding back. Fuck me," she begged.

That was all I needed to hear. I pulled out of her, until just the tip of my cock was nestled in her entrance, before slamming home. Sitting back on my heels, I grabbed her ankles and held her legs against my chest as I continued to slam into her.

She screamed my name again as she began to come again. This time, I couldn't hold back and I groaned as my own orgasm hit me in a rush.

My cock spurted deep inside Brooklyn, my orgasm being practically squeezed from me as she ground against me through her own orgasm. I panted and slowly slipped from her, collapsing next her. I grabbed tissues from my nightstand and softly cleaned my fluids from between Brooklyn's legs.

She grabbed my hand and stopped me.

"You're just going to turn me on again. Let me handle it," she laughed, breathlessly.

Carefully, she got out of bed and went into my ensuite. When she came back she cuddled up next to me and let out a loud yawn.

"Every night cannot be like this. I'll never survive," she said.

"I mean, you would, that's what naps are for," I replied.

"We can't all be self employed and make our own schedules," she said, poking me in the ribs.

"We'll work on that. First big bed. Second nap times for Brooklyn," I said.

She just giggled and laid her head on my shoulder. Her breathing changed and I knew when she fell asleep. I laid staring at the ceiling, just listening to her and smelling her. I knew it was creepy as all hell, but I hadn't felt this with someone in a really long time. I tried to pull memories into focus, but even then I couldn't compare Brooklyn to any of it. This felt like a different league completely.

In the morning, my alarm woke us both. Brooklyn stretched, gloriously naked next to me. I eyed her and went to pull her into me, but she scrambled from the bed.

"Not gonna happen big guy. I gotta get ready for work," she laughed.

She picked up a shirt from the floor, what she must have worn to my room last night. I smiled when I realized it was the t-shirt I had lent her. She blew me a kiss and left quietly. I stared at the closed door longer than I'd care to admit, before getting up and going through my own morning routine.

Typically, I don't rush off to an office or anything in the morning. I would usually go downstairs and workout, take a shower, and then maybe head into the club to go over numbers and personnel details. Or, I'd never leave the house and just work from my station in my room.

Today was different. I was playing personal security for Brooklyn, a role I was going to take very seriously. I knew she wouldn't want me hovering in her office, but I would be walking her to and from the door, to ensure there was no one and nothing waiting for her when she got there. We couldn't take chances, now that Lyle had gone as far as breaking into her apartment.

That thought had me pausing as I was pulling my damp hair into a bun. The video surveillance from Brooklyn's front door was puzzling. Granted, I hadn't scoured every inch of footage to see if someone had been casing the apartment. But it seemed like the person definitely knew there would be a camera outside.

Then there was the stature of the person. I couldn't be sure if that was a man in the hoodie and it got my wheels moving thinking about if Lyle had an accomplice. If he did, then there was someone else out there that we wouldn't know to look for.

Lyle could have easily made it to the apartment between the time Brooklyn saw him at the gala and when she got home. However, the extent of the damage, felt like it took time to complete. That pointed more toward Lyle having at least one partner.

I dressed in dark dress pants and a button up shirt, professional, yet not restricting if I had to be physical with anyone. I also didn't want to embarrass Brooklyn in her place of work. Explaining our relationship would likely not be something she wanted to do. So I would play the friend, and behave professionally.

In the kitchen, I walked in on the most domestic scene this house had ever seen. Brooklyn was there, dressed in the new clothes Oliver had ordered for her. He had her style right. Her pencil skirt was a slate with thin pinstripes. It hugged her curves in the perfect ways and when I glanced around at my brothers, I knew they had noticed as well. She was also wearing a high collared shirt, something she always did when working. She was barefoot, her pink polished toenails, catching my attention.

She moved around the kitchen, comfortable in her surroundings. When she saw me, a smile appeared and she turned toward the coffee pot. She stood on her toes to reach where the mugs were stored and Jaxon almost fell off his stool, trying to lean and see her legs. I smothered a chuckle, so as to not give away that I saw him.

Brooklyn put a mug of coffee by an empty stool and motioned for me to sit. She then sat the cream next to Aiden, who was trying to read the paper.

"You don't need to wait on anyone," he said in a growly voice.

Brooklyn stopped her movements and turned around to look at him.

"Aiden, not a morning person. Got it," she said.

Oliver choked on his coffee as Aiden flicked down the edge of the newspaper and glared at Brooklyn. She gave him a sickly sweet smile and sat on a stool next to his.

"Why are you reading a physical newspaper, anyway? Wouldn't it be easier to read it digitally?" She asked.

"There's nothing like holding a newspaper in your hands. I like the tradition of it," he replied, shrugging his shoulders.

The truth was, Aiden had gotten a paper everyday for as long as I had known him. When we were kids, he used to read the classified ads and the obituaries. It took a few years, but I eventually figured out he was looking for his real father. He wanted to believe the man knew he existed and would look for him and in Aiden's young mind, the newspaper is where you went to find things.

Of course, none of that would come out of Aiden's mouth, not to Brooklyn. She was still an outsider for Aiden. And the story wasn't for any of us to tell. Now, I knew Aiden was just in the habit of having the paper in the morning, while he drank coffee and ate breakfast. While the rest of us wouldn't press him on the subject, Brooklyn had no such limits.

"Just seems outdated. Most of what is in the newspaper has been online for 24 hours already," she said.

I saw Aiden stiffen. Though, I could suggest to Brooklyn it was time to go to the office, I was curious to see how far he'd let her go before shutting down her questions. When he didn't reply, Brooklyn looked at his profile for a beat, before turning to her own coffee. As she sipped, she sighed and a smile appeared on her face. The look was closely similar to the one she had after I made her come twice in my bed. I couldn't help but grin at the thought.

After coffee and a small bagel breakfast, we all broke from the kitchen to go our separate ways. Jaxon pulled Brooklyn into an embrace and told her to be careful while not at home. She nodded, but didn't say anything. Oliver was next, kissing her hard on the mouth, then making some comment that if she kept herself safe he'd do the thing with his tongue she liked so much again. That had her laughing and blushing.

I had called a town car for the day, not wanting to wind

blow Brooklyn on the bike when she had to be in the office. In the back of the car, she went through her briefcase quickly, ensuring everything she needed was there. I watched her methodically go through her purse as well, before setting them both on the floor at her feet.

Her hand came down on mine on the seat and she intertwined our fingers. I looked down and her and she smiled and rested her head against my shoulder.

"I thought we'd get to ride the bike today, I was kinda excited," she said.

"I didn't wanna muss you up before work. Plus, I'd have to take you to an alley or something, because having you wrapped around me like that just makes me wanna sink into you," I replied.

Her hand squeezed and I didn't miss the way her thighs shifted under her pencil skirt. My girl liked the idea. I filed that away for another time, when I wasn't supposed to be acting as her private security. Getting caught with my pants down, wasn't the way I wanted to be attacked, because I knew if my cock was buried inside Brooklyn, my mind wouldn't be on anything else.

Brooklyn

GIDEON INSISTED I wait in the town car as he went up to my office alone, to ensure there were no surprises waiting. He was back within ten minutes, his hand offered to help me out of the back of the car. He reached in and pulled out my purse and briefcase and held them both out to me.

"Everything is clear upstairs. The receptionist isn't in yet, so I don't think anyone saw me checking the office. I'm going to be down here, so I don't cause a scene for you. But if you see anything or even feel something off, you call me," he said.

"Thanks big guy. I'm sure it'll be ok. Security is pretty decent at this building," I said.

He didn't respond, instead crashed his mouth to mine. His arm banded around my lower back, pressing me forward. I almost dropped my things, but he pulled back and left me breathless. A small smile formed on his face and he winked at me. When I turned to go, he swatted my ass and I gasped. When I looked back, he was already climbing back into the car.

In the elevator, I had to think about calming myself down. What was with these guys and not being able to keep their hands to themselves. I wanted to blame them, but it was really me. I couldn't control my libido when they were in the vicinity. Thinking about the sex fest last night, I could feel a blush rushing up my neck. I had more sex in less than 24 hours than I could remember having in years. And I wasn't going to complain.

On my floor, I stepped out just as the receptionist was getting settled. She smiled and greeted me and I waved as I went beyond her desk to the hall that held my office. Even though Gideon had checked the room, I entered the office hesitantly. A flash of the murdered rat entered my mind as I looked around.

Nothing was amiss. Part of me wondered if Lyle had found a way to get to my office as well. I guessed it was too much of a risk coming to such a public place. With that in mind, I set up my laptop and put away my purse. My calendar was full of follow up from the gala, as well as a debrief meeting with the president about the fundraiser results.

The meeting was up beat, as we recounted the highest fundraising results ever. The president was pleased with the success. No one mentioned the fifty thousand dollars that were a large part of why we were so far over our previous record. And no one brought up how strange it was for Aiden Knight to bid that amount on a dance, after donating the location, food, drink and staff.

When we were walking out of the meeting, I let out a sigh of relief, glad I wasn't going to have to answer any questions about my connection to Aiden. What was I going to say? I'm in a relationship with his three brothers, yes all of them, yes at once. I didn't want to imagine how that conversation would go.

As I walked toward my office, my assistant came from her desk to stop me.

"Hi, Brooklyn!"

"Hi, Pam. What's up?"

"I was thinking, it's been awhile since we've gone out to lunch. There's this new little cafe a few blocks down I wanted to try out. You up for a lunch date?" She asked.

Her smile was so huge, I couldn't exactly say no. Pam and I were the closest to a work friendship as I had. She was very efficient with handling my calendar and was one of the best gatekeepers I'd ever met. It was true, we hadn't gone to lunch together in awhile. Her exuberance for lunch, made me feel a little guilty for not nurturing the relationship.

"Sure, Pam, that sounds like a great idea. Just let me grab my stuff," I replied.

She did a little clap and went back to her desk. Pam had never been so excited for lunch before and I started to think she wanted to ask me about the gala dance. I started to think of excuses I could give to why Aiden would bid such a large amount of money on me.

In my office, I realized I had to let Gideon know I was leaving the office. I picked up my cell and pulled up his contact. He answered on the first ring.

"Brooklyn?"

His deep voice came through the line, causing a shiver to run through my body.

"It's all good, big man," I said.

I heard a deep breathe on the other end of the phone and I knew Gideon was wound tight, even just sitting in the parking garage of the building.

"So listen, my assistant wants to have lunch. Do you think that would be ok?" I asked.

Silence was all that came across.

"Gideon? Did I lose you?" I said, pulling my cellphone from my ear to look at my service.

"You can't just order in, stellina?" He asked.

"I can't just stay inside for the rest of my life, Gideon. What are you going to do, shuttle me from your place to the office everyday? No where else, until Lyle is found?" I asked.

"If I asked for that, would you do it?" He asked.

"It's not about would, Gideon. It's about if I could handle it. And I can't. I absolutely will not lose everything I've worked so hard for. And my sanity is one of those things," I replied.

Another deep breath, though this one wasn't him relieved that I was safe. This breath was definitely exasperation.

"So, now that we have that straight. I know you aren't going to let me go alone. Can you follow, like without follow-ing? I'm not really sure how to explain you yet. I already know there's questions about the dance at the gala," I said.

"You're embarrassed," he said in a tight voice.

"God, no, Gideon! Never. I have just barely started to come to terms with our relationship. I'm not ready for that to be under a microscope with other people," I replied.

"Ok," he said, though his voice hadn't changed.

"Thank you. We'll come out the front doors in about five

minutes. The cafe she wants to go to isn't far from here," I said, my voice soft.

"Ok," he said before clicking off the call.

"Ugh!" I exclaimed and looked up at the ceiling, as if I was looking for answers.

It made me sad that Gideon didn't understand how I was feeling. Though, when I thought about it, feelings hadn't really come up in the short time we'd all been seeing each other. Being swept off my feet by anyone seemed ridiculous. But I was already deep in with my men. It hadn't occurred to me any of them would be insecure about that.

Picking up my purse, I came out of my office just as my assistant was about to knock.

"Ready to go?" She asked.

"Lead the way!" I replied, adding extra excitement to my voice.

We took the elevator to the lobby floor. As we walked out, I waved at the nice security man that sat at the desk. I rarely saw him, since I passed a different guard coming from the parking garage. When he saw me, he stood and tipped an imaginary hat, making me laugh just as we walked out the door.

Pam turned left out of the lobby doors and I looked toward the way I figured Gideon would come up from the garage. There he was, in all his dark, brooding glory. His hair was slicked back in his bun and he wore dark sunglasses to shield his eyes from the sun. I sent him a smile, that he didn't return before I followed Pam.

As I turned I had to walk fast to catch up with Pam, and she realized I had fallen behind.

"Sorry! I'm always in such a hurry. We should be walking slow and enjoying this beautiful weather," she said with a laugh.

"It is gorgeous out," I agreed.

"So, we haven't caught up in so long. You're such a busy lady," she said, nudging me softly with her shoulder.

"I know. I'm so sorry. I feel like everything has gotten away from me with the gala happening," I said.

"I'm just glad it wasn't me!"

"Oh, of course not, Pam. You're wonderful. How do you think I even made it through all of this?" I said with a laugh.

We walked in silence for a few blocks, until Pam pulled up a door of a hole in the wall cafe. The outside wasn't much to look at, though they had a few wrought iron tables under umbrellas. Inside, the restaurant was adorably decorated to look like it had vines and had twinkle lights strung up around the room.

I was about to suggest and outdoor table, but Pam asked the hostess for something inside. I looked out the window and saw Gideon walk by the cafe and look in the window. He waited a beat before coming into the cafe as well, but from my table I heard him ask the hostess for a table outside.

Pam and I ordered iced teas while we looked over the menu. They didn't have a huge selection, being a small boutique cafe. Each of us ordered different salads and gave the waitress our menus. Pam took a sip of her drink and I looked up to find her studying me.

"What?" I laughed.

"You know what I'm going to ask, right?" She asked with a smile.

"The dance at the gala?" I sighed.

Pam nodded her head. "I mean, fifty thousand dollars! It was ten times what anyone else bid during the auction. How do you know Aiden Knight?"

"We're, friends, I suppose," I answered lamely.

I felt like I was caught between a rock and hard place. If I said I was dating his brother, Pam would want to know which one. Then I'd have to decide if I would have a public relationship with just one Knight. How could I do that without hurting the other two? And how would Aiden feel about 4K being associated with a poly relationship like ours.

Thankfully, Pam didn't ask to elaborate. Her eyes shifted around the cafe, as if she was looking for something. I turned to glance over my shoulder, not seeing anything or anyone we knew. I could see Gideon through the front window and he was blatantly staring at me. I felt a slight blush and I turned to drink my tea, hoping the cool drink would keep me from flaming like a tomato.

Pam accepted the friendship about Aiden, but she dropped a few comments about how sweet our dance was. I didn't go into detail about how I felt at that moment, on the dance floor, in Aiden's arms, surrounded by his expensive cologne and having his hand on my bare skin. I had tried to not put much thought into the feelings that arose that night from that dance. Not only the physical feelings, but how I felt about Aiden coming to my rescue.

I was saved from more conversation when our salads were served. The food was delicious and we ate in peaceful silence for a while. I couldn't help but wonder why Pam kept looking around us, but I chalked it up to her just investigating the new cafe. When I glanced over my shoulder again, I saw that Gideon was sipping from an espresso cup, which looked tiny in his large hand. I couldn't ignore the fact that my big man had style.

After paying our check, I excused myself to the bathroom. I could feel Gideon's gaze on me as I walked to the back of the cafe. I slipped into the women's bathroom, which held three stalls. I went to the last stall and shut myself in. As I sat on the toilet, I heard the door open and someone go into the first stall in the row. After flushing and leaving my stall, I went to wash my hands.

The sound of the other stall door opening, without a flushing sound, had me looking up. I froze with my hands under the water as I looked into the mirror and saw the face of the person leaving the stall. For a moment, I mentally shook myself, to snap out of it, but instead I started to shake. Lyle walked forward, until he was standing behind me and looking me in the eye in the mirror.

His limp brown hair was grimy and slicked down, with the cowlick he always had in the back sticking up. He hadn't shaved in quite a while, however the hair on his face didn't grow evenly. His clothes were rumpled and dirty. The entire look made him look like a homeless man you'd walk by in an alley. But the steel in his eyes was the same as I knew from the past.

"Well, well, Bee. It's good to see you, again."

His voice seemed to break something in me and I darted toward the bathroom door. His hand snapped out and grabbed my hair, yanking it from the bun it was in, and pulling me back to him. His other hand came around my waist, holding me to his body as I tried to think of a way out of the hold.

"You've become quite the whore, B. I thought I taught you better than that," he whispered in my ear.

I shuttered as I felt the heat of his breath across my cheek. He ran his nose along my neck, taking in a deep breath.

"Three men? You couldn't satisfy one, let alone three. I can't imagine the game you're playing," he said.

His hand tightened in my hair painfully, making me cry out. He turned me toward him, keeping one arm tight around my waist so I couldn't just take off. His mouth was on mine before I realized what his plans were. When he tried to force his tongue into my mouth, I did the only thing I could think of and bit down hard, tasting the tangy flavor of blood against my own tongue.

Lyle yelped and pulled back. His eyes were full of fury and he stepped back and backhanded me, causing me to trip on my heels. As I went down, I tried to use my hands to break my fall, but my head smashed into the counter before I fell. Blackness started to invade my vision, but I tried to fight it. I couldn't be unconscious near Lyle, there was no limit to the things he would do to me. And his face wouldn't be the last thing I saw before I died.

I tried to crawl away, but heat began to flow down my face and blood ran into my eye. I tried to swipe it away, but Lyle was on me, dragging me to my feet. My vision lurched and my stomach somersaulted. He pulled me to his face again and sneered.

"Don't do that shit again," he growled.

Just as he tried to kiss me again, the bathroom door opened. A woman took in the scene in front of her and she paled at the blood on me and the floor. With the door open, I took a chance and screamed at the top of my lungs. The sound caused pressure in my head that made me want to faint, but all I could think of was Gideon, my beast of a man. He would come.

Gideon

I WATCHED Brooklyn as she made her way to the back of the little restaurant. She smiled at me as she went, but I kept my face straight. I didn't know why, but I was really bothered by her not wanting to be seen with me. Did she feel the same way about my brothers or was it just me? I usually didn't suffer from insecurities, but this woman got to me.

Her assistant stayed at the table, but she had the same squirrelly behavior I had noted from the beginning of lunch.

The woman seemed to be waiting for something or looking for someone. And I didn't like the feeling it was giving me. I knew from the background I had done on Brooklyn, her assistant had been with her a long while. So she wasn't someone I'd normally suspect. However, her behavior was saying something else.

I looked back to the bathroom and wondered how long it could really take a woman to pee and powder her nose, or whatever else they did in the bathroom. Another woman went toward the bathroom and I tapped my foot waiting for Brooklyn to appear. I looked back at her assistant but the woman was looking at her phone.

Suddenly a muffled scream came through the restaurant. The assistant's face instantly snapped up and looked in the direction of the bathroom. That was all the confirmation that I needed that Brooklyn was in trouble. I jumped from my seat, knocking the little metal chair across the patio in my rush to get inside.

My legs ate up the distance between the door and the bathroom, cutting off the assistant who now was making her way toward the bathroom too. The woman that had walked into the bathroom came running out screaming herself now.

"He's killing her!"

My blood went cold. A scared waitress went running by and the restaurant started to break into chaos. I slammed into the bathroom door, knocking if off a hinge. There was Brooklyn, her hair in disarray, blood flowing down her face and a man standing with his back to me. He slowly turned to me and his gaze was evil and he took me in and turned to slam something into Brooklyn's gut.

I didn't take stock of what was happening, before ripping Lyle away from Brooklyn and slamming my fist into his weasel face. I felt a tooth rip in my knuckles as I hit him again.

He threw a punch into my ribs, but I didn't feel anything. Trying to avoid my fist, he grasped me around the waist, but he was too small to control my body. I lifted him and threw him against the open doorjamb.

As I walked toward him, I heard Brooklyn's assistant come in and she screamed, shaking me from the red fury I was seeing. Looking back over my shoulder, I saw Brooklyn standing, clearly in shock, as she pulled a knife from her stomach. Blood immediately began to stain her shirt.

"No!" I exclaimed.

I rushed to her, just as she started to fall. Catching her, I lowered us both to the ground. I ripped off my shirt and pressed it to her stomach. She looked up at me, her face covered in blood and getting paler by the moment.

"Call 9-1-1!" I roared.

Brooklyn flinched in my arms and I cradled her with one arm, while keeping pressure on the stab wound.

"I'm sorry, stellina. I'm sorry. I should have been right with you," I stammered.

"I knew you'd come," she whispered.

"Of course, of course I did. As soon as I heard you," I replied.

One of her hands came up, to tug lightly on my beard.

"Love this. And your hair. Don't cut it, k?" She muttered, her eyes fluttering.

"No, Brooklyn, you stay awake. You hear me!" I yelled.

Her eyes came open again, but there was so much pain on her face, I felt bad for yelling.

"I'm sorry, I know it all hurts, stellina. But I need you to stay awake. Until the paramedics get here, ok?" I said.

She tried to nod, but she froze and grimaced. I tried to look at her head but couldn't make out the wound with all the blood and hair matted in it. I hoped it wasn't as bad as it seemed. I had experienced plenty of head wounds and knew even the minor ones bled like crazy.

Looking around the damage to the bathroom, I saw blood on the bathroom sink and tried to piece together the events. I wanted something to tell the paramedics. And the cops. Suddenly, thinking about the police, I swung my gaze over to where I had left Lyle. The little shit was gone, in the wind again, running and hiding from us. I immediately knew I should have just killed him on the spot. I chastised myself for not just wearing a jacket so I could carry my sidearm.

The room was suddenly full of people as men in white uniforms rushed in and tried to take Brooklyn from me. I growled at them and they stepped back for a moment. It took me a long moment to accept they were with the paramedics and not someone working with Lyle coming after my girl.

At the instruction of the lead paramedic, I lifted her from the floor and carefully placed her in the gurney. They immediately started pushing her shirt up and packing gauze against her knife wound. I was covered in blood and there was a small puddle on the floor, making me panic about how much she had lost.

I followed the paramedics out and her assistant rushed to my side.

"Who are you?" She demanded.

"Her friend," I said absently. Then I rounded on her. "Why did you suggest this cafe? Who else did you tell you were coming here?"

"I, uh, I thought that I was doing something nice," she stuttered, avoiding my eyes.

"Wha the fuck does that mean?" I demanded.

My harsh tone made her flinch and continue to look away.

"Her old friend called. She said they lost touch in college. She wanted to surprise her," the assistant said.

"She?" I asked.

"Yes. It was a woman," she replied.

She finally dared to gaze up at me, just as the paramedics were putting Brooklyn into the ambulance. I followed and turned back to the assistant.

"I need the contact information for this old friend. Send it to 4K. Put Gideon in the subject line, it'll get to me. Wait for the police, tell them to come to the hospital to speak with me. I know who did this."

Turning back to the ambulance, I started to climb in. One paramedic, who clearly didn't value his life, put his hand up to stop me.

"Are you family?"

"I'm all she has. And if you think you're going to stop me, you have a death wish," I growled.

The paramedic had the smarts to blanch and move his arm, allowing me a spot next to Brooklyn's head. During the trip to the ambulance, Brooklyn had passed out. The paramedics didn't seem concerned, as they continued to work on stemming the blood flow from her stomach.

"Is she going to be ok?" I asked to no one in particular.

"She's lost a lot of blood. We don't know if there's any internal injuries. We'll do what we can while we get her to the hospital," a paramedic answered.

I took Brooklyn's limp hand in mine. I rubbed my fingers over her skin, trying to get rid of all the blood on her. But I did nothing but smear it around more. I leaned down and pressed a light kiss to an area of her forehead that wasn't covered in blood.

I moved to her ear, hoping she could hear me even in the darkness she must be in.

"Stellina, you need to be ok. You can't do this to us. Not when we've just found you. Please. You can do this."

I felt her fingers flex against mine and I squeezed her hand softly to reassure her I was right there with her. The wail of the sirens were comforting as we sped through traffic that parted for the ambulance. When we screeched to a stop, the back doors were thrown open by the paramedics and doctors rushed out.

"What'da we got?" A doctor asked.

"Stabbing, stomach wound is all we see that's from a knife. She also has a gash on her head," a paramedic rattled off.

I climbed out of the vehicle, still holding Brooklyn's hand, as they rushed her inside. The paramedic rattled off stats to the doctor and they switched her to another bed in the trauma room. Nurses and doctors flooded the area.

"Sir, you need to let her go and move back, so we can take care of her," one nurse said.

I glared down, but the woman looked at me with such sincere compassion that I swallowed the nasty reply that was bubbling out. I allowed the woman to guide me back, to where I could still see Brooklyn, but I was out of the way.

When she didn't move away I looked at her again and saw she was studying me. I suddenly remembered I was shirtless and covered in blood. Looking down at myself, I looked like I walked out of a slasher movie.

"Is any of this yours?" She asked.

I shook my head. I was aware of the ache on my knuckles from beating on Lyle, but it wasn't something that needed attention. They all needed to focus on Brooklyn. Abruptly an alarm started to sound in Brooklyn's room and the movements of the doctors became more erratic.

They called for blood from a blood bank. Scans and tests were talked about that I couldn't decipher. When they started pumping on Brooklyn's chest, my knees almost buckled. The small nurse in front of me, put her shoulder under my armpit, as if I wasn't twice her size. She led me to a chair that was outside the room and made me sit down.

"Is there anyone I can call for you?" She asked kindly.

I shook my head, fishing my cellphone from my pocket. This was a call I had to make myself. I was afraid to tell my brothers that I had let Brooklyn get hurt so badly. However, if she wasn't going to make it, I couldn't let them miss the chance to say goodbye.

The thought had me squeezing my phone until a crack sounded. Looking at it, I realized it must have gotten cracked during the fighting somehow and now the screen was cracked all the way across. Luckily it was still working and I called Jaxon.

Ten minutes later, all three of my brothers were running through the hospital, sliding to a stop in front of me, just as they wheeled Brooklyn's bed out of the trauma bay. I stood, ready to follow, but the same nice nurse stopped me. She looked up at me and then looked at my brothers and she nodded before speaking.

"They're taking her to surgery. She has internal injuries that need to be fixed, as she's bleeding into her abdomen. That's the first problem that needs to be addressed. Her head wound is an unknown right now. But that will be looked at after the bleeding is controlled," the nurse explained.

I was trying to understand what the woman was telling me, but Brooklyn was out of sight and I felt fear clawing at my throat. I wanted to barrel down everyone in my path to keep her in sight. The last time I let her out of my sight, she ended up like this. It was my fault.

The nurse seemed to see my thoughts, as she held up her hands, just in front of me, but not touching me.

"She is safe here. The doctors are the best at what they do.

Let them do the work. I will find you the moment you can be with her," she said softly.

I nodded but didn't sit back down. My head hung. The nurse walked away and suddenly Aiden was standing in front of me.

"Gideon, what the fuck happened?"

I studied him for a moment. He looked wrecked. His normally perfectly done hair was mussed as if he had been running his hands through it. He was dressed more casually than normal, clearly coming straight from home. He was even wearing flip flops, which he usually reserved for the pool.

I turned to see Oliver looking pale and stoic. Jaxon was pacing in front of him, his stature tense. I slumped down in my chair again, knowing I was going to have to go over everything with them and then again with the police.

The story burned my throat as I told it. I didn't leave out any details, being clear that she wasn't far from me the entire day. And then telling them everything that happened in the cafe bathroom. When I got to the part of her pulling the knife from her stomach, Oliver gasped and covered his face. Jaxon froze his steps and stared at me. Aiden's hands gripped his hair, showing how it had become so disastrous in the first place.

"Lyle has a partner. And she's a female," I finally said.

"How do you know that?" Aiden asked.

"The assistant, the one that suggested the cafe. She told me before we left in the ambulance, a woman called, claimed to be a friend from Brooklyn's past. Said she wanted to surprise her. I knew the assistant was acting strange, but she's not been on my radar. I don't think she knew what was really happening. She thought she was surprising Brooklyn with an old friend," I explained.

"She was positive it was a woman?" Aiden asked.

I nodded. "I told her to send the contact information for the woman to the general 4K email. Hopefully, by the time the police get here, the information will be in the inbox."

The nice nurse came back with a wet towel and a scrub uniform top.

"I'm guessing you won't go home to clean up. There's a bathroom down the hall and this was the largest scrub top I could find. If it fits, you're welcome to it."

I nodded, taking the items. Hesitating I looked at my brothers and the panic that was on all of their faces. Failing Brooklyn also meant I failed them. I was supposed to protect the person that was becoming so important to three of us. I sighed and started to walk away, but Jaxon called out to me.

"This isn't your fault, Gideon. You couldn't have known this would happen."

I hunched my shoulders, not acknowledging his words as I went to the bathroom. Inside I looked at myself in the mirror. I could see why the nurse wanted me to clean up. I looked like a horror show. Brooklyn's blood was streaked across most of the front of me. I scrubbed at myself with the towel, being rough with my skin until it was clean and pink with my own blood rising to the surface.

The top barely covered me, ending right at my pants, looking fairly ridiculous. It wasn't the biggest concern on my mind, so I went back to find my brothers. A doctor stood with them and I could hear Aiden firing questions. By the time I joined, the doctor had smiled and excused himself.

"It's her spleen. It's bleeding into her abdomen. They're trying to fix it. If it's not fixable they might have to remove a piece of it," Jaxon explained to me.

"Did the doctor think she was going to make it?" I asked.

"He seemed positive. Said the fact that you kept pressure on it the moment the knife came out are a big difference. And the ambulance was fast. The prognosis should be good. The big question is if she has to live without a spleen," Aiden said.

He started clicking around on his phone and I glanced over his shoulder, seeing him searching for the ways to live without a spleen. It seemed our brother, who tried to keep so much distance, might care for Brooklyn more than he was letting on.

CHAPTER
Thirty-Five

Jaxon

SITTING NEXT to Brooklyn's hospital bed, the events of the day played through my head over and over. The doctors had told us that she should wake up within a few hours and that they were giving her pain medication to make it easier for her once she did wake. They didn't have to take her spleen, which was the biggest concern.

I sat staring at the doctor, as he threw medical jargon at us. Most of which I didn't recognize, but I understood that she didn't have to lose an organ from her body. Beyond that, nothing mattered, as long as she woke up and wasn't permanently injured. The doctors seemed positive and insisted we leave for the night. Once Gideon said no, they didn't try to move us again.

Gideon hovered outside the room, mentally punishing himself for what had happened. I had tried to tell him it wasn't his fault, but he wasn't hearing me. Aiden even tried to pull him aside, but their conversation ended in an argument with Gideon disappearing for thirty minutes.

Aiden paced the small room, clicking away on his phone. I wanted to throw it against the wall, to stop him from working, even when we were all in the hospital waiting for Brooklyn to wake up. However, he turned to Gideon and they discussed something quietly and I realized Aiden wasn't doing normal work.

"Lyle is in the wind again. My detective friend caught him on camera running from the back of the cafe, but they lost him in some blind spots," Gideon said.

"What can we do, to stop this motherfucker from coming near her again?" Oliver asked.

It was strange to hear his normal jovial attitude ground to dust. This morning, we woke up to an empty bed, but the smell of Brooklyn was still on the sheets between us. The mood was happy and domestic as we showed her where we kept the coffee and she started to take over the kitchen. Having her there felt like a missing piece was clicking into place.

When she left for work, we kissed her, believing she'd be back with us in the evening. The threats from Lyle were serious, but we were mistaken in believing he wouldn't physically go after Brooklyn. There were no doubts for us now, the scum wanted our girl dead.

I touched her hand, thankful for the warmth. I imagined

her blood, moving through her veins, going to all of her major organs, keeping her breathing and alive. I bent and pressed my lips to her skin. It didn't smell like her now that she had been sterilized through surgery and the trauma unit. But it didn't stop me from wanting to kiss her and reassure her we were here with her.

"She had a permanent restraining order, but really that's going to do nothing to protect her. If the cops can't catch him, they can't arrest him," Aiden said.

"Arresting him isn't going to be the end here," Gideon said quietly.

I didn't look over at him, didn't need to confirm what he was saying. If Brooklyn was going to be protected, it was going to have to be us that did it. We couldn't rely on the city police or Gideon's inside people to take care of Lyle. It was going to have to be us. It wasn't the first time we had to get our hands dirty in our lives, but this was definitely a different time and situation.

"Agreed," I said.

"Whatever it takes," Oliver added.

"Aiden?" Gideon asked.

I looked over then, to gauge Aiden's reaction. Oliver and Gideon also watched him. We all stared, waiting for his answer. He looked into each of our faces, before nodding once and we knew he was in.

Silence fell in the hospital room, as we just waited. A commotion outside, pulled my attention from Brooklyn's form and I saw a woman gesturing wildly with Gideon in the hallway. She clearly wanted by, but Gideon wasn't allowing it. I stood from my bedside chair, to find out what was happening.

"She's my friend. I never would have done something to hurt her on purpose!" The woman was exclaiming.

As I got closer I recognized the woman as Pam, Brooklyn's assistant. Gideon's face was set in stone, fury in his features. I knew that look and I knew he needed to beat something to a pulp to unleash all of the emotions he was keeping bottled in. I had to give Pam some credit, that didn't stop her from trying to argue her way into Brooklyn's hospital room.

"Here, I brought the contact information for the woman I told you about. Look into it, give it to the police. I didn't bring her to that cafe on my own," Pam said.

"That's fine. But until we know what's going on, no one is going near her," Gideon said, grinding out the words through clenched teeth.

"Hi Pam. Maybe we can take this conversation away from the room. I really don't think Brooklyn needs to wake up to arguing," I said, trying to calm the situation.

Pam's eyes flew to me. She looked back to Gideon and then at my other two brothers inside Brooklyn's hospital room. Her eyebrows shot up as she tried to put together the situation she was seeing. Oliver was sitting on the opposite side of the bed from where I had been. He was brushing Brooklyn's hair out of her face, with his eyes glued to her. Aiden was still pacing erratically. I tried to imagine what was happening in Pam's head.

"You all do some business with us and now you think you have some sort of right in Brooklyn's life? I've worked for her longer than you all have been around. So I'm not sure what makes you think you can stop me from seeing her," Pam said. She put her hands on her hips, her stance defiant.

Just then, as if to save the day, Gideon's detective friend came out of an elevator down the hall and quickly made his way to us. Gideon's eyes snapped up to him and then he put his hands on Pam's shoulders and physically turned her until he could shove her toward the detective. I grimaced, thinking he could have been a bit kinder with the woman, but I kept my mouth shut.

"Lee, this is the woman that took Brooklyn to the cafe, under a rouse to surprise her," Gideon bit out.

The detective nodded and motioned for Pam to follow him back down the hall. But she stopped and whirled back on Gideon.

"I would never have hurt Brooklyn on purpose. I'm devastated by this, just as clearly you are. She is the kindest soul I've met in this god awful city. I will be back to see her and you won't be able to stop me forever," she said.

"We'll see about that," Gideon replied.

Pam stomped away, following Lee to wherever he was taking her for questioning. I watched until they disappeared from sight and turned to Gideon.

"You don't really think her assistant did this on purpose, do you?" I asked.

"It's not high on my list, but I'm not ignoring the possibility that's right in our faces. Lee will sort her out. I still didn't want her hysterics near Brooklyn before she's woken up," he replied.

He glanced behind us at Brooklyn's still form and his head hung. His hair was down from his normal bun and he kept running his hands through it, making it look wild.

"I know I already said this, brother. But I'm gonna repeat myself. This wasn't your fault," I said.

"I couldn't tell her no. When she said she wanted to go to the cafe with her assistant, she asked me to watch from a distance. She didn't want to explain me to Pam. I should have told her no. But I have no willpower when it comes to her," he said.

I chuckled softly. "That seems to be the power she has."

"But I knew she was in danger. I didn't anticipate it being

so soon, but I knew Lyle would be out there waiting for her," Gideon said.

"Sure, you knew. We all did. But, Gideon, how could you possibly know Lyle would be in that bathroom today? You can't hang that responsibility on your neck. It's too heavy, brother," I said, reaching out to put my hand on his shoulder.

I pressed on him, guiding him back to the entrance of Brooklyn's room. As soon as we entered, I noticed Brooklyn's eyes starting to blink.

"She's waking up," I said softly, rushing over to the chair I had vacated.

Gideon stayed glued to the doorframe, watching Brooklyn. His face was haggard and nervous. Aiden hung near the foot of her bed, looking just as concerned, but not within reach of her. Oliver held her hand that didn't have needles in it. I brushed her cheek with my finger, just trying to bring her back to the surface.

"Come on, love. We're here. Wake up," I whispered.

Brooklyn blinked her eyes, frowning at the ceiling. She finally focused, but she didn't look around the room. I could see her face start to crumble and the tears started to leak from the corners of her eyes. Oliver jumped to his feet to lean over her.

"Babe, are you in pain? Aiden, get the doctor," he said.

Aiden rushed out of the room, bumping into the tree that Gideon had become. Brooklyn began to shake her head, crying in earnest. Oliver looked over to me in panic and then at the machines she was hooked up to. The beeping hadn't changed since she came in, but none of us were doctors so it meant nothing to us.

I stood up and took Oliver's place over Brooklyn's face. When she wouldn't focus on me, I gently grabbed her chin and stopped her head until she had no choice but see me above her. She frowned for a moment and then more tears poured from her eyes.

"Brooklyn, are you crying because you are in pain?" I asked.

She shook her head slightly.

"Why are you so upset, love? Tell us, so we can help," I said.

"I...Lyle...I tried to get away," she whispered.

"Of course you did. You didn't do anything wrong," I said.

"He stabbed me, didn't he?" She asked.

"Yes, love, he did," I replied quietly.

"Oh god," she whispered, crying harder.

She brought her hand to her neck, touching the scar that was clearly visible with her hospital gown. She tried to tug the material up to cover more, but I stilled her hand.

"There's no reason to hide, Brooklyn. No one is judging you. No one is staring. Please just take a deep breath and try to calm down."

We were interrupted by a doctor that came to Brooklyn's side so she could easily see him. He checked her eyes and the monitors as well as listened to her heart. He turned to look at Oliver, Aiden and myself that were crowding her bed.

"You're going to have to leave so I can examine her surgery site," he said.

I began to shake my head and was about to argue when Brooklyn spoke up.

"They can stay. I need them to stay," she said.

I wasn't sure she realized that Aiden was also in the room, but he was clearly not leaving either. Gideon stepped just inside the door, so it could be shut, but he didn't come any closer to Brooklyn's bed. He adjusted slightly, watching all of the doctor's movements, but he hadn't said a word to Brooklyn herself.

The doctor carefully lifted the side of her gown, clearing the way for the incision site. He slowly pulled back the tape of the wound covering that had been applied. Just under her ribcage on the left side a long stitched surgery opening could be seen. Slightly lower was where the knife entered her, which had to be more carefully stitched due to the jagged edges of the wound. However, everything seemed cleaned up as good as it could be.

Brooklyn tried to look down, but the gown was in her way. She tried to move things and I could see she was panicking without seeing what the doctor was seeing. The monitor that was hooked to her heart rate started to beep faster and the doctor looked up from her chart.

"Ms. Reeves, are you in pain?"

"I can't...I can't see what happened," she said.

He looked at her oddly for a moment and then looked around the room at us. Suddenly, it dawned on me what was going through her mind. Her scars. They were the leading character in all of her worst stories. And now she was going to have more of them, reminding her of yet another nightmare she had to live through.

"I can take a photo and show you," I said.

She looked over to me and nodded gratefully. I centered the wounds in my cellphone camera and snapped the photo. Before showing it to her, I leaned down to whisper in her ear, so the doctor didn't hear us.

"Your scars do not define you, Brooklyn. They are nothing but reminders of the times you survived because you're amazing. I think they're beautiful, strong and amazing."

When I pulled back her eyes were full of tears again but she tried to smile at me. I pulled up the photo and looked at her, making sure she was prepared. I held the phone up so she could see it. She took a deep breath and her lips began to tremble. I pulled the phone away and kissed her forehead, trying to console her somehow.

"Ms. Reeves, are you up for an update?" The doctor asked.

Brooklyn's hand came up and gripped my arm as she nodded to the doctor. I stayed where she held me in place. I wanted to pour my support directly into her, however I could. As the doctor began to talk, her fingers dug into my arm as the doctor began to explain everything they had to do to save her life.

CHAPTER
Thirty-Six

Brooklyn

THE BEATING of my heart in my ears made it hard to focus on the doctor's words. I dug my fingers into Jaxon's arm, keeping him close. His warmth, his smell, I needed the calm feeling he brought to me, to handle what the doctor was saying to me.

"Ms. Reeves, I first want to say, you're going to be fine. We were able to repair the damage done to your spleen from the knife wound. The knife was serrated, causing a jagged entry wound below the spleen. However, the angle of the attack, caused it the puncture the organ and cause internal bleeding," the doctor said.

I stared at him. He was an older man, gray hair and balding at the top. He wore wire glasses to read my chart, but looked at me over them. I would ask later, but the idea that he performed my surgery had me slightly panicked.

"Due to the emergency situation, we had to perform an open surgery. Which means we'll need to keep you in the hospital for approximately a week to keep an eye on your progress. You also suffered a blow to the head. Tests are showing that you likely have a decent concussion, so we want to watch that as well."

Emergency situation, was a really polite way of talking about being attacked by my ex-boyfriend in a bathroom. When pieces of memories came back to me, I had to take a deep breath and close my eyes for a moment. The doctor paused, watching me.

"I'd ask if there's anyone I could call, but your room is already quite full," he said with a chuckle.

That had me looking around, more than I had since I opened my eyes. All four Knights were in the smallish hospital room. Oliver grinned at me from his place near my legs. He had to give up his spot for the doctor to do his work. Jaxon just leaned on the bed on the other side, where I had grabbed him. Aiden was at the foot of the bed, looking worried and stressed. Gideon stood near the door, looking ready to bolt. I studied him, but he refused to meet my eye.

"There's no one to call. They're all here," I said quietly.

The doctor checked the monitors, took additional notes, let me know how to contact the nurses and then excused himself from the room. The silence was deafening as the guys all waited on edge to see what I would say.

"Can I speak with Gideon alone, please?" I said.

Jaxon looked down at me, nodding. His eyes were under-standing and it told me more of what I needed to know. It was clear Gideon was beating himself up, avoiding any direct contact with me. And I knew if we didn't address it now, everything would just fester until we couldn't undo the damage. Oliver and Aiden filed out after Jaxon without argument. Gideon's eyes followed them, but he didn't try to stop them.

"Big man, please come here. Sit with me," I said.

Reluctantly, Gideon moved forward and pulled the chair back slightly, so he was sitting away from the bed. I tried to plan what I wanted to say in my head, but the way he was pulling away from me was only annoying me.

"I'm on drugs right now, so I'm going to be mean, and I'll use that as an excuse," I started.

Gideon just stared at the end of the bed, still not looking me in the face.

"Gideon, I need something from you," I said.

That had him turning to look at me. I knew even with the distance he was trying to put between us, he would still do anything he could for me.

"Kiss me," I said, repeating the request I had the first morning we woke up together in my apartment.

I knew he remembered that moment, it was the beginning of us. I watched as uncertainty hung in his face, but he stood and moved toward the bed anyway. When he lowered toward me, I lifted the hand that didn't have an IV and anchored my fingers in his free hair. I pulled his face to mine, to make sure he didn't try to pull away.

When his lips touched mine, electricity passed through us, a feeling I had become used to when any of my men kissed me. His lips were soft and exploring, but I demanded more, running my tongue along the seam of his lips, until he relented and gave me access. As soon as I rubbed my tongue against his, he moaned and his hand came to my cheek.

Our kiss continued, until he pulled away, leaving me breathless. I could feel a blush in my cheeks, but also could feel a bit of pain in my stomach. I took a few deep breaths, trying to control the pain, without needing additional meds. Gideon watched me, as he pulled the chair closer.

"You need to stop blaming yourself. Don't argue, I can see what's going on in your head," I said, holding up my hand as he opened his mouth.

"You can't know everything, Gideon. At some point Lyle was going to come after me. I was lucky you were right there, to stop him from doing much worse."

"Worse? You could have died!" He exclaimed.

"But I didn't. Because you were there, to stop the bleeding until I could get here and the doctors did their thing. Am I upset? Yes. With you? No. Am I scared? Shitless. But knowing you, Oliver and Jaxon have my back, the fear is a bit more manageable. But I can't feel that way, if you pull away and put distance between us. This wasn't your fault," I said, reaching my hand out to him.

He hesitated, before taking my hand. He cradled it between his, before dropping his forehead down, resting it against my hand and staying there. His hair curtained his face, so I waited, hoping he would talk it through with me. When he didn't speak, I decided to take the reins. He was the only one that could tell me what happened in the cafe and I could only remember bits and pieces.

"Can you walk me through what happened, from your point of view? Some of it is a bit hazy. It might help me if we can compare what you know to what I can remember. These drugs, they're real good," I giggled quietly.

"There's one thing, you should know," he started.

As he told me about Pam and the arrangement she thought she was setting up, I turned to stare at the ceiling. I felt partially at blame for the whole event. If I had been honest and told my coworkers at least some of the truth about my past, Pam would have known to be more cautious about a random person from my past. I had to wonder who the woman was that Lyle had found to help get me alone in the cafe.

"She's being questioned by detectives. Hopefully there's a lead they can tug there," Gideon said.

When I looked over at him, he had his elbows on his knees, his chin propped on his folded hands. I then noticed the tight shirt he was wearing, a nurse's scrub top. The sleeves cut into his muscular arms, looking very uncomfortable. In the back, I could see the material raising up at his waist, exposing his lower back. I grinned at him and he looked at quizzically.

"Nice shirt, big guy," I said.

"It was the biggest one they had," he grumbled, trying to pull the material down to cover more.

The sour look on his face had me laughing. But then I was gripping my side, gasping and trying not to laugh. Gideon looked at me in panic.

"Calm down! You're going to bust a suture!"

I took some deep breaths and lowered my laughter to a little giggle. Gideon finally relaxed and sat back. He waited and once I was calmed down I started to explain what happened in the bathroom. His face became stony against as I recounted what I could remember. When I mentioned Lyle hitting me and me hitting my head, Gideon paled. Things got fuzzy once Gideon came into the story.

He cleared his throat and his leg began to bounce. I wanted to go to him, to comfort him. But my body wasn't ready to get out of bed. I waited for him to fill in the gaps of the story. I wanted everything out between us, so we could move on and heal together.

"When I came in, he had his back to me. I waited too long to act, because he stabbed you just before I grabbed him. I got a few hits in on him, before I saw you pull the knife from your stomach. I had to let him escape so I could put pressure on the wound," he explained.

"You saved my life," I said.

"I never should have let you be put in the position where it needed to be saved," he said.

"You were only doing what I asked you to do. If anything, this is my fault."

"I could have said no. I knew it was a bad idea. I underestimated this guy. That's not how I normally operate," he said, his voice sounding miserable.

"Look, let's just make an agreement? I'll be better about listening to your security advice until this is all over. And you'll be better about telling me the risks and your concerns. We can work together," I said.

He looked at me for a long moment. His scrutiny made me squirm. I couldn't read his expression. He finally nodded his agreement with a large sigh that made the scrub top tighten on him again. I almost burst into laughter again but remember my pain and swallowed it down. I did have a huge grin and Gideon just shook his head at me.

I started to feel drowsy and Gideon had the rest of the guys come back in. Jaxon looked at us both and nodded his head, happy with the results of our discussion. Oliver came to my side, leaning down to kiss me soundly on the mouth. He leaned back slightly, so he could study me, his blue eyes behind his glasses looking deep and concerned. I smiled at him and reached up to touch his face.

I fell asleep with them surrounding me. I felt safe in the

hospital. The pain meds were doing their job and for twenty-four hours I was in and out of a drug induced sleep. I was often woken by nurses checking vitals and making sure my pupils were still reactionary. Having a light shined in my eyes after waking wasn't exactly my idea of a good time, but I didn't argue.

At some point, I awoke and the room was dark, except the monitors surrounding me. I finally felt rested, but I couldn't tell what time it was. I started to shift, but I felt something against my hip and I froze. In the light of the monitor, I could see Oliver's sleeping form. He was sitting in a chair next to me, bent over with his head resting on his arms right next to me.

I softly ran my hand through his curls, the hair soft and silky against my fingertips. His breathing changed and he gasped awake, sitting up quickly. He grabbed my hand and kissed it before standing up and coming closer to my head.

"Babe? You ok?" He asked, his voice groggy.

"Yeah, I'm sorry I woke you. What time is it?" I asked.

A light shined as he checked his watch, illuminating his face for a moment. He squinted without his glasses on.

"2 am," he replied.

"Crap. My sleep is all off. I finally feel awake," I mumbled.

Without complaint, Oliver went to the bathroom and turned on the light. He closed the door so it wasn't too bright, but we could see each other more clearly. He went to a small table and poured some water for me, bringing a straw to my lips. I drank, enjoying the refreshing feeling in my mouth and down my throat.

"Doctor said your throat might be sore, from the tube, during the surgery," Oliver said.

"I think it's the least of my worries," I replied.

I shifted in the bed, moving to one side. Oliver rushed over, trying to help me. Once I got settled again, I was out of breath. I realized the feeling of being awake was limited and not at all the same as feeling healthy.

"Come lay with me," I said.

"I can't. You'll get hurt," he said.

"I'm the patient. I want you to lay with me," I argued.

Oliver grinned at my demanding attitude. He nodded and lowered the rail on the one side of the bed. Very carefully he climbed onto the half of the bed I had moved from. He laid on his side, as there wasn't enough space for him to lay on his back. I scooted closer, until I could nuzzle my head under his chin. Oliver always seems to smell sweet, like vanilla and it felt real and reminded me of what I had.

Tentatively, Oliver placed his hand on my hip, afraid of touching me anywhere else. I found his free hand and laced my fingers with his. The comfort made me feel more drowsy and I yawned.

"We can't sleep like this, the nurses are mean," Oliver whispered.

"Awe, is my man afraid of some little nurses?" I joked.

My joke was met with silence, and I wondered what I had said wrong.

"Is that what I am? Your man?" Oliver finally said.

"What do you mean?" I asked tentatively.

"You pushed us away. I get that it was all a lot and it was fast. I also want to act like I'm some tough guy and that it didn't hurt when you pushed us away. But being honest with you seems to be the only thing I can do. And it did hurt. Badly."

I squeezed his hand and tilted my face to softly kiss his neck, before nuzzling back into him.

"I'm sorry. I didn't want to hurt you. I think I had myself

convinced that it didn't matter. That we didn't matter. I'll be honest too. I was miserable. I missed you too much," I said.

"So, babe, what do you want?" He asked.

"Us, what we are together. You, Jaxon and Gideon," I replied without hesitation.

"Good. Now, sleep. It's the middle of the damn night," he said.

I giggled lightly, being aware of my surgical site. With Oliver's warmth surrounding me, his thumb rubbing against my hip and his fingers tightened around mine, it was easier to drift into a comfortable sleep.

Brooklyn

THE DAY I was discharged from the hospital, all four Knights were there, waiting for me to complete my paperwork. Jaxon had already filled the prescriptions that were given to me. Gideon waited with a wheelchair. Oliver leaned against the wall, oblivious to the stares he was getting from the nurses behind the desk. And Aiden was being his disconnected self, standing near the elevator with his cellphone pressed to his ear.

Gideon carefully pushed me to the elevator with a nurse trailing behind us. The wheelchair escort was insisted upon, even though I was positive I could walk. Gideon said my butt would be in the chair or he would carry me, which would only embarrass me more. I huffed, but sat in the wheelchair.

A limo was waiting in the front of the hospital. When the nurse raised her eyebrow at me, I felt myself go crimson. The Knights didn't do much halfway. And apparently I needed to go home in style. Oliver held out his hands to help me stand and carefully climb into the limo. The four men climbed in after me.

Aiden was still on a business call and sat near the privacy screen at the front of the vehicle. Jaxon and Oliver sat on either side of me, with Gideon on the side seat. The ride to their home was quiet. My mind was in a different place, trying to figure out what I was going to do long term.

Ash had called while I was in the hospital. She was devastated by the news of the attack. I apologized about bringing the problems into her home, but she stopped me and said it was just stuff. And really, Lyle hadn't touched anything other than my room.

She wanted to come home immediately. I reassured her that I was being well taken care of by the guys and she needed to finish her work. I didn't tell her that I didn't want to worry about her safety as well as my own.

The fact that I was staying at the Knight estate had her worked up beyond everything else. She wanted to come home, just so she could visit me to see where the elusive business men lived. I had to keep myself from laughing, so I didn't cause more pain, as she went on and on about how I had no idea how many women would hate me for taking my place in the family. She wasn't concerned in the least about the fact I was actually with three of the four men. Ash figured I should add Aiden to the list and make it a full deck.

As I watched said man in the limo, I knew the idea had crossed my mind before Ash had even said it. Aiden exuded strength and control. Sometimes I saw a break in the business only behavior from him, when he'd laugh at the dinner table with his brothers, or when he saved me at the gala. But after the first day after my attack, I rarely saw Aiden at the hospital and it seemed his feelings for me didn't go further than an acquaintance, sleeping with his brothers and currently living under his roof.

When we arrived to the house, Gideon carefully helped me out of the car. I stood up straight, taking a deep breath, testing what limits I may have. I felt good, sore, but good. I smiled up at my big man and I got one of his rare grins in return. Holding my hand, he brought me to the front door.

After unlocking it, I heard a beeping and saw Aiden punching numbers into a pad I hadn't seen before.

"You had an alarm installed? You already have a wall around the entire place," I said.

"Extra security can never hurt, stellina," Gideon said.

"You think he'll come here?" I asked quietly, looking at my feet.

Aiden's shined wingtips came into my vision and I looked up quickly, to see him standing too close to me. Gideon was watchful from beside me, but he didn't say anything in response to my question. Aiden's eyes pierced mine and I felt unable to look away for a moment.

"Do not for one moment think this is your fault. You are the victim here. You are not responsible for Lyle's actions. Do I make myself clear?"

I just nodded, not really sure how to respond to the anger dripping from Aiden's voice. His words weren't to attack me, but he was clearly furious about Lyle. If nothing else, I knew Aiden would have my back, should it ever come down to it. And that made living in the huge house feel a little more comfortable.

I watched him storm away and decided to ignore the pang in my chest. Gideon held his hand out to me, leading me toward the stairs. By the time we got to the top I was completely winded and a headache was forming behind my eyes. Gideon slowed down,

In the guest room, it was clear the guys had been busy. There was a mini fridge in one corner, with a glass set on the top. Pain medications, vitamins, heating pad and more random medical items were on one night stand. Extra towels were piled up on the bathroom counter and the shower even had a chair in it.

"I'm not a complete invalid," I exclaimed, turning to Gideon.

He glanced in the shower and rolled his eyes.

"I'm sure that was Oliver," he said.

"What was me?" Oliver's voice came from behind us.

I frowned at him and pointed at the shower. He didn't even look before cracking up into laughter.

"Well if anything, it could make showering a bit more fun," Oliver said, wiggling his eyebrows at me.

"Hold your horses, joker. I'm in no shape for all that," I said.

I turned back to the bedroom, to stare at the furniture that now dominated the room. The previous guest bed had been replaced by a massive four poster bed that had to be as wide as two king beds next to each other. It was piled high with pillows and a pale yellow comforter.

"Uh, how did you find linens to fit that?" I asked.

"You'd be surprised what you can have custom made," Oliver said.

Jaxon walked in then with my prescriptions, adding them to the night stand. He shook out a pill from one bottle and pulled a bottled water from the mini fridge. Handing me the pill and the bottle, he waited.

"What is it?" I asked.

"Your antibiotic," Jaxon replied.

I did as I was instructed and then looked at the three of them hovering.

"I'm ok. You don't need to stay here and watch me."

"We just want to make sure we're here if you need help," Gideon said.

"I appreciate that. But really, right now, I just want a nap."

Going to the dresser, I pulled out a random tank top and short set that Oliver had stocked me with. When I tried to lift my arms to remove my shirt, I hissed out in pain, which caused all three guys to rush forward. Gideon reached me first and he pushed down my arms.

"Just let us help," he said quietly.

Closing my eyes for a moment, I just sighed and nodded. I was at a moment of weakness and I knew I needed to accept their assistance. Even if another part of me screamed that I needed to be strong and handle things on my own. Oliver stepped up behind me and started to lift the hem of my shirt, while Gideon carefully bent my arms to guide them through the arm holes.

I stood in front of the men, completely naked. However, they all moved around me clinically. Jaxon softly touched my bandage, checking the edges and smoothing it down carefully. Gideon brought the tank top forward, putting it over my head first. Oliver tapped my ankle, to indicate I needed to lift one foot and then the other.

Completely dressed again, the three of them stood back to assess their work. I started to cross my arms across my chest, but realized that hurt too, so I just put my hands on my hips.

"You three are starting to freak me out. Can you stop staring?"

"Sorry, babe. Hard not to stare at you," Oliver said with a small sexy smile.

"Normally, I'd appreciate it. But, right now it's all serious and not hot and sexy. I miss hot and sexy," I said with a pout.

Jaxon came to me and kissed my temple, before leading me toward the massive bed. He pulled back the covers and Gideon came to my side. Using his arm, I carefully climbed up into the bed and he helped me lay back without using my abdominal muscles. Once I was laying down, Jaxon smoothed the blankets over me.

I felt the bed dip next to me and I looked over to find Oliver getting settled. I raised an eyebrow at him.

"Who doesn't like a nap in the middle of the day?" He asked.

I just giggled lightly and scooted over so I could press the side of my body to his. He turned and kissed my jaw before letting me tuck my head under his chin. Gideon closed the blackout curtains, plunging the room into darkness, except the light that was still on in the bathroom.

My big man came to me and kissed me softly on the mouth. I reached up and tugged on his beard lightly.

"I really miss hot and sexy," I said softly.

"We miss it too. Believe me," he said gruffly, standing up and walking to join Jaxon at the door.

I snuggled into Oliver's side, careful to not bump into my surgical site. Being in a real bed, in clothes that I could call my own, behind the walls and safety of the Knight compound, I was able to finally fall asleep without worry. Oliver's deep breathing came quickly and I knew they were all just as tired from taking constant shifts with me at the hospital.

Though sleep came quickly, my dreams were turbulent and dark. I was standing in my apartment, looking in my bathroom mirror and suddenly Lyle was behind me. In my dream I couldn't understand his words, but the fear felt real, causing me to gasp awake. My stomach hurt, from the sudden movement of me sitting up in bed. Oliver had rolled away slightly and I sat quietly, making sure I didn't wake him.

I knew I wasn't going to easily fall back asleep. Looking at the clock, I saw it was dinner time. My stomach chose that moment to growl and I slipped from bed to investigate what was in the kitchen. I tried to be quiet as I snuck downstairs, not wanting to disturb anyone in the house. If one of the guys found me wandering, they would go into overprotective, provider mode. That was cute for a minute, but it was going to make me feel like a complete invalid.

The kitchen was dark and empty. Barefoot, I padded across the tile to the kitchen. The light from the fridge illuminated the room and I caught movement from the corner of my eye. I spun, faster than I should have and started to lose my balance. Arms came around me, pulling me into a hard chest before I tumbled. I looked up into Aiden's face, finding a furious concern wrinkling his forehead.

"What in the world are you doing?" He asked.

"I...well...what are you doing sitting in the dark?" I stuttered.

"Everyone is sleeping. I was just being quiet and enjoying the peace," he said.

"Oh, sorry," I said, starting to pull away.

"For what?"

"Interrupting. I couldn't sleep, so I thought I should eat something," I said.

Though, I tried to pull back from his arms, Aiden didn't losen his grip. He was dressed casually, something he only seemed to do on the weekends. Even during the week, it was a variation of suit jackets, dress pants and dress shirts. On the weekends, it was a pleasure to see him in distressed jeans and t-shirts. This evening, he was relaxed, wearing gray sweat pants and a black v-neck shirt.

My gaze couldn't help but wander down to his chest, and the piece of skin that showed at his collar. I could see a sprinkling of dark hair, but his skin was olive and smooth. I could feel the bands of his arms around my back, holding me to him, but not so tightly that he was pressing against my injury. I let my hand move down from his shoulder to his forearm, feeling the heat of his skin under my palm.

"You're always apologizing, aren't you sweetheart?" Aiden asked.

I cocked my head at him, thinking about the question. It was normally my first instinct, to apologize, for whatever I had done. My therapist had addressed it with me a few times in sessions, but I often slipped back into old habits. She told me that it was a trained behavior, caused by the fear of domestic violence.

When she said that, it had made perfect sense. However, it wasn't a conscious fear. I had no reason to be afraid of any of the Knights. None of them would hurt me, I knew that with my entire being. But the fear of loss, the fear of upsetting someone else, it was always in the back of my mind.

"Old habit," I mumbled.

His hand came up, to cup my chin and using his thumb, he pushed my chin up to force me to look into his eyes. In the darkness, it was impossible to read his expression. His face was incredibly close, I could feel his breath against my own mouth. Neither of us moved, caught in an intense moment of insecurity and unknowing. I couldn't be sure what Aiden felt for me or wanted from me. But, as his hand moved to the nape of my neck, tangling in my hair, I knew I was about to find out.

"I've been trying to resist you. I should have known, once my brothers brought you here, I would lose the fight," he murmured, his lips grazing mine as they moved with his words.

"Why? Why did you need to resist me?" I asked.

"You're dangerous," he replied.

Before I could think of a decent response, his lips softly pressed against mine, in a testing kiss. As his lips moved against mine, I pressed up on my toes, to get closer to him, my right arm coming up around his neck. My left hand stayed on his arm, knowing it would only hurt if I tried to raise it.

Aiden pulled away for a moment and I wished for a light, just so I could read his expression. I had a feeling it was fierce and passionate, because a breath of time later, his mouth was crashing back onto mine. We battled, lips teeth, tongues. Aiden fought against me, as if he was still fighting his attraction to me. My fight was to keep him with me, kissing me senseless in the dark kitchen.

Suddenly, the kitchen illuminated brightly and I jumped in Aiden's arms. However, Aiden wasn't letting me go. I looked over toward the kitchen entrance and there was Jaxon, a smile on his face. Aiden's mouth went to my neck and I shivered with Jaxon watching the whole scene.

"She's still healing, brother. You should let her go," he said, jokingly.

Aiden's kisses slowed and I wanted to protest. But my body was sore and I could tell pain meds would be fed to me soon by Jaxon. Once I took those pills, I would likely go back to bed. For the moment, I was stuck in a vicious cycle of trying to heal. Which also meant, my men couldn't or, more likely wouldn't, touch me.

I lowered back to the sole of my feet, letting my head lay on Aiden's chest while I caught my breath. Jaxon came to us, and he kissed my cheek before going to the fridge and pulling out the makings for sandwiches. My stomach audibly growled just then and Aiden actually chuckled.

"You did say you were hungry," he said.

"I sorta forgot for a moment," I said against his chest.

Using his arms and body he moved me to the nearest stool and helped me sit. I leaned my elbows on the island, planting my chin on my hands, while I watched the two of them move around the kitchen. A glass of sparkling water was sat in front of me, which I sipped gratefully. Aiden stood behind me, rubbing my arms as we both watched Jaxon fix me a sandwich.

Once the food was in front of me, both of them sat across from me and watched. I felt heat rise into my cheeks as they followed each bite I took. There was a look of satisfaction on Jaxon's face when I finally finished the meal. Then, as expected, a pill appeared next to my glass of water. I didn't bother to ask, giving over my care to the men that seemed to want the task so badly.

Brooklyn

"ARE you sure you're up to this?"

I spun to face Gideon, who had a worried crease across his forehead. Reaching up, I rubbed at it, until he relaxed. I tugged on his beard, pulling his face closer to me, so I could plant a smacking kiss on his mouth.

"If one of you ask me that one more time, I'm not going to put on a pretty dress for you," I said.

He grumbled but started to back out of the bathroom. What

I wasn't going to tell him was I also wasn't going to wear any panties under said dress. Currently, I was wrapped in a fluffy robe as I swiped eyeshadow across my eyes. I went with a dark smoky eye, since the guys said we were going somewhere dark and fancy.

I had been on the road of healing and perfect recovery for three weeks. Which meant three weeks of four hot as sin men waiting on me hand and foot in all ways, except sex. Aiden kept his distance, claiming he was going to take his time with our relationship, but that would have to wait until I was healthy. The other three took turns sleeping with me in the huge bed, but they never touched me beyond a kiss goodnight or a momentary snuggle.

It couldn't have been easy on them. More than once I watched them leaving the room with a hard on I would have gladly cared for. But none of my advances worked. They kept putting my recovery first. Yes, that sexually frustrated me, even if it was incredibly sweet and caring. The sweet and caring behavior was making me want them even more.

Ash would be home in less than three weeks. I couldn't believe her Europe trip was almost over. During my time off from work, Jaxon helped me work to get my apartment bedroom cleaned and all evidence of the break in fixed and wiped away. Though, it didn't matter. When I walked into the apartment, all I saw was Lyle's fingerprints everywhere. It was a discussion Jaxon had tried to have with me numerous times. I did agree to stay at their house at least until Lyle was caught. It just felt safer that way.

Finally, the guys were willing to let us have a little fun. Oliver started the plan, deeming the evening our second official date, since the only one I had been on with them was our business dinner that didn't end in a business like way. I was super excited for the evening and had taken the longest shower shaving and exfoliating all the important bits.

I slipped a red strapless mini dress over my head. It had a double pointed neckline and boning in the front that pushed my breasts up and gave me the perfect cleavage. I wore a single pendant that fell right above, pulling the eye right to where I wanted. I didn't bother hiding my scar anymore. The Knights knew about my physical scars as well as my emotional ones and they hadn't run from me yet.

In the closet, were boxes of shoes that I hadn't even had the chance to open. Oliver had gone a little crazy with what was supposed to be a wardrobe just to get me by until I could go shopping. I found a pair of black stilettos, in the perfect size and slipped them on. The height made my legs look a mile long, with the dress barely falling below my ass. Checking myself out before leaving the room, I knew my guys couldn't tell me no tonight.

As I made my way down the stairs, I knew the moment I was spotted. Oliver's mouth physically hung open. Aiden was looking at his phone, but when he glanced up, he stopped scrolling and stared. Gideon wasn't looking my way and it took Jaxon pounding on his arm to get him to spin. Once he did, both he and Jaxon stood stock still, staring at me.

"Oliver, where did she get that dress?" Aiden growled.

"I'll take your thanks now," Oliver shot back.

Jaxon came to the stairs and held out a hand to me, helping me down the last few.

"You look amazing," he said.

"Thanks," I replied, beaming up at him.

The four of them looked rather delicious themselves. They were all wearing various shades of dress pants that hugged thighs and asses perfectly. I needed to thank their tailor, because they left just enough to the imagination while allowing enough to be seen. Aiden and Gideon were both in white button up shirts, top buttons undone like always. Gideon had his sleeves rolled halfway up his forearms and suddenly I realized I had a thing for muscular forearms. His tribal tattoo coming down one arm definitely helped.

Oliver and Jaxon seemed a bit more relaxed, wearing what looked like expensive v-neck t-shirts. The shirts both sat untucked, however they hugged their torsos in the sexiest way, just begging to be peeled off. I gripped Jaxon's tattooed fore-arm, excitement racing through me.

"Where are we going?" I asked.

"You'll see, love," he replied with a smile.

We chatted and laughed in the back of the limo as it drove through the city. I didn't bother trying to guess our destina-tion. It really didn't matter. All I cared about was being near them. My heart did a little patter in my chest, trying to tell me it was more than that, but I pushed it down. It was too soon to be thinking and feeling that way.

When we pulled into the familiar back alley of Club 4, I looked around at the Knights with a questioning glance. No one gave me an explanation and I wasn't going to argue if the night was going to start with sweaty dancing that lead to sex in a dark office. As I looked at Gideon, I added stairwell in my head and I could see his mind was in the same place mine was.

We entered through their private backdoor and immedi-ately I knew something wasn't the same. It was Friday night. We should be able to feel the throb of music in the stairwell. But I didn't say anything as they didn't take the stairs, but instead led me to the first floor. I was picking up nerves from them and I wasn't quite sure why.

Inside the main floor of the club, it was clear the building had been transformed once again. There wasn't another soul inside. The interior was dim, lit only by two chandeliers and hundreds of twinkle lights that had been strewn from each post, balcony and staircase. A dining table was off to the side of the dance floor, with two large candelabras, lit with white candles.

I turned around in a circle, taking everything in. The Knights stood off to the side, just watching my reaction. I could feel tears springing to my eyes and I blinked quickly to keep them from falling. I didn't need my perfect makeup ruined and I wasn't going to let tears ruin the moment.

"This is beautiful, but it's Friday. Shouldn't the club be open?" I asked quietly.

"Special event. Closed to the public," Aiden said with a smile.

"You closed the club, on a Friday? You guys are crazy," I said.

"We wanted to eat and not be bothered by other people. Where else could we do that?" Jaxon said.

With that, a waiter came out with a tray of drinks and we each took a glass. The Knights led me to the table and before we sat Jaxon held up his glass.

"I just wanted to make a toast, to Brooklyn. For bringing light back into lives."

A lump rose in my throat as I tried to smile, again with the waterworks trying to force their way through. The four of them looked at me and raised their glasses. I did the same. Taking a sip was hard, through my emotions that wanted to sit in my throat and chest. A small part of me shook with panic, not knowing if I was ready to have this in my life. Though, I already knew how miserable I was without them and I wasn't ready to do that to myself again.

Oliver pulled out my chair for me and I sat just as another waiter entered the room with appetizers that were put in front of us. The seating was close and intimate with us sharing the meal family style. I had noticed over the last few weeks that a lot of what the guys did was very family oriented. It was clear they had created a family, one they didn't have growing up, one that could be all the things they wanted it to be.

The meal was delicious, each course perfectly prepared and served by quiet waiters with smiles on their faces. At some point Aiden picked up an iPad and after a few clicks, quiet music came from the club speakers, creating a soft ambiance to enjoy each other's company.

Dessert was a variety of pies, which we all took turns taking bites from. Laughter bubbled as Jaxon and Gideon fought over the last bite of key lime pie, while Oliver and Aiden took bets on which of them would bite the other to win. I sat back, enjoying my drink, watching my men be relaxed in a way they rarely were. It made my heart feel full and happy.

Once the pies plates were taken away, Aiden turned up the music slightly and Jaxon stood, coming to my side. He held out a hand and I took it, allowing him to pull me to my feet.

"We decided that since Aiden got a special dance with you, it was only right, the rest of us did too," Jaxon said.

The first guitar strains of "Poison and Wine" by the Civil Wars began to flow through the club speakers as Jaxon pulled me into his arms. Now, without pain, I was able to lift both arms around his neck as he wrapped his arms around my waist. As we moved together I laid my head against Jaxon's neck.

"We each chose a song, specifically for tonight," he whispered.

I pulled back to look up at him, listening to the lyrics as they moved around us. *I don't have a choice, but I'd still choose you,* hit me hard as Jaxon stared down into my eyes. The song was sad but also about a love that would always be there, a song about always loving. My heartbeat sped up as we moved and I felt speechless.

As the last strings of the song faded, Jaxon pulled me into his chest, hugging me tightly. He bent to kiss me, just below my ear, before turning away. I stood in the center of the dance floor, shivering slightly from the emotions roiling inside me. A hand slid along my shoulder, turning me.

Oliver smiled warmly at me as he opened his arms. I rushed into him, needing to grip onto someone. He hugged me for a moment, before music started again and he spun me away from him in a playful manner. "Dive" by Ed Sheeran was Oliver's song for us, the first line making me laugh. *Maybe I came on too strong*, making me think of that first night in the club and then the business dinner that didn't exactly go that way.

In his arms, Oliver slid his hands up and down my back, looking down at me with a sexy smile.

"I'm really glad I listened to Jaxon that night, and followed him down to the dance floor. I couldn't imagine it would turn out like this. But I'm damn thankful it has," he said.

"Me too," I said with a smile.

When the chorus of the song played, Oliver's face got more serious and I knew what his message was with the song. *Don't call me baby, unless you mean it. Don't tell me you need me, if you don't believe it.* Oliver, my silly man, wore more of his heart on his sleeve than he liked to believe. He seemed to have been more hurt by me pushing them away, than I had realized.

I smiled up at him, before laying my head on his shoulder, as we danced. He had one arm around my waist and the other around my shoulders, hugging me, and moving our bodies together. His chest rubbed deliciously against mine and I could feel my nipples harden. It wouldn't take much to get me hot and bothered after the last few weeks.

As the song ended, Oliver's hands came up to my face. He looked down at me seriously, before bringing his mouth to mine. The kiss was innocent and soft at first, but when I sighed, his tongue took the chance to slip into my mouth and move against me. The kiss sent heat flickering through my entire body, pooling in my core.

Oliver pulled away with a devilish grin on his face, knowing exactly what he had done. He turned and went back to the table where Aiden and Jaxon were sitting, watching everything unfold. Gideon approached and clapped Oliver on the shoulder when they passed.

"My turn," he said when he got closer.

"All yours, big man," I said with a hand on my hip.

"Don't look at me like that, I might have to drag you to the stairwell," he growled near my ear, as he took my hand in his. I squeaked in surprise as his other hand gripped my ass, before going to my waist.

The first strings of a country song started to play and I was surprised that it was Gideon's style of music. It made me think of all I had to learn about the guys. Their likes, their dislikes. What relaxed them, how they like to spend their free time when they weren't with me. So many things flooded my mind and I felt a sense of excitement with the prospect of learning them all inside and out.

The chorus of the song caught my attention and Gideon brought our joined hands to his chest, pulling me in tighter to him. *In case you didn't know, Baby, I'm crazy 'bout you* the song went and my heart did the flipflop thing again. I tried to swallow down the lump in my throat as I absorbed each word of the song Gideon had chosen. His big body wrapped around me, making me feel like there was no one else around.

"What's this song called?" I asked quietly.

"In Case You Didn't Know, by Brett Young," Gideon replied.

"It's wonderful," I said,

"I'm not like Jaxon, with all the perfect things to say. Or Oliver, who can make a joke about anything and everything. I just hope, that in someway, you know how I feel," he said.

I pulled back, so I could look up into his face. His eyes were serious as he studied me right back. I slid my hand up to tug lightly on his perfectly trimmed beard, that I loved so much. I could see his emotions written on his face, even if he didn't have all the words to speak them. I pushed up on my toes, so I could wrap my arms around his neck. I kissed him hard.

"I know, babe. You show me all the time," I said.

When our song came to an end, Gideon took my hand to walk me back to the table. But Aiden came to stop us. I looked at him quizzically, since technically he had his dance when he paid fifty thousand dollars for me. He held out his hand and I slipped my fingers into his palm.

"I know I paid for a dance, but I think it's only fair I get a second one with a song of my choosing," he said.

I nodded, as I wasn't going to argue the chance to be close to Aiden. He had helped take care of me the last few weeks, but he kept his attention clinical more often than not. I couldn't help but lose myself in the memory of the kiss in the dark kitchen the night I had come home from the hospital.

Aiden looked over to motion to Jaxon, who tapped on the iPad. "Falling" by Harry Styles started to play. This song I definitely knew and I immediately found it an odd selection by Aiden. I knew I was frowning, when he turned me toward him on the dance floor. He pulled me into him with one hand, his other still holding my hand. I let my free hand rest on his shoulder, looking into his face, trying to figure out what he was telling me.

What if I'm someone you won't talk about, Harry's voice crooned and I started to shake my head at Aiden, not liking the feeling I was getting from the song.

"Don't misunderstand," he said.

"Then tell me," I replied.

"You're this bright thing, beautiful, strong and despite everything you've been through, pure. I'm not sure I'm good enough for all of that," he said quietly, never breaking eye contact with me.

I searched his face, trying to think of the right response. *What if you're someone I just want around?* Aiden smiled with that lyric and I felt the vice in my chest release slightly.

"I think I'm too selfish though, to let you go," he continued.

I nodded, happy with that for now. Though I knew the truth about Aiden. The man who donated to causes because he wanted children to not suffer the way he did. The man who threw down fifty thousand dollars to save me from the panic he could see me struggling with. The man who opened his home to a practical stranger, because she was in danger. Aiden was a lot of things. Not good enough wasn't one of those things.

Aiden

THE MOMENT I saw the red dress on her, I knew the night was going to go a very specific way. Dancing with Brooklyn, in the empty club, was more romantic than I had prepared myself for. I hadn't been ready for the emotional impact. Holding her close to me, as we danced, I made some decisions, sorting through my conflicting thoughts.

"Stay with me tonight," I said.

Brooklyn looked up at me, her icy blue eyes, warming as

she studied me. She nodded, but then looked over at my brothers.

"I'll talk to them. They'll understand. I need time with you, alone," I said.

A blush started to bloom on her face and I leaned down and kissed one of her heated cheeks. She turned her face to catch my mouth with hers. I slipped a hand to her throat, tilting her chin so I could more deeply kiss her. She tasted sweet like the cocktails she had been drinking as well as the slices of pie we had shared.

We had stopped dancing and she was on her toes, her arms wrapped around my shoulders. I nipped at her bottom lip and she gasped. I swallowed her moan as our tongues tangled and the kiss became more heated. I slid my hand down her waist, cupping her ass and pressing her against me.

I started trailing kisses down her neck, grazing across the tops of her breasts. Her head was thrown back, her hair tickling the back of my hand that was still on her ass. Straightening again, I wrapped her hair around one of my hands, keeping her head pulled back. Her eyes were closed and her mouth was parted. I kissed around her mouth, before kissing her hard again.

"Take me home," she moaned.

"Don't have to ask me twice, sweetheart."

With my arm around her waist, we turned toward where my brothers were lounging around the dinner table. Oliver had a stupid smile on his face. Gideon and Jaxon both had content looks on their faces. I knew the three of them never doubted I would be interested in Brooklyn. She had a way of drawing you in and not releasing you.

"I called a car," Gideon said as we got close.

Brooklyn looked from them back to me, confused. I just nodded.

"We'll see you at home, later," I said, putting emphasis on the word later.

The three of them nodded and I led Brooklyn toward our private door. She twined her fingers with mine, her heels tapping along as she worked to keep up with my strides. When we exited the club, the limo sat waiting. The driver popped out of his door and opened the backdoor for us. I guided Brooklyn to climb in and followed quickly behind her.

Once the car engine started, the driver put up the privacy screen. I grabbed Brooklyn by the waist and dragged her into my lap. She shifted and straddled me, her dress pushing up her thighs. My hands immediately went to her exposed skin, squeezing her beautiful legs. She pressed closer to me, grinding against my cock.

Tenderly, I grabbed her throat and pulled her forward. I crushed her lips against mine and she immediately opened, granting my tongue access to her mouth. I slid my tongue along hers, causing her to moan and grind against me harder. With my free hand, I inched up her skirt further. When I didn't encounter any panties, I pulled back to look up at her. A sexy smirk appeared on her mouth and I knew she had thoughts for tonight.

I slid my fingers along her folds, finding her soaking wet. I growled against her lips, before diving into her for another bruising kiss. Her pulse pounded against my fingers on her throat. I circled her opening with one of my fingers and she tried to get me where she wanted me.

Without hesitation, I slid a finger into her. Brooklyn's hips jumped and then pressed back against my hand. Slowly, I fucked her with my finger. Adding a second one, I curled them and slid my thumb against her clit. She cried out and ground against my hand harder. The walls of her pussy clamped down on my fingers as she fell over the crest of her orgasm.

She reached down and started to unbuckle my belt and unbutton my trousers. Once she had access, she slid her hand into my briefs and palmed my cock. She stroked me, as her tongue invaded my mouth, moving seductively against mine.

"Now, Aiden. I need you now," she begged against my lips.

"Take what you want, sweetheart."

Shifting back on my thighs, she released my hardness from my briefs. She looked down at me hungrily, before sliding off of my thighs to the floor of the limo. On her knees, she leaned over me and took my cock into her mouth.

"Fuck, Brooklyn," I growled out, gritting my teeth.

My hips bucked up, pushing deeper into her mouth and she moaned. I took a hold of her hair, thrusting shallowly into her mouth, feeling her tongue massage the head of my cock. Knowing I wasn't going to last, I pulled back and she released my cock with a pop.

"Sweetheart, I can't last. I need to be inside you."

She scrambled to climb back onto my lap, straddling me and lining my cock up with her hot center. As she slowly lowered herself down, impaling herself, we both moaned loudly. She was burning hot and tight, squeezing my cock.

"So full," she moaned, as she full seated herself.

I gripped her hips, lifting her slightly and slamming her back down. She thrust her hips, rubbing herself in all the right places. Her pace began to increase and I knew she was getting close to the peak again. I reached between us and found her clit and the moment I put pressure, she exploded and her pussy became a vice on my cock.

She rode her way through her orgasm and her movements began to slow. However, I wasn't done with her. I knew we had to be getting close to home, but I wasn't getting out of the car until I had filled her up with my cum. The idea almost had me exploding on the spot.

Gripping her under the ass, I turned us, so she was on her back on the seat. I pulled out of her tight channel, until just the tip of my cock was at her entrance, before slamming deeply into her. She cried out and arched her back, lifting her hips to give me more access to her.

"You are so fucking tight, sweetheart," I groaned.

"Please, Aiden. Baby, fuck me," she cried out.

Hearing my name tumbling from her lips, was all the encouragement I needed. I picked up the pace and began to fuck her in earnest. Chasing the mountain of my own orgasm, I could feel her pussy beginning to tremble around me again. As she found her pleasure once more, I couldn't hold back as her channel tightened on me. I spilled deeply inside her, holding her close as we both came down.

As I came back to my senses, I realized the limo was still, though the engine was still running. Our drivers were smart and discreet. They enjoyed the perks of working for 4K and would keep their mouths shut regarding what happened inside the vehicles. Carefully, I pulled out of Brooklyn. She shimmied to pull her dress down and tried to fix her hair.

"Don't bother, I'm not done with you, yet," I said with a grin.

Her smile was radiant. She had the perfect just fucked look and she seemed to glow with the attention. We climbed out of the limo and she practically ran for the front door, embarrassed to face the limo driver. Inside, I disabled the alarm before swinging her into my arms and starting for the stairs. She laughed and began to kiss my neck. When she got to my ear, she nipped at it before sucking the lobe into her mouth to sooth the sting.

I went to her room, knowing eventually my brothers would come to find her. The big bed would make it easier to share, without having to actually leave her. While I headed straight for the bathroom, she kicked her heels off. I put her on her bare feet which made her more than a head shorter than me now. She immediately started to unbutton my shirt and yanking it from my pants.

"I've really been wanting to do this," she murmured.

I couldn't suppress the shiver that ran through me as she scraped her nails down my chest, over my nipples and down my abs. I hadn't fixed my belt before climbing out of the limo, so she just went straight to the button and zipper. Pushing my hands into her hair, I pulled until she was looking up at me. Her pupils were blown and her face was flushed.

Our lips met softly at first, but I tightened my hold on her hair, causing her to moan. I deepened the kiss and she sucked on my bottom lip. Sliding the zipper down on her dress, she stood still as I pushed it down over her hips. She was gloriously naked in front of me and I had to take a step back to admire her.

The wounds from the knife attack and surgery were healing nicely, but she would have two additional scars. It was clear how much that bothered her in the hospital. However, as she stood in front of me now, she didn't have any such self consciousness. She was bold and sexy. I ran my fingers over the new wounds and she watched my face closely. Then I let my fingers trail down the scar from her ear to above her breast. Lastly, I ran my fingers up her thigh, over the raised burn scar, before reaching the apex of her thighs and sliding a finger through her wetness.

Her hands came up to grip my shoulders for support as I slid a finger into her. I didn't hesitate to add a second one as she looked up at me, her mouth parted as she panted.

"You're perfect," I murmured.

"Aiden," she moaned, as I picked up speed and added my thumb to her clit.

"Tell me, sweetheart," I whispered into her ear, as I leaned down to run my tongue along the shell.

"So close, don't stop, please don't stop," she panted.

"You're beautiful, riding my hand," I said.

Her hips bucked against my fingers, pivoting as her release built in her. I knew the moment she was close because her walls began their small spasms, so I quickened my pace and put pressure on her clit. Her nails dug into my skin as she exploded and her knees threatened to give out. I wrapped my free arm around her waist, pressing her close to me. I could feel her little breaths against my chest.

Once I was sure she wasn't going to fall, I led her to the shower and turned on the large rainfall shower head. The guest shower had multiple shower heads, for whatever you were looking for. But I wanted to see the water falling on her from above. When the water warmed, I kicked off what was left of my clothes and we stepped into the stall together.

CHAPTER
Forty

Brooklyn

THE HOT WATER sluiced over our already heated skin. I pulled Aiden to me, under the waterfall shower head. The water soaked his hair and ran down his body, and my eyes followed the flow down his taunt torso. Looking at a naked Aiden wasn't a chore and I took in my fill while I had him to myself. It was clear he spent time in the gym, his arms bulged and his stomach was a cut washboard. His lean hips had the delicious V and I ran my fingers over each side.

Aiden's slow pace with me hadn't been my first choice, but I respected what he needed. I also needed time to heal, but that didn't stop my attraction to him. Aiden commanded attention when he walked into a room, even when he wasn't intending to. When he was near me, I swore there was a crackle in the air, demanding my obedience. I wanted Aiden to control my body, I wanted to give myself over to him.

Date night had gone better than I could have expected. The length the guys had gone to, for us to have a private night, had made everything feel so special, had made me feel important and cherished. Aiden being the one to take me home wasn't what I had anticipated, but I wasn't complaining.

It was the first time Aiden had seen all of my scars and at one time. The way he touched each one, then making me come on his hand, telling me I was perfect, made me fall deeper for him. I didn't feel the need to hide myself from the Knights. Even before Aiden had seen me naked, he was aware of my history. And he didn't make me feel less for any of it.

I ran my hands up his chest, until I could circle my arms around his neck. I pulled him down to me and crushed my lips to his. His fingers dug into my hips as he groaned and deepened our kiss. My breasts pressed against his chest, my nipples teasing along the sparse hair there. I could feel his hardness pressing against my stomach and even after all of the orgasms I'd had during the night, I wanted him inside me again.

Sliding my hands from his shoulders, I pulled back slightly, so I could wrap my hand around his length. I twisted my fist around his plush head, before stroking down and squeezing at the base. Air hissed out between Aiden's teeth and his head fell back under the water spray.

Suddenly, Aiden pushed me back against the shower wall, one of his muscular thighs coming between my legs, rubbing against me. His hand came up to circle my throat, something he had done before. Instead of feeling the fear I expected, I was turned on beyond belief. His thumb rubbed against my pulse, and I knew he could feel the increased speed.

He pushed me harder against the wall before attacking my mouth with his. His mouth burned a path down my throat, across my collarbone, until he captured one of my nipples in his mouth. I gasped out and my hand flew to his head, burying my fingers into his dark strands.

Aiden moved us toward the chair in the corner of the shower. Oliver had thought it was a hilarious addition. All I had used it for was shaving my legs, as I had never found myself too weak to shower on my own. Not to mention one of the guys was always sitting in the bathroom while I was getting clean, to ensure I didn't pass out.

At the chair, Aiden spins me, pushing my shoulders down until I rested my palms on the seat of the chair.

"Hold on, sweetheart," he growled.

I curled my fingers around the edges of the chair, as Aiden pushed my thighs further apart. I felt his hardness prod my entrance and I lifted on my toes, encouraging him to hurry.

"Aiden, I want you inside me," I moaned, as he ran his tip through my folds, teasing me relentlessly.

Gripping my hips roughly, Aiden slowly slipped into my channel, inch by inch, until he was full seated. He held us still, his hands tight on my skin.

"Is this what you wanted?" He asked.

I tried to nod, but he pulled out and slammed back into me, causing me to scream his name. The position allowed him to plunge deeply into me, causing pleasure to course through me with every thrust. I held tightly to the chair, using it to keep me still for his steady rhythm. He leaned over my back, running his tongue along my skin, until he got to my ear.

"Touch yourself, sweetheart," he demanded.

Shakily, I released the chair with one hand, and slid it between my legs. I could feel his hardness as he thrust into me. Finding my clit, I circled my fingers around it as he hit the spot inside me that was guaranteed to get me off.

"Aiden, oh god, baby, I'm going to come," I cried out.

"Come on my cock, sweetheart. Let me feel you," he groaned.

His words were all I needed to fall right over the cliff again. He continued to slam into me, pushing my orgasm further, my head becoming foggy with pleasure. Moments later, I felt him spilling into me again and his legs shook against mine.

"You'll be the death of me," he said against my back.

"We can die together," I murmured.

We spent the rest of the time in the shower, slowly cleaning each other, kissing and enjoying the afterglow of multiple orgasms. When Aiden turned off the water, he grabbed a towel and kneeled in front of me, drying each inch of my skin before getting his own towel.

In my room, he stood looking at the bed for a moment and I saw indecision flash across his face.

"You'll stay with me tonight, won't you?" I asked.

"Of course, if that's what you'd like," he replied.

"Yes. That is what I want. Why would you think different-ly?" I asked.

"Sharing a relationship with my brothers, is something I'll just need to get used to again. That's all."

"Is it a problem?" I asked.

He shook his head and smiled at me.

"Not at all. I just have to remember to not be greedy with you," he said, pulling me close to kiss my bare shoulder.

"You can be greedy, once in a while," I said with a laugh.

We climbed into the center of the huge bed. I stretched and let out a small yawn. Aiden held out an arm and I immediately curled up on his chest. I tried not to focus on all the naked skin we had pressed together, I was too tired for another round.

I fell asleep pretty quickly, the warmth of Aiden and his fingers playing with my hair pulling me. As I dozed I heard murmuring voices and woke to see the rest of my men in the room. I couldn't quite wake up enough to voice my wants.

A kiss landed on my shoulder as another body slid in next to me. The bed dipped as another leaned over me and kissed my temple. A third feathery light kiss slid along my lips. I knew they were all there, in my bed, as close as they could be.

The next morning I woke to a completely empty bed. Slipping on shorts and a tank top, I went in search of my guys. As expected they were all in the kitchen. I stood near the entrance, observing them before they knew I was there.

Gideon had his back to me. His muscles moved as he stirred batter which looked to soon be waffles. His hair was pulled back in a messy bun, making it easy to see the tattoo on his neck. The tight tank top he wore his more details of his back but I knew the feel of every muscle under my fingers.

A laptop was open on the island counter, with Oliver tapping at the keys. He was wearing his glasses and his face was creased in concentration. A goofy exterior that he often used to hide his true feeling. Laughing with Oliver always made the situation feel less heavy. But the serious moments, when his mouth was on me or he stared into my eyes while he was inside me, those moments were my favorite.

Jaxon was shirtless, which quickly made my mouth water. He stood next to Gideon pouring coffee, with gray sweatpants slung low on his hips. His normal stubble was a bit longer than usual and his short hair was mussed from sleeping. It made me want to run my fingers through it. I had a sudden thought about the dark hallway at the restaurant when I would have let Jaxon have me against a wall. Looking at him now, I'd still let him have me wherever and whenever he wanted.

Of course Aiden was the first to spot me. As if he was drawn to me, his eyes came up from his newspaper to land on my face. The normal tension I was used to seeing on him was relaxed. A sexy smile spread across his mouth as he let the paper fall and he stood.

Coming to me, Aiden cupped my cheek and looked into my eyes. His thumb swept along my cheek softly and I couldn't help but smiling up at him. He leaned down and kissed me softly.

"Sleep well?" He asked.

"Perfectly," I replied.

And things did feel perfect. Sitting down to eat waffles surrounded by four men who wanted me, felt close to perfect. It wasn't conventional, explaining our relationship wouldn't make sense to anyone. But then, I thought, I didn't have anyone I had to answer to. No parents, no extended family. The only close friend I had was Ash, and she was already weirdly thrilled for me.

I looked around the kitchen island at each of my guys. Aiden was laughing at something Oliver said. Oliver met my gaze and threw me a saucy wink. Jaxon had a thoughtful look on his face but he smiled at me as soon as I caught his eye. Next to me, Gideon put a hand on my bare thigh, causing sparks to lick up my body.

Perfect wasn't a word I used often. What I had around me, was exactly what I needed in my life. I only wanted to focus on that, what was right at that table. The happiness I was finding with the four Knights. The rest of the world and worries could wait.

CHAPTER
Forty-One

Lyle

SHE THOUGHT she was so smart, so safe. I had given up looking at the mansion with binoculars. The building was too far from the wall and they kept windows covered most of the day.

My phone rang and I looked at the screen. I couldn't help the disgusting sigh that left my mouth. I swallowed back my annoyance and tapped the button to pick up.

"Yeah?" I said.

"Hey baby," the female voice purred across the line.

"What's up?" I asked.

These calls happened too often. I didn't have time to entertain a woman that wasn't my ultimate goal. But this chick was a means to an end. I had been clear with her in the beginning that Brooklyn was my goal, that I would get her back where she belonged. I realized too late that fucking the woman was going to make her clingy.

"Are you there again?" She whined.

"She has to leave the house at some point."

"If she sees you, you're gonna end up back in jail. You should've just killed her," she said, hotly.

"She's no good to me dead," I snarled.

Stabbing Brooklyn had been an emotional response. My anger had been brewing as I watched her flaunt her shit with the rich assholes. Whenever she left her apartment with one of them, I would see red.

That day at the cafe was supposed to be easy, she was supposed to just cower and obey. Instead, she tried to run. Then she screamed for the big asshole. I didn't even remember making the decision to slam the knife into her.

Now she was back behind the walls and protected by the security these rich fucks could provide. Brooklyn didn't know anything about money or having it. And I was going to remind her where she came from.

"So, what's next," the annoying voice on the phone asked.

"I think it's time for you to play a more active part in this show," I replied.

The woman giggled which only made me grind my teeth together.

"Will I see you tonight?"

I didn't bother responding, I just clicked end on the call. I lifted the binoculars to my eyes again, only confirming that I couldn't see anything in the upper floor windows. Night was coming and there were soft glows around some of the window coverings. But the house gave nothing away.

These men had pasts that weren't much different than what I came from. I had done my research. So why did they get to become high and mighty, be called the Club Kings of the city? What did they have that I didn't?

I asked the question but I immediately answered it. Nothing. These fucks didn't have anything I didn't have. And they wouldn't be keeping my woman either. Brooklyn would come home to me, willingly, or not.

A little something extra...

CAN'T WAIT for more of Brooklyn and her men? Click on the link below to receive a bonus scene, only available here!

https://charlottest-pierre.eo.page/j3wxz

Acknowledgments

Thank you so much for reading Taming Brooklyn, book 1 of The Club Kings Series. I hope you enjoyed the story of Brooklyn and The Knights finding each other and their blossoming relationships. If you'd like to follow my upcoming works find me on Facebook at https://www.facebook.com/charlottestpierreauthor or at my website https://charlottestpierre.com/ .

This book wouldn't have been made possible without my editor DJ Cooper with Angry Eagle Publishing. She has been an inspiration, a sounding board and great friend through this writing process!

Also a huge thank you to JS Designs for the beautiful cover that perfectly fit the story of Brooklyn and her Knights. Thank you to my family for all of the sacrificed weekends and evenings where I was doing nothing but typing away. I couldn't do anything without you and the belief you have in me. If you were interested in any of the music listed in the book, it has all been compiled on one playlist for you, that you can find by scanning the below QR code -